CW01560555

CHRISTMAS WITH THREE COWBOYS

A CONTEMPORARY REVERSE HAREM ROMANCE

KAI LESY

**Three rugged cowboys.
One unforgettable Christmas.**

After being framed by my ex, I spent years behind bars for a crime I didn't commit.
Now, with Christmas around the corner, I've been granted an unexpected miracle—a fresh start on a remote Nebraska ranch.

What I didn't expect was to be snowed in with three dangerously handsome cowboys.
Colton and Ethan Avery are twin brothers, all muscle and grit, with piercing eyes that strip me bare.
And Mitch, their dark and brooding adopted brother, whose smoldering stare sets my soul—and my body—on fire.

Their heated touches and whispered promises awaken desires I thought were long buried.
And before long, the snow isn't the only thing melting.

But just as I begin to believe in love again, my past comes crashing back.
The man who destroyed my life isn't done with me, and this time, he's brought powerful enemies with him.

To make things even more complicated, I'm pregnant.
With twins.

Now, the three men who've claimed my heart will have to fight to protect me, our babies, and the future we're building together.

Will this Christmas bring the happily ever after we've dreamed of?
Or will the ghosts of my past destroy the only family I've ever truly wanted?

This is a sizzling, stand-alone reverse harem romance packed with sexual tension, suspense, and all the Christmas magic you can handle. Featuring dangerously sexy cowboys, plenty of banter, MFMM and ménage scenes so steamy they'll melt more than just the Nebraska snow. Blistering heat, heart-pounding danger, and an HEA guaranteed!

PROLOGUE

"You're still nervous," Colton murmurs, his voice low and soothing as he plants soft kisses across my face. His hands skim over my skin, calming me and igniting me all at once.

Mitch steps closer, his presence impossible to ignore. My gaze travels over the sharp lines and curves of his naked body, each muscle carved and taut. His broad shoulders taper down to a narrow waist, and his powerful thighs flex as he moves, drawing my eyes lower until they lock on the throbbing length between his legs. My lips part, and I can't help but lick them as I look up at him, awestruck.

"I've never done this before," I whisper. "All three of you?"

Mitch cups my face with a gentleness that surprises me, his thumb brushing my cheek. "You don't have to do anything you're not ready for," he says softly.

But I am.

Ethan moves in, his hands steady as he starts unbuttoning my shirt, while Mitch and Colton work in sync to peel away my clothes. Every layer they remove feels like they're uncovering not just my body, but a part of me I've kept hidden for far too long. I shiver as the cool air meets my bare skin, but it's nothing compared to the heat pooling low in my belly as they take their time exploring me with their eyes and hands.

I reach up and put my arms around Mitch's neck. We kiss and let our hands roam everywhere while Colton and Ethan take their sweet time touching me, exploring me with their lips and their fingertips. I melt against Mitch's rock-hard pecs, his cock throbbing against my womb as Colton spreads my legs and lets his tongue slide through my wet folds, fingers digging into my butt cheeks at the same time.

"Oh!" I gasp, the sound muffled as Mitch captures my mouth again, his kiss demanding and tender all at once, while Colton licks me into a trembling frenzy. Ethan's hands slip around the front, kneading my breasts as my head falls back, and Mitch brings his hand between us until he finds my clit.

Colton licks my entrance with burning enthusiasm.

Mitch flicks my swollen nub, teasing and adding tension to my core.

Ethan pinches my nipples, tighter and tighter until I squirm.

I lose myself and disappear somewhere in the dark pools of Mitch's eyes as he pushes me over the edge. I begin shaking, arousal flowing freely as my pussy clenches in its tempestuous release. Mitch keeps flicking my clit, pressing and rubbing until my senses dissolve entirely.

"That's it, baby, come for me," he says, his voice hot and harsh.

Colton's fingers slide in, pumping in and out of me until I come a second time, quickly after the first. I cry out, gushing like a fountain and holding on to Mitch for dear life while Colton bites my ass cheek and Ethan kisses me.

Hungry.

Desperate.

Needing more. So much more.

"Oh, God," I manage, unable to stand.

They guide me to the bed, and as soon as I lie on my back, Mitch is on top of me, pinning me into the mattress with his full body weight.

Colton and Ethan climb up, kneeling to my left and right, their sturdy, veiny, delicious-looking cocks mere inches from my lips. I surrender to my instincts, my most primal desire, and I reach for them. My fingers lock tightly around the base of their thick shafts.

"That's my girl," Colton groans, his hand tangling in my hair as Ethan watches with hooded eyes, his own cock throbbing in my grip.

I don't know how the night will end, but right now, with Mitch's body grounding me, Colton's taste on my tongue, and Ethan's quiet intensity beside me, I know one thing for certain.

This will be the best damn night of my life.

MELISSA

"Carson!"

Bucky's voice cuts through the thick noise of the cell block, sharp enough to pull me out of the paperback escape that's been my salvation for three long years. In here, books are more than pages—they're lifelines, a fragile tether to sanity in a place that does everything it can to strip it away.

"Yeah," I reply, slowly getting up. I hide the book under my pillow. "What's wrong?"

"Nothing's wrong," Bucky says, half-smiling as he unlocks my cell.

Bucky's one of the nicer guards. He knows how to keep the other women in the correctional facility in check—especially the ones with gang affiliations. I'm pretty sure he was the one who made sure I didn't have a cellmate. Bucky knows I'm better off on my own, keeping my distance from everyone else. I just want to finish the last two years of this prison sentence so I can start over.

"Are you sure?" I ask, my brow furrowed.

"Yeah, the warden wants to see you."

"There's nothing wrong, but the warden wants to see me?"

"Relax," he says as he unlocks the door. "No one's in trouble. Deep breaths, Carson. Don't overthink it."

Deep breaths. Sure. Like that ever stops the what-ifs from running wild in my head. The warden's attention on me always triggers an unpleasant feeling. I stay out of trouble. I keep my nose clean. Hell, I shouldn't even be here in the first place, but I keep my head down and tread carefully every day.

"What does he want?"

"I don't know, Mel, but for what it's worth, he didn't seem angry when he called me into his office earlier. If anything, he was pretty upbeat."

I follow Bucky down the hallway, feeling momentarily safe behind his burly figure. This part of the cell block is always a hot mess. The inmates get into fights a lot; they're cranky and itching for conflict, lashing out. I often take the stairs at the other end of the corridor to avoid running into them.

Passing by one of their cells, I see Ramona, my nemesis, and she sees me. She smirks, but she knows she can't touch me anymore. The last time she tried to rope me into one of her so-called turf wars, she ended up spending two weeks in solitary.

"Lookin' good, Mel," Ramona snickers. "On your way to the principal's office, huh?"

"Give that bitch detention!" Gloria, one of her acolytes, calls out from the neighboring cell.

She's a big lady with tattoos everywhere and rabid pink hair. "Nice to see you too, Gloria," I mumble.

"Fuck you, bitch!"

"Mind your business, inmates!" Bucky shouts, and there's instant silence in his wake.

I can almost hear them growling from their cells, but they can't touch me. Not today, anyway.

"You've been a model prisoner," Bucky tells me as we continue walking.

"I was a model citizen, too," I scoff. "Look where that got me."

"Good behavior might still get you an early release," Bucky says.

"I've got two years left on my sentence and a shitty lawyer who hasn't even returned my calls the past couple of months."

Bucky gives me another smile before he opens the door to the warden's office. His teeth are stained from coffee and cigarettes, but his pale blue eyes and rosy cheeks liven him up when he smiles. He has a way of reassuring me without saying anything.

Bucky has often been kind and patient with me although he intimidates most of the other inmates. Then again, he's right. I have been a model prisoner, avoiding conflict and keeping to myself.

"You're gonna be alright," he says, then nods at the warden. "Got Melissa Carson for you, Warden Jeffries."

"Ah, Carson. Come in," Jeffries says.

"Sir?" I ask, my voice barely a whisper as I stand before his desk, fingers fidgeting behind my back. At least Bucky didn't cuff me, which is the usual procedure when stepping out of the inmate-reserved areas.

"Have a seat, Carson," Jeffries replies.

"Is everything okay, sir?" I ask meekly.

He gives me a surprised look. "Why would you ask that?"

"I'm in your office."

"Oh." He opens a green folder, flipping through several printed pages with renewed interest. I don't have a good line of sight from where I'm sitting, so I can only rely on his often-unreadable facial expressions to try and figure out what's going on. "You've been a good inmate."

I blink a few times, briefly lost as I take deep, calming breaths. "Thank you?"

"I'm serious. You've been a model inmate. I'm sure Bucky and the other guards have told you that."

"Yes. Is there a 'but' coming?"

"No." He pauses to look at me. "Do you remember the Path to Freedom Initiative?"

"The inmate reform program, yes."

"You applied for that."

"Every year, sir. But I was never considered." I pause as my eyes widen with understanding. "Sir..."

Jeffries offers a broad smile. "Congratulations, Carson. You have qualified for a precious slot in the Path to Freedom Initiative."

I want to jump out of my seat and squeal with joy. My heart is so full, I'm terrified I'm dreaming. But I pinch myself until it hurts and find myself awake, so I take a few more deep breaths in order to contain my excitement while Jeffries holds back a chuckle.

"You've earned it."

"Thank you, sir. I can't thank you enough."

"You'll finish the rest of your sentence outside this correction facility," he says, "as a live-in ranch employee."

"A ranch employee?" Panic takes over. "But I don't have any experience on a ranch."

"Believe me when I tell you that I picked the best option for you. The Avery Ranch outside of Long Pine is in need of kitchen staff. Specifically, they need a decent cook."

"Oh, I can do that."

Jeffries smirks. "Did you think I was going to have you roping calves and shoeing horses?"

"I wasn't quite sure what to expect."

"You never really belonged here, Carson."

I nod in agreement and bite my tongue. The last thing I want to do right now is go on a tirade about how I was unjustly imprisoned. I'm too tired for that. Besides, it's been three years. Jake is in the wind, and I had to pick myself back up after he let me take the fall for him. I can't change the past. I can only reclaim my future. And this Path to Freedom Initiative is precisely what I need.

"Thank you, sir."

"I think you're going to like the Avery Ranch. They recently signed up with the program, and they provided us with all the documentation necessary for your transfer," Jeffries continues. "The facility gets a cut from your salary, but you will retain up to about seventy-five percent of your earnings whilst in their employment."

"While living on the ranch."

"Yes. It'll get you set up for the future"

"I'll be able to set some cash aside, yes sir."

"Of course, you won't have access to it until you finish your sentence," he bluntly reminds me. "Your living expenses will be covered by the ranch and this facility in equal measure. We'll also cover your medical expenses, should you need it. Your earnings will be deposited into a bank account that you'll be granted access to upon being discharged from the corrections system."

Another deep breath. None of that matters. I'm getting out of here. That's all that matters.

"Understood, sir."

"Good. If you have things to pack, now's your chance," Jeffries replies.

I give him a confused frown. "Excuse me?"

"You're leaving tomorrow."

TWENTY-FOUR HOURS LATER, I get out of Bucky's prison-assigned black van. Before me, the truck stop stretches lazily against the November morning sky while rain drizzles over the metal roof and drips into dark puddles. The snows will come soon enough, but until then, everything is grey and drab—yet I love the view.

I love it because it's not the courtyard of a prison. I love it because I'm not going back to my cell, to those grimy walls and that awful single bed. I'm not free yet, but this is as close as I'm going to get to real freedom for the next two years, and it's better than the previous three.

"Are you going to be okay?" Bucky asks as he joins me outside, my paperwork stuck to a clipboard for my new bosses to sign as part of the process.

"Yeah, why?"

"You look like you're about to cry."

I stare at Bucky for a long second. Indeed, tears are pricking my eyes, and I have a hard time describing the emotions behind them. "I'm not sad or anything," I say. "It's just that it's been a while since I've worn anything other than a prison jumpsuit, so I'm a little choked up." I chuckle dryly.

"And you've lost a little bit of weight," he replies.

My grey hoodie and jeans do fit looser than the last time I wore them—the night I was arrested. I lost my appetite from the moment I heard the judge deliver my sentence. I remember looking around the courtroom. Jake was nowhere to be found. He testified against me. He lied. He let me take the fall for him and ran like the coward he is.

"Anyway, thanks for everything, Bucky. But I hope I never see you again."

"I know what you mean," he sighs deeply. "I hope I never see you again either, Mel." He glances to our left. I follow his gaze and see a red pickup truck pull into a parking spot. "That's your ride."

A woman in her mid-sixties gets out of the truck, cursing under her breath when she notices the rain drizzling and causing her blonde hair to frizz. She looks pretty spry for her age, clad in denim and a plaid shirt underneath a camel-brown coat with woolen lapels. Her boots tap on the pavement as she walks toward us.

"That's Darla Avery, the owners' aunt," Bucky tells me. "She's going to take you to the ranch. Seemed like a nice lady over the phone."

I keep my mouth shut until Darla reaches us. She gives me a curious, suspicious glare, her hazel eyes scanning every inch of my face, making me feel like an ant under a magnifying glass before it burns up.

"You're Bucky?" she asks.

"Yes, ma'am. Robert Strickland, Ridgeboro Correctional Facility. Pleasure to meet you. And this is Melissa Carson."

"Carson, eh?" Darla seems to have taken a dislike to me already or maybe I'm just being paranoid. "Are your folks from the area?"

"No, ma'am. Lincoln."

"Alright. Get in. It's not a long ride, but the weather is shit and traffic's gonna be a bitch 'til we get past mile marker twelve."

Bucky gives her the clipboard along with a pen. "Just need you to sign here and here."

"Sure," Darla mutters, her gaze never leaving my face. She must've read my file. She knows why I'm doing time, so she

has a right to be a little suspicious. I should be more understanding, at least until they get to know me enough to understand that I'm not a threat even though I'm a prison inmate.

"You got any luggage, Carson?"

"No, ma'am, just this bag," I reply, turning so she can see the
duffel hanging from my shoulder.

The rain starts to intensify. I enjoy the feel of it. I welcome
the sensation—yet another testament to my semi-freedom.

"Got any sharp objects in there? Any weapons?"

"No, ma'am," I say, feeling slightly insulted.

"Mrs. Avery—"

"Ms."

"Ms. Avery, she just came out of a correctional facility,"
Bucky says. "And her charges never involved any kind of
dangerous weapons. The Path to Freedom Initiative would
never—"

"Hey, I don't give a rat's ass about no Path to Freedom whatever," Darla says, cutting him off again. "I watch out for my
nephews and my ranch, and I ask whatever questions I
wanna ask."

"I don't carry knives or guns or anything that could be used
as a weapon," I calmly reply. "You have nothing to worry
about, Ms. Avery. I'm here to work and finish the rest of my
sentence period."

"Good. Come on."

She heads back to the truck while I give Bucky one last smile
and mouth a "Thank you" before I rush after Darla. Once
we're in the pickup truck, seat belts on, and the open road

ahead, a heavy kind of silence settles between Darla and me. Traffic is bad, just as she expected. Ahead of us, all I see through the rain-speckled windshield is a river of red tail-lights. On either side of the road are empty pastures, fenced in to keep the cattle in and trespassers out.

"The boys won't be expecting someone like you," Darla says out of the blue.

"Someone like me?" I ask, hands neatly folded in my lap.

"Honestly, you're not what I expected, either," Darla mutters. "When Colton signed the ranch up for this whole Path to Freedom Initiative, I warned him. I warned him it could be dangerous. I don't believe people can change."

"Ma'am, I—"

"That being said, we all thought they were going to send us a tatted-up goon from a men's prison," Darla continues.

I can't help but laugh lightly. She seems irritated and intrigued at the same time. "I'm sorry," I say, trying to find the right words. "It's just that… this whole inmate program is really hard to get into. You need to be a low-risk, model prisoner. They won't let in anybody sentenced for violent crimes or for burglary and theft."

"Right. You're just a drug dealer."

I feel my face burn. I stopped touting my innocence about six months into my sentence when I realized it wasn't going to do me any good. Whether I was guilty of the crime I'd been convicted of made no difference. I had a label, and I had to own it.

"I never hurt anybody. I never stole anything. And I've been a model prisoner from day one, Ms. Avery. Also, I'm not a fan of tattoos."

"Can you cook?"

"Yes, ma'am. It's why the program paired me with the Avery Ranch. I spent two to four hours a day in the prison kitchen cooking alongside the staff and catering to three thousand inmates."

"Good. We only have seven people on the ranch, so it'll be like a walk in the park for you," Darla replies.

Again, minutes of awkward silence go by. She's either warming up to me, or she's running out of reasons not to like me. Either way, her body language does most of the talking for her. She seems more relaxed than before.

After a while, she takes a tight right turn onto a dirt road. Around us, mellow hills rise, parts of them covered in thick woods. It's been a while since I've been in rural Nebraska. Even before prison, I was mostly a city person, and my life in Lincoln was anything but exciting. Jake made it exciting, and then took it to an extreme.

"If you don't mind me asking, who are the seven people I'll be feeding?"

"There's Colton, Ethan, and Mitch. They're my nephews and run the ranch. There's me, of course. Sammy, who's been around for decades. He's the ranch manager. I'm the administrator. And we've got Kyle and Jason, our ranch hands. That's all the crew we need for the winter season."

"I see. Did you have a cook before?"

Darla gives me a sour look and releases a heavy sigh. "Yeah, me, but I can't taste much anymore."

"I don't understand."

"I've got some kind of neurodegenerative disorder or disease or whatever. My taste buds don't work right. I can barely taste anything. I damn near slipped into a diabetic coma 'cause I couldn't taste the sugar in my coffee for weeks on end. So, I can't be in charge of cooking anymore."

"I'm sorry," I reply. "That can't be easy."

"It isn't. A whole life of loving sweets, and now I can't taste them anymore. I can only chew food for the nutrients. Fuel for the body and all that crap."

"Isn't there a treatment?"

Darla shrugs. "Not that they know of. It's a rare affliction, so there isn't much data on it. For now, we all agreed we need a cook on the ranch, and the boys thought it would be a good idea to give back to the community with this Path to Freedom Initiative thingy. Two birds, one stone."

"That's good of them. I'll always be grateful."

"Here's the ranch," she says as we pass through the front gates, which open automatically. Ahead, the two-story ranch house stands proudly. It's painted a creamy white with brown shutters abutting tall windows. A wide porch stretches out in front supported by sculpted-wood pillars and topped with a second-floor terrace. It's beautiful, and by its perfectly weathered look, it's been around for a few generations at least.

"I've never seen a ranch house like this before," I mutter as Darla pulls up to the front and parks next to several newish pickup trucks and a sleek-looking grey SUV.

"Nor will you. Colton had it remodeled ten years ago. That top floor is new," Darla replies.

"I see. That makes sense."

"It was cheaper than spreading out and losing good dirt."

"Good dirt?"

Darla turns the engine off and motions for me to get out. "Yeah. For the back garden, for everything else. Come on, the rain's about to get worse, and I don't wanna end up looking like a drowned rat this early in the day."

From the little I can see as we rush toward the house, the ranch is surrounded by rolling, hills and tall trees and I catch a glimpse of a creek in the distance.

It must be beautiful in the summertime, I think. *I hope I'm still here to see it.*

For now, I take a deep breath and catch a whiff of wet dirt and manure. I thought the smell would be nasty, but it's quickly growing on me, maybe because it doesn't remind me of the inside of a prison cell.

"So, before we go in," Darla says, stopping at the front door for a moment. "There are a few things you should know."

"Okay, I'm listening," I reply, my bag on my shoulder.

"The Avery Ranch has been around for generations," Darla explains. "It's worth a lot, and prospectors often come with offers. Others try to force their way onto our turf. It never works out for any of them. We aren't selling. Ever. We live on several acres of pure green gold, and the climate here loves us. We roll with it."

"That's pretty cool," I say, smiling slightly. "There's a legacy to be passed on."

Darla sighs deeply. "Yeah, provided my boys settle down and get married. That hasn't been in the books for them for one reason or another." She pauses and shakes her head slowly, and I guess there's a history I'm not yet privy to. "So, bottom line, we don't let anyone on the property if we don't know who they are or what they want. The boys will instruct you further on the matter."

"I understand."

"Second, the ranch is run by my nephews. Their parents passed away some years ago while they were still deployed. They came back to take over."

"The boys. What are their names again?" I ask.

"Colton and Ethan. They're twins. There's also Mitch, their adopted brother. The three of them have the final say on everything. Remember that."

"Yes, ma'am."

She nods once, satisfied with my responses so far. "Good. Come on."

I follow her inside and find myself instantly mesmerized by what they've done with the decor. They've kept it rustic yet modern, stylish yet cozy.

And the men who come to greet us have my full and undivided attention.

I recognize the twins quickly, even though they're not identical. Tall as mighty oaks, with broad shoulders and the kind of arms that could easily snap me in two like a twig. The third one is different but just as gorgeous and superbly built, and they're all in their early to mid-forties—I can tell by the fine lines around their eyes and the specks of silver in their hair and beards.

"Fellas, here she is. Your new cook," Darla announces. "Melissa Carson, meet Colton and Ethan Avery, and this is Mitch Teller, your new bosses."

I stand in the middle of the open living room, my eyes wide and my lips sealed shut as I try to think of something remotely clever to say. My brain refuses to cooperate, so all I manage to do is reach my hand out.

"Nice to meet you all," I mumble.

Colton is the first to approach me, a curious twinkle dancing in his blue eyes. He's wearing a wool sweaters and loose jeans, but they're not loose enough to hide those linebacker thighs of his. His blonde hair is slightly longer than his brother's, and he's one of the few men I've seen to look phenomenally good with a short stubble and a mustache, given his bone structure.

"You're different from what we expected," he says, his voice causing me to exhale sharply, and try to at least offer a light-hearted laugh. But at the same time, he shakes my hand, and the physical contact is so electrifying, I can barely register my own existence.

"Ms. Avery mentioned that. I'm sorry I'm not a big, bulky tatted-up gang member," I finally reply.

"That's okay. I think we prefer you," Mitch cuts in, half-smiling as he, too, comes closer to shake my hand. "Please, tell us you're a good cook."

"I'd like to think I am. I've never had any complaints."

Mitch's handshake is firm, but the way his thumb lingers over my knuckle while his dark brown eyes seem to pierce through to my soul rattles me.

Mitch is slightly shorter than the other two, but still a head taller than me. He's bulkier as well. His skin is a tad darker, his black hair short and his massive chest makes my knees quiver discretely. "Welcome to the Avery Ranch, Melissa."

"Thank you, sir."

"No sir in this house," Ethan says. But he doesn't move from his spot by the fireplace. Clean shaven and stockier than his brother, Ethan has the same devastating blonde hair and blue eyes as his brother. He and Mitch are both in plaid shirts, though I don't mind the way the fabric clings to their torsos. "You can call us by our first names, and we'll do the same."

"Yes, sir. I mean, okay, Ethan."

Darla gives me another one of her hard looks. "The boys like to have breakfast early in the morning, which means you need to be up at about five to make sure the table's ready by half past six."

"That's fine," I say.

"Aunt Darla, go easy on the girl," Colton chuckles softly. "Let her dry off from the rain before you throw her into the kitchen."

At this point, I think she can throw me pretty much anywhere she wants as long as I get to be around these gorgeous men. Prison isolation seems to have done quite the number on my libido.

The way they look at me spells trouble. There's an underlying darkness, a hunger I can't quite place, but it lingers between us, unspoken yet noticeably intense. Perhaps I'm losing my mind. I'm just the convict who will be cooking their meals.

It's going to be a long two years.

2

MELISSA

olton takes the lead in showing me around while
Ethan and Mitch handle the day's chores with their
ranch hands. Darla has errands to run, so I'm left with
Colton to teach me the ins and outs of the place. I'm excited,
not just because Colton is simply a pleasure to be around, but
also because I'm surrounded by hills and the Nebraskan
countryside. I'm almost a free woman, and it feels like a
dream come true—even though I'm only getting a spoonful
of it for the time being.

"How do you like it so far?" Colton asks as we walk across
the pasture.

The rain has stopped, and I've been given a spare pair of
boots, two sizes too big, for this particular segment of the
tour, but I'm loving every second of it. "It's beautiful," I say.
"And it must be a whole lot of work."

"It is a lot of work, hard work, although in the winter there's
less to do," he says. "We still let the cattle out for a bit,
though. It keeps them healthy and does the same for us. The

winters haven't been as harsh lately anyway. We've had entire weeks in December when there were still patches of grass left for them to graze."

"And it's just you guys."

He nods once. I can see the creek ahead; its crystalline water shimmers in the sunlight that peeks through the clouds.

"We hire a few more guys during the summer. If this whole Path to Freedom thing works out for us, we might use the program for that, too," he replies, then gives me a long, curious look. "I understand you've got two years left on your sentence."

"That's right."

It's not my favorite subject, and Colton can clearly tell, but it doesn't stop him from probing deeper. I can't really hold it against him. I am a criminal in the eyes of the law, and they're taking a huge leap of faith by welcoming me into their home.

"You were a drug dealer?" he asks.

"My sentence was for possession with the intent to distribute."

"You felt the need to specify that," Colton smiles. "Why?"

"Because details matter, at least to me they do."

He nods slowly, never taking his eyes off me. Something in his gaze is enticing and makes me want to know more about him. The spark of a youthful soul is wrapped in the hardened body of a man in his mid-forties who has likely seen his share of hardships. Darla said they were deployed. So, military men, all three of them. That means they're disciplined and strong-willed, unlike like my usual choice in men.

For once, I'm drawn to someone who isn't an emotional disaster and in need of fixing. Not that I could fix anyone. That was the biggest mistake of my life, imagining I could fix Jake Miller, that true love would change him. Boy, was I wrong...

"So, you were in possession and you intended to distribute, but you weren't actually distributing," Colton says, picking apart my statement.

Suddenly, I feel anxious and I take a few deep, calming breaths. I can't fall apart now; I've come too far, and tomorrow marks my first day on the job. I cannot appear troubled in any way.

"I was in possession, yes, but I wasn't distributing. The judge decided differently," I reply.

Colton stops me in my tracks. "You don't agree with his verdict."

"There's a lot I don't agree with, but I can't change the past. All I can do is look forward." I offer a faint smile. "Darla said you guys were deployed?"

"You're not much for changing the subject, but I'll give you a free pass." He laughs lightly, then leads me along the banks of the creek.

"I mean, if you're worried about me and any potential criminal activities, please don't," I say. "I have absolutely no intention of dealing drugs. Never did, never will."

"So, then what were you doing with – how much did they find in your possession again?"

"Four kilos." I say absently, trying hard not to dwell on the worst night of my life. "But it's a long story and I'd rather not get into it."

"Alright, alright, I get it," Colton says. "It's about building trust. Yes, we were deployed. Ethan, Mitch, and I served in the same unit for about twelve years."

"That's a long time. How many tours is that?"

"Five. But we changed locations."

"Marines?"

"Even better," he chuckles softly, and his gorgeous smile makes my skin tingle all over. "Rangers. Leading the way."

We move downstream, then take a right along one of the many paths in the pasture. It leads us back to the ranch house just as the sun vanishes beyond the hills.

"Can I ask you something?" I say after a long silence.

"Sure."

"Darla said she can't cook for you anymore. She has a condition…"

"That is correct. The doctors are still running tests and monitoring her on a monthly basis, trying to figure out what syndrome they're dealing with, but it's definitely something neurological," Colton says. "Her bloodwork is fine, and her blood pressure puts the rest of us to shame. Darla's a strong woman, and there's a good chance she'll outlive us all."

I smile. "Yeah, she's a dynamo."

Colton grins. "We could handle the cooking ourselves, but we have other work to do. We could potentially do the cooking during the winter, but if a blizzard hits, we've all go to pitch in to make sure we don't lose any cattle. And when summer comes, we're busy most of the day, which leaves no time to cook. I barely manage to whip up a few eggs for myself in the morning, let alone breakfast for the whole crew."

"I understand why you need a cook."

"Yeah, the last time Darla tried to handle our breakfast, it went sideways."

I give him a curious look, further intrigued by the amused look in his blue eyes and the way he smiles, revealing two rows of perfectly white teeth. Damn, this man turns me on, and I'm not sure that's a good thing.

"We still kid her about that particular incident just to rile her up once in a while. You know, I should mention…" He gets in front of me again, but this time he's closer. Much closer. So close, in fact, that I smell in his musky scent and briefly imagine myself wrapped in his strong arms. "Darla might come across as a hard woman, but she's a softie on the inside."

"I know she doesn't trust me," I say, lowering my gaze.

But Colton gently clasps my chin between his thumb and index finger, causing me to look up at him. His touch reverberates across every inch of my skin, and it quickly becomes evident that I am not imagining any of this. He is close. He is touching me. His lips are dangerously close to mine.

"Darla doesn't trust anybody, regardless of their background. All you have to do is be consistent. Let your words match your actions, and she'll see you precisely for who you are."

"You seem more trusting."

"I've read your file, Melissa. You didn't even have a criminal record before you went to prison," Colton replies, his gaze darkening for a moment. "There's a story there, and you're not ready to share it with me. I get it. Like I said, it's about building trust, but I'm willing to wait, especially if you wish to carry out the rest of your sentence on this ranch."

"I do."

"Good. We look out for our own," he says.

"I'll do my best not to disappoint."

"I have no doubt." He smiles and changes the subject. "Mr. Jeffries had nothing but glowing reviews about your culinary skills. We know what we signed up for."

THE NEXT DAY, I wake up feeling like a new woman. The bed was comfy and my room is huge compared to my tiny prison cell. I bask in the hot shower of my ensuite bathroom, then pat myself dry and put on a pair of jeans and a grey shirt Darla left for me on a chair by the dresser. I'm looking forward to dabbling in the brand-new kitchen. They had it refitted and modernized, and it is beautiful.

I notice a note in the front pocket of my shirt. *I'll take you into town tomorrow to get you some new clothes*, it says. *Expenses covered by the ranch. D*.

I smile inwardly as I pull my long black hair into a tight bun, then apply some moisturizer to a face that already seems ten years younger. It's a new day. Yet as I reach for the door, a claw reaches into my chest and clutches my heart, its grip tightening until I can't breathe from the pain.

"Oh, shit," I manage as I struggle to breathe. The last thing I need is a panic attack coming out of nowhere. But my knees buckle nonetheless, and I fall to the floor. "Come on," I wheeze. "You've got this…" The pain in my chest fades and the room comes back into focus.

Yeah, I've got this, I tell myself, determined to power through the first part of the day without falling apart again.

As soon as I reach the first floor, I'm hit with the unmistakable scent of freshly brewed coffee. Walking into the kitchen, I find Ethan in front of the espresso machine, waiting for another coffee to finish dripping.

"Good morning," I say, stealing a quick glance at him before I step into the cooking area.

"Figured you could use it," Ethan replies without looking my way.

I take out plates and bowls from the cupboards below the counter island and lay them out, then dive into the fridge for my ingredients. Colton provided me with a full list of culinary preferences and dietary restrictions—Sammy is the only one who needs to watch his cholesterol, so I'm delighted to find a package of turkey bacon in the fridge with his name on it.

"Thank you," I say to Ethan as I get to cracking the eggs in one of the bowls, my hands moving automatically throughout the rest of the process. "It does smell nice."

"How'd you sleep?" he asks, setting my mug on the table in the breakfast area.

"Like a baby," I chuckle as I whisk my eggs, adding a bit of milk in along with the seasoning to make the perfect scramble. The bacon is frying in the pan in the meantime. "It's awfully quiet out here."

Ethan nods slowly as he takes a seat by the window. He looks dangerously hot in that white, long-sleeved shirt, his blue eyes scanning me from head to toe. I feel awfully self-conscious, briefly trying to imagine the kind of woman that men like him and his brother would go for. I think of a blonde, the all-American type with a perfect body and toned arms.

I don't see myself in that image with my thick thighs and plump behind. I've always been on the plus side—which is probably why I settled for someone like Jake Miller in the first place. He was a walking red flag, yet I went all-in because, deep down, I was scared I'd end up alone.

"You'll get used to the quiet," Ethan says. "I like it. It beats gunfire and bombshells."

"I don't know what those sounds are like in real life, but I've seen my share of movies," I mutter as I take the bacon out and pour the eggs over the grease in the pan.

My back is to Ethan, yet I can feel his gaze still very much on me. It makes the hairs on the back of my neck stand up, a tingling sensation unraveling down my spine.

"It's not something I'd wish on anyone," Ethan says, his tone clipped.

A minute passes in heavy silence while I listen for noises throughout the house, hoping the others might join us soon. It feels awkward. I'm not sure if Ethan likes me or if he's just studying me like I'm some sort of critter the cat dragged in.

"I read your file," Ethan finally says.

"I figured you would," I reply, already knowing where this conversation is going. I've already danced this jig with Darla, then Colton. I'd hoped one of them would bring the others up to speed, but I've got a feeling that each of them wants to personally test me in one form or another. "I appreciate this opportunity and won't let any of you down."

"Can you score something for me?"

I almost drop the wooden spoon as I whirl around to give him the nastiest, most appalled glare I can muster. "Excuse me?"

"Good reaction." Ethan smiles and takes a long sip of his coffee.

My blood is boiling. "That's not funny and I don't appreciate it."

"Tough shit, Melissa. You're in my house now. I need to make sure I can trust you."

"I thought Warden Jeffries clarified any doubts you might've—"

"I don't care about your warden's opinion," Ethan shoots back. "I build my own, based on what I see and hear right here."

I need a deep breath for this. "My eggs. Shit," I mumble and turn back to the stove, rushing to stir and keep the scrambling at the appropriate softness before I dump the whole pan into a separate bowl.

He's still watching me.

Heat pools between my legs.

"My methods may be unorthodox, but I know what I'm looking for."

"And what are you looking for?"

I turn around again, this time to get a clean pan on the stove while the other goes into the sink.

"Someone we can trust with our most vulnerable side," Ethan says.

"Your stomachs?" I chuckle softly as I start mixing the pancake batter next. My recipe is quick and simple, so about one minute later, I'm pouring the first pancake into the simmering pan.

"We can start there, yeah," Ethan's voice tickles my ears.

I didn't even hear him get up, let alone walk over to my side of the kitchen and get so close to me. "What do you mean… start there?" I manage, afraid to turn around.

I get a whiff of his soap, and my fingers tingle with the thought of touching his skin.

I glance over my shoulder and see him leaning against the counter island. There are several inches between us, but the air feels thick enough to slice as I try to focus on preparing the rest of the pancakes.

"I'm not sure yet," Ethan says, his voice sounding like a purr in the back of my head. "I guess we'll figure it out as we go along as long as you don't betray our trust."

Instantly, my back stiffens, and I answer him curtly. "I have no intention of going back to prison," I tell Ethan. "As a matter of fact, I have no intention of ever getting on the wrong side of the law ever again."

"That's good," he says, a hint of amusement in his voice.

I glance back and catch my breath. He's so tall that he towers over me and when Colton enters the kitchen I can note how the resemblance between him and Ethan is striking.

Unlike Ethan, however, Colton seems to be in a better, brighter mood. "Good morning, Melissa," he says. "Hope you slept well."

"Like a baby," Ethan replies in my stead as I finish flipping the last of the pancakes.

"Glad to hear that," Colton chuckles and stops by the coffee machine first.

"Who slept like a baby?" Mitch asks, coming into the kitchen.

"Melissa," Colton tells Mitch.

"Ah, good. That's a new bed, by the way," he quips, patiently waiting for Colton to brew him a cup as well. "We got it especially for you."

"I'm beyond grateful," I reply, half-smiling as I place the pancakes on a large platter, then drizzle maple syrup on top, followed by a sprinkle of powdered sweetener and handfuls of berries and roasted pumpkin seeds.

The food catches Colton's eye. "That looks incredible."

"And edible," Mitch adds, equally enthralled.

"It's settled, then," Ethan says. "She can cook."

Sammy, the ranch manager, comes in. I need no introduction to recognize him. He's as scrawny as Darla described him—though I did catch the affection she has for this kind of man. Sammy may be of retirement age, but he is as spry as Darla and just as hell-bent on living to a hundred.

"What the hell are you three doin'?" he barks at the Avery brothers and Mitch.

"Waiting for breakfast, obviously," Ethan retorts, his brow slightly furrowed.

"Help the girl out and put those plates on the table," Sammy says. "Mitch, get the cutlery out of the drawer. Y'all hired a cook, not a servant. Come on!"

I suppress a giggle, flustered and flattered by the old man's rough chivalry. He comes over and offers me his hand. "I'm Sammy Winston, sweetheart. It's a pleasure to meet you."

"Likewise, sir, and thank you for the support. It's greatly appreciated," I reply, surprised by the firmness of his handshake. He could easily break every bone in my hand if he wanted to.

"Oh, don't you worry about a thing, darlin'," he says. "These boys still need a whippin' once in a while. Nothing I can't handle."

Colton chuckles as he helps Ethan and Mitch with setting the giant, cherrywood breakfast table. "Look at him, treating us like we're the same sixteen-year-olds he used to kick in the ass whenever our paths crossed."

"Pop and Ma are probably laughing up in heaven," Ethan adds with a subtle smile. I note the hint of sadness in his voice. "Here, Sammy," he says, pointing at the table, "are you happy?"

I let the men talk while I prep and carry the platters to the breakfast table one at a time, followed by the fresh fruit bowls and a pitcher of freshly squeezed orange juice. As soon as I'm done, I get to cleaning my workstation and rinsing the pots and pans before I load them in the dishwasher.

Kyle, Jason, and Darla come in, their eyes sparkling with excitement upon being greeted with the wonderful smells of a freshly cooked breakfast.

"Morning," Darla says to me, then stops by the counter with an inquisitive look. "How'd you fare?"

"So far, so good." I give her a soft smile. "Let's hope they like the food."

"It looks great," she says with an appreciative nod, sadness enveloping her face. "It's a shame I can barely taste any of it."

Kyle and Jason step to her side, both flashing their broadest, friendliest smiles. Kyle is in his early twenties, skinny, with shaggy brown hair and wide eyes. Jason is thirtyish, chunky, and dark-haired, with equally big, equally warm eyes.

"I'm Kyle, ma'am."

"Jason. Nice to meet you."

"Likewise," I say, shaking their slightly trembling hands. "I look forward to working with you all."

Darla rolls her eyes. "Wait until they start dragging all that mud from the pasture in on their boots. You're not gonna love them then."

They join the others at the table, and I notice that Ethan moved my coffee to the edge of the counter island. I give him a gracious nod and proceed to take the longest, most heart-felt sip. It tastes fantastic, with hints of berries and burnt wood. This is the fancy kind of coffee, not the inky crap I had in prison.

"What the hell are you doing over there?" Sammy asks me.

I'm somewhat confused. "Well, I finished cooking breakfast. Do you need me to do anything else?"

"Yeah, join us," Colton replies, his eyes fixed on me, which makes my heart do flip-flops.

"Oh."

"We look after our own, remember?" Colton says. "You cooked, and now—"

"You eat," Mitch adds, already loading a plate for me.

Ethan pulls the last of the chairs out. "Sammy nailed it. You're not a servant, you're part of the crew."

"And you eat with us," Darla says.

I give a grateful smile and sit down to eat. I'd almost forgotten what it's like to be treated like a human being.

A few hours later, I handle the guys' lunch with the same kind of ease.

The weather is growing colder, and since they're taking the cattle out for one last graze before the first snowfall, I make sure their lunch is hearty and loaded with protein and good fats.

"What's on your mind?" Colton asks.

I just finished loading the dishwasher, so deep in my thoughts, I barely noticed Ethan and Mitch heading out.

"Oh, just the usual," I say, half-joking.

He gets up from the table and brings the last of the dishes over. "What's the usual for you, Melissa? I'm genuinely curious."

"Why, though? I'm just the kitchen staff. You don't have to be friendly out of some kind of obligation."

Colton frowns slightly, and I feel as though I keep saying the wrong things out of a fear of attachment.

"Just because you're a Ridgeboro inmate doesn't mean you're not worthy of my respect," he says. "You're already doing a great job here, and the guys are happy." He tilts his head as he looks at me curiously. "Are you afraid you'll get sent back to prison if you get too friendly with the boss?"

"Pretty much."

"Well, don't be," he says. "And don't ever feel like you have to be friendly with us either. You just strike me as the warm type, that's all. If I'm wrong, and if you want me to keep my distance, say so. I won't hold it against you."

"I'm sorry," I reply, turning around to face him. He moves around the counter and comes closer, yet I cannot read his expression. He's got one hell of a handsome poker face. "I don't mean to be antisocial. It's just that I've been keeping my head down and my thoughts to myself for three years now. I've apparently forgotten how to interact with people."

"It's alright, Melissa. You have nothing to apologize for. I get it."

"You do?"

"We practiced something similar during our service with the Rangers," he says. "Once we started losing some of our guys in the battlefield, Ethan, Mitch and I decided we were better off on our own, just the three of us. We wouldn't let anybody get close to us because we didn't want to suffer through the pain of another loss."

He does get it, albeit from a different perspective. His fear was of losing someone, mine was of losing myself.

"But then we came back here and had to bury our parents," he adds with a bitter smile. "And we weren't at war anymore. The people here needed us. We needed them. It just took some time to bring our spirits over to the ranch along with our bodies, so to speak."

"I'm sorry about your parents," I say. "May I ask what happened?"

"Car crash," he sighs deeply. "A drunk trucker t-boned them in Long Pine."

"Oh, God…"

He shrugs slightly. "It was over ten years ago. Time has a way of healing all wounds. It will do the same for you, Melissa. But I'll say it again, for your peace of mind: On this ranch, we're all equals, no matter where we come from."

"Even if it's Ridgeboro?" I say jokingly.

"Did you see Kyle? How skinny and fidgety he gets when he sits down at the table?"

"Yeah."

Colton smiles. "He had a choice when the sheriff caught him abusing oxy. It would've been his third strike. He could either go to jail or come work here and start attending NA meetings. We supported him through every step, and now Kyle is three years sober. He's still restless and anxious, a remnant of his uglier years, but he's working through it. We keep him riding and we work him hard. And every night, he goes to bed a sober man. So, yeah, no matter where you're from, once you're on the Avery Ranch and as long as you respect and honor the place and its people, you're one of us. Period."

"Thank you. That means a lot," I mumble.

"Don't you worry. I reckon we'll grow on you soon enough," he says, then brings a hand up to tuck a lock of hair behind my ear. His touch is subtle yet electrifying. My heart goes galloping again like a furious mustang. "I can see it in your eyes."

"What do you see?" I manage.

"You crave human contact," he replies, blinking slowly as the blue pools of his eyes darken. "It's a good thing. It means you're a red-blooded woman. Your heart's not made of stone."

That I can confirm. It's beating a thousand miles per minute.

Colton clears his throat and takes a few steps back. "I'll be out for a while, but I'll see you later. Can't wait to see what you've got lined up for dinner because breakfast and lunch were top-notch."

I chuckle softly as I watch him leave, his massive frame receding into the deep shadows of the hallway. As his footsteps fade, I'm left on my own, taking copious breaths as the ghost of his touch lingers on my earlobe.

* * *

LATER THAT AFTERNOON I'm upstairs in my room and somewhat frustrated by the absence of hot water in my bathroom. Darla took me shopping for new clothes shortly after lunch, and I want to take a bath, but the water is ice cold.

"Dang it," I mutter as I try to find a solution to my problem.

I go downstairs to check the kitchen faucets first. Maybe it's an issue with the entire house, and then I can text Sammy to let him know. If the heating system is acting up, they need to deal with it before winter sets in. We're nearing the end of November already. But there's hot water in the kitchen.

A few moments pass, and I get a not-so-bright idea—but it's one that makes sense. I go to Colton's bathroom and let out a delighted squeal as I feel the hot water running down my arm. It's risky to be in here but I do need a hot bath and they won't be back for another hour at least. Why waste this golden opportunity?

I let the hot water run and fill the tub, then peel my clothes off and get right in. As soon as I sink into the water, I feel my muscles instantly relax. I welcome the sensation and revel in every minute, scrubbing myself squeaky clean, then washing my hair. Alas, I didn't think to bring a towel or my toiletries downstairs in this operation, so I use a bit of Colton's shampoo.

"Oh, it smells nice," I whisper as I lather my hair, then sink under the water for that ultra fresh feel. The scent of cedar-wood feels like a warm hug as I come out of the bath and wring the excess water from my hair before I clean the tub, my body emanating a most delicious kind of heat.

The sound of approaching footsteps startles me, and I scramble to reach for a towel, but it's too late. I freeze as Colton comes into the bathroom with a confused look on his face.

"Shit," I say.

Colton stands in the doorway, his jeans hugging him tightly —too tightly around the crotch area by the looks of it. My nakedness had an instant impact on him, and I press my lips into a tight line as I struggle to drag my gaze away from that ginormous bulge.

"Melissa."

"Colton," I manage. "I… I can explain."

"Please, do, but take your time. I'm in no rush."

The shadow of a smile dances across his face, and my core ignites. I need to pull myself together. This is completely inappropriate, no matter what my body is shamelessly hinting. "Could I maybe get that towel first?"

Again, he smiles. "It's a gorgeous view. Why would I want to obscure it?" Again, my body reacts in a way that is not suited for this moment. Maybe that's his intention. Making this situation worse, just for kicks. He's messing with me. But the hunger in his eyes is real. I recognize the desire, the crackling fire burning just beneath the surface. I recognize it because I feel it, too, with equal intensity.

This is dangerous. He's my boss. I'm an inmate. This can't happen. It shouldn't.

"Please?" I try again.

"Well, since you ask so nicely," Colton replies, then grabs the towel from the wall-mounted drying rack and brings it over. I'd hoped he'd toss it instead because the close proximity is making my blood simmer and my head dizzy. "Here you go."

"Thank you," I mumble and quickly wrap it around myself. "I'm so sorry. There's no hot water in my bathroom. I just came in to see if the problem was general—"

"There's no need to apologize. I forgot to mention that the upstairs pipes are iffy sometimes. Sammy will take a look at it when he gets back."

"Oh. Okay."

He steps even closer. I should push back. Run away.

But I can't. I don't want to.

"What are you doing?" I whisper, startled by the fact that I can feel his hot breath on my face, and it's doing one hell of a number on me.

"Testing a theory."

"What theory?"

He cups my cheek with one hand. I don't resist. God, it feels incredible. It's as if my whole body is opening up to him, desperate for his undivided attention. "I told you... it's written all over your face."

Without hesitation, he kisses me.

My lips part eagerly, and his tongue rushes in to taste and explore me. I welcome him and taste the subtle hints of mint and coffee.

My mind goes haywire, his body so close but not close enough.

I need more. I'm blind and melting as I take the final step and let my full figure press against him. Colton reacts instantly, his arm snaking around my waist. He pulls me even closer, his breath ragged as he deepens the kiss.

"This is wrong," I manage, but his lips conquer me again.

His hand moves from my cheek, working its way down, his fingers recording everything along the way while I let mine run through his rich, blonde hair. He tastes like a lazy morning, but the throbbing erection nestled against my belly speaks of something much more fiery and all-consuming.

Instinctively, I part my legs for his hand to freely explore.

His long, nimble fingers sneak past the towel, finding me slick and eager for more. My clit swells under his touch, every stroke bringing me dangerously close to something I've only managed to experience by myself in the dark solitude of my cell. He's doing everything right, though, starting little fires everywhere as he devours my mouth and my soul at the same time.

"Shit," Colton gasps and suddenly pulls back, his eyes wide and glassy. "I'm… I shouldn't have. I apologize."

There it is. The reality. It's coming back to bite me in the ass. I already miss his touch.

My face feels hot as I try to remember where I am and what I was doing. "No, I apologize. For everything. Excuse me," I reply and run out like my feet are on fire.

"Melissa!" he calls out, but I'm already up the stairs, my eyes blistering with tears of shame.

"Sorry!" I shout and lock myself in my room.

Panting, I need a moment to pull my thoughts together. They all unraveled somewhere along the way, and I no longer know what to do with myself. My core feels tight. My pussy aches, clenching in a slow and steady rhythm. I look at the bed and realize I need a release so I can think clearly again.

I remove the towel and lay on the bed, letting my fingers do the rest of the work.

With fresh memories of Colton's sizzling touch forever embedded in my very soul, I use one hand to squeeze my breast and pinch the nipple until it stings, while I let the other work my clit closer to that much needed edge. Closing my eyes, I can almost feel Colton on top of me, the weight of his hard body pinning me against the mattress.

I slide two fingers inside my pussy, tasting him on my lips.

My release comes hard, and I shudder as I explode, rippling like a newborn sun as I imagine him pumping me full of him, fucking me until I'm breathless and senseless.

I ride that wave for as long as I can.

Then reality comes crashing back down around me.

3

MELISSA

T he next morning, I stand in the kitchen, flustered as I carry platters of a rich breakfast over to the table.

They're all here, eager to eat. Darla's got an eye on me. I wonder if she knows something or if I'm just being paranoid.

"Here you go," I say, my voice trembling as I place the fruit platter at the center of the table. Colton moves some of the other plates to make more room. "Thank you."

"You're most welcome, Melissa." Even my name sounds different rolling off his tongue.

I give him a slight nod and go back to the kitchen counter, loading the dishwasher with shaky hands. I can feel Ethan's eyes on me. Mitch's, too.

"I tell ya, that heifer is gonna be the death of me," Sammy says with a laugh, breaking the silence.

From what I gather, they're having trouble with some of the younger cows, but it's to be expected. They're new to the herd—recent acquisitions from an auction in Long Pine.

Colton keeps looking at me. Darla keeps looking at him. I think she's picking up on the subtle signs because her gaze shifts to me, and I just want the floor to open up and swallow me whole.

"Melissa, you need to eat," she says, her tone rather commanding.

"I'll eat after you guys are done. I still need to clean this pot," I reply, grabbing a brush to do something a round in the dishwasher could easily fix. I just need to keep myself busy until they all leave the kitchen.

If I let enough time pass and never mention it again, Colton won't bring it up either. If there's one thing I cannot afford, it's to lose this job and go back to prison. I can't. I don't want to squander this little slice of paradise I've found.

Listening to bits and pieces of the conversation, I focus on scrubbing the pot, my body slowly releasing some of the tension through deep sighs.

"What's up with her?" Darla mutters.

"She's conscientious. Leave the girl be," Sammy cuts in.

"And you've got quite the attitude problem since Melissa came in. You got the hots for the girl?" she snaps, prompting the others to burst into a heavy round of laughter.

Sammy slaps the tabletop, doubling over. "My God, woman, I can't believe it. You're jealous?"

"Why would I be jealous?"

"You miss me. Admit it."

"I'd rather be dragged by that heifer you hate so much all the way to Long Pine before I'd admit such a thing."

Colton laughs. "Oh, come on, Aunt Darla. We all know you two are itching to get back together. Why don't you?"

"In your dreams," Darla snaps and gets up from the table and exits the kitchen, leaving an awkward silence in her wake.

I glance back and notice how Kyle and Jason are quietly eating, their eyes darting from one Avery to another, while the brothers, Mitch included, keep smiling at Sammy.

The old man grumbles as he stabs his eggs with a fork. "What?"

"How long are you two gonna pretend you don't belong together?" Mitch asks.

"It's complicated, boys. You know that. Just leave it."

Colton grins coolly. "You started it."

"Yeah, well, I was stupid. Not the first time. Won't be the last either. I should've known better."

"You gotta make it up to her," Ethan says.

"Some flowers might do the trick," Mitch suggests.

"She'll just shove 'em down my throat. I blew my chances with her. It's my fault. Just leave it at that," he says, then exits the kitchen as well.

Kyle and Jason are busy scarfing down their breakfast, while Colton, Ethan, and Mitch discuss the situation. They would very much like to see Darla and Sammy get back together, but they know it's entirely up to their aunt. Colton keeps glancing my way, making my heart buck with each gaze.

I try to be professional and find ways to stay busy until they all leave, but the universe is not on my side. One by one, the others go to help with the cattle.

Sammy stops by the counter and leaves his empty plate. "Delicious as usual. Thank you, Melissa."

"You're most welcome," I reply.

He gives me a faint smile, then heads out.

"You deserve a prize for these eggs," Mitch says. His smile makes my shoulders drop, obliterating my defenses as I giggle softly.

"Oh, no need. It's my pleasure. I'm glad you like them."

"I'll figure something out, don't worry," he says. He leaves me with an unspoken promise as he follows Ethan out the door.

And then I am alone with Colton.

I hold my breath as I feel Colton cautiously approaching me. His very presence is enough to scramble my thoughts, making it increasingly harder for me to focus on the dishes. But I can't ignore the elephant in the room any longer, so, I turn the water off and dry my hands with a towel before I turn around to face him.

Time seems to stand still.

He's close. Too close and with no regard for my personal space. But honestly, I don't mind it. If there were no repercussions, I'd get naked with him right then and there. But there *would be* repercussions.

"Hey," I mumble. "What's up?"

"What's up?" He almost laughs, the tension suddenly fizzling away between us.

"I don't know what else to say."

Colton gives me a warm smile, hands deep in his jeans pockets as he shifts his body weight from one leg to the other. "We need to talk about yesterday."

"I was afraid you'd say that."

"Don't be afraid. I was out of line. It won't happen again. No matter how I feel, it was completely unprofessional and disrespectful. Rest assured, your position here is in no jeopardy whatsoever."

I give him a surprised look. "You're not sending me back to Ridgeboro?"

"Honestly, I've only known you for a couple of days, but I can already tell you have no business being in that place," he says. "So, no, I'm not sending you back. It's my fault, anyway. You're safe here; I just need you to know that."

The knot in my gut begins to slowly unravel, and I let out a loud breath—the one I'd been holding since this conversation started.

"Thank you, Colton. For what it's worth, I'm partly to blame, too. I didn't stop you. If anything, I was an eager participant. So, if you want to deduct something from my pay, go ahead and do that."

"That's not gonna happen," he says and smiles, his gaze softening as it searches my face for… something. "You're full of surprises, I'll give you that."

I watch him confidently stride out of the kitchen, his broad shoulders back and his head held high. He must be pleased with how the conversation went, and frankly, so am I. It's nice to feel safe after so long, but still, there's that lingering anxiety about being sent back to prison. It affects my every interaction. Of course, it's not healthy to indulge that fear, but it's hard to control when so much is on the line.

The worst part is I that I keep thinking about Colton's kiss, about the way his hands felt on my body, of how his fingers spread me open and explored me. Maybe it's because I've been celibate the last three years, but I felt a connection there —a chemistry between us.

And then there's Ethan's dark gaze and intense allure. And Mitch's boyish smile and spicy humor. Alone, each of them is irresistible. But together? Holy shit, how could any woman *not* fall head over heels for them.

And that is precisely what I can't do. I can't let my desire take over. I need to keep a professional distance—my head down, my nose clean, just like Bucky said. It's the only way I'll get to finish my sentence on the ranch instead back at Ridgeboro. That's the simple truth.

Too bad it's easier said than done.

* * *

I'M CHOPPING carrots and sweet potatoes for a veal stew when I find my thoughts once again wandering back to yesterday's events, and the memory of Colton's touch triggers a variety of heated sensations throughout my body. I weigh the idea of going upstairs to finish myself off to take the edge off. But Darla comes in, and I revert to full, professional work mode, chopping away with a faint smile on my lips.

"How's it going?" she asks, stopping by the coffee machine first.

"Good, thank you. I'm using that veal you bought yesterday for a nice stew."

She nods while waiting for her coffee to brew. I'm starting to really enjoy the buzzing sound of the espresso machine. It's the kind of sound that soothes my brain.

"Sounds wonderful. Do you have everything you need?"

"Yes, ma'am. I've taken the liberty of using some of the frozen tomatoes you saved over the summer for the red sauce instead of the usual canned stuff. Hope that's not a problem."

"Not at all. That's one of the reasons I stacked them in the freezer, to be honest," Darla replies. "I doubt I'll ever get to enjoy a red sauce again, but it doesn't mean to rest of y'all can't enjoy it for me."

"What did the doctor say?" I ask.

Darla takes a seat in one of the tall chairs by the counter island, sipping her coffee as she watches my hands work. "We're still waiting on a round of tests to figure out if it's a bacterial infection. It's a possibility, given how bountiful life on the ranch can be in that sense."

"There's bacteria that messes with your sense of taste?"

"And smell. Yeah. There are viruses that do the same. So, they're testing for everything. Frankly, I'm getting tired of all the poking and prodding. All the needles and MRIs…"

"So, it's not necessarily a neurodegenerative condition?"

Darla takes a deep breath and lets it out as slowly as possible. I know that look on her face. Its exhaustion combined with frustration. I understand the feeling perfectly, albeit under a different set of circumstances.

"They're still testing for that, too. I reckon it'll be a couple more months, at least, before the doctors are able to give me a clear diagnosis. In the meantime, they're trying different treatments to see what works. I'm just grateful they're letting me do it as an outpatient, otherwise somebody in that hospital would end up dead."

"Oh, dear." I giggle.

Darla changes the subject. "How are you settling in, Melissa?" I notice the subtle shift in her tone. It's not as stern or as rough as it was the first time we met. She seems a tad softer, and I welcome the change. Maybe she's getting used to me. "Everybody treating you okay?"

"Yes, absolutely," I reply, struggling not to think of my session with Colton for the purpose of this conversation. "They're all good people, kind and welcoming and patient. I like it here, to be honest. It's peaceful, and there's plenty of work to keep me busy."

Darla takes another sip of her coffee, her attention focused on me. She makes me feel like I'm under a microscope lens, but I keep reminding myself it's in her nature to be cautious, suspicious, and protective of the ranch, of her family, and her people.

"Were those your drugs you got busted for?" she asks, changing gears yet again.

"Wow."

"I need you to tell me the truth."

"I could lie."

Darla flashes a cool grin. "I'd know if you were lying."

"Fine," I say, taking a deep breath. "No, they were not my drugs."

"Whose, then?"

"My fiancé, Jake. I didn't even know he was dealing," I reply. "He told me a story about him running an independent delivery service for local pharmaceutical companies."

Darla chuckles dryly. "Technically speaking, drugs are drugs, no matter who distributes them."

"Yeah, but class A narcotics aren't just any drugs," I sigh deeply. "One night, he asked me to pick up his van from somewhere and drop it off at a different address across Lincoln. He'd been drinking, he said, and a client had called for a last-minute delivery."

"And you believed him."

I shake my head slowly. "I was stupid and deeply in love. Granted, I knew he was troubled. I think that's what drew me to him. I thought I could fix him, show him what real love was."

"Oh, Melissa. You weren't stupid. Most of us find at least one such project to emotionally wreck us in our lifetime." She laughs, but the bitterness in her tone is unmistakable.

"That's right. And I've spent the past three years working on precisely that aspect."

"How'd you get such a harsh sentence then?"

I lower my gaze in shame. "The cops pulled me over. I showed them my driver's license. The van didn't have all the necessary paperwork. I didn't know that. Five minutes later, they got a call through the station and started going through the van. They found the drugs, and I was speechless, shocked. I couldn't even react."

My breathing quickens.

"Are you okay?" Darla asks, instantly noticing the change in my voice. A panic attack is hovering at the edges of my consciousness. "You look pale."

"I'm fine," I mumble. "I get anxious when I think about that night and what followed."

"So, you got arrested for possession."

"Yes, ma'am."

"What happened next?"

"You're really digging into it here," I say with a nervous laugh.

Darla's expression doesn't shift. "It'll help you focus and avoid a panic attack. I know what that looks like. Come on, think back. Tell me about it."

"I was arrested. Entitled to a phone call, so naturally, I called Jake. He wouldn't pick up. I spent the night in jail," I say, following her lead. "He didn't show up at my arraignment either. I couldn't reach him at all. I couldn't afford a lawyer, so—"

"One was appointed to you, and I'm guessing he was a stooge."

"He wanted me to agree to a plea deal," I say and exhale sharply. Lo and behold, I soon realize Darla was right. I do feel better, calmer. My breath is even once more. "It wasn't until I was standing in front of the judge that I realized what was going on. I insisted on my innocence. Then the prosecution brought Jake in as their witness. He told them quite the story. He even had proof, though it was circumstantial and easy to disprove if you're a good defense attorney, but my guy..."

"Your guy was shit." Darla curses under her breath. "Damn, girl, you really got the short end of the stick there."

"I did, yeah. They gave me five years in a low-security facility because I didn't have a record or a history of violence."

"I'm sorry," Darla says.

I give her a surprised look. "You believe me?"

"I told you. I'd know if you were lying. So don't ever lie to me."

"Wouldn't even think of it," I say. "Thank you, Darla. Thank you for believing me."

While we chat, I transfer the chopped vegetables into a bowl, leaving them to soak in cold salted water for a while, then open the cans of pre-cooked peas and beans and strain them in the sink.

"You should get another lawyer and appeal the verdict," Darla concludes after sipping her coffee. "It's not too late. You could get the sentence vacated and sue the state. You'd be entitled to quite the settlement. They'll never take it to court if the evidence is compelling enough to throw out the original verdict."

"I've got two years left. Might as well get it over with."

"That record will haunt you forever," she replies.

All I can do is shrug. "I don't know, Darla. Lawyers are expensive. Right now, I'm dirt poor. All the money I make here goes into an escrow account until I'm released."

"There are plenty of lawyers who do this sort of thing pro bono."

"Why are you pushing this?" I ask her.

Darla thinks about it for a moment, her eyes darting across the counter as she seems to search for the right response. "You don't deserve to pay for a man's crimes. I think you should fight this with everything you've got. It'll be better for you in the future. Your employment opportunities will be different. You may feel like you deserve this, somewhere deep down, like you deserve to be punished for having believed in and loved that prick. But it wasn't your fault. And ruining your life over this just doesn't feel right."

"You're way nicer than I originally thought." I chuckle lightly, trying to ease the tone of the conversation because I'm uncomfortable with the truth she just delivered. At least I'm able to recognize a hard truth when I hear it. If that's not a sign of growth, I don't know what is.

"The guys would agree, too," Darla insists.

"The guys?"

"Colton, Ethan, Mitch. Hell, they've got some great lawyers working for the ranch. They're close friends with them, too. I could—"

"Maybe it's best if I keep my head down and just finish what I started here."

Darla offers a wry smile and finishes her coffee. "For what it's worth, Ethan almost got court martialed while they were serving with the Rangers. He was accused of something another member of their platoon had done. Colton and Mitch went to hell and back to prove his innocence."

"Where are you going with this?" I ask.

"You need a smidge of faith, Melissa. It'll take you far; trust me."

"What crime was Ethan accused of?" I ask, more curious about their history than I am eager to revisit mine.

Darla lowers her gaze for a moment. "Murdering a fellow Ranger, not that he doesn't have a dark side and not that he hasn't killed, but never outside of duty."

"Oh…"

A different kind of shiver travels down my spine. What Darla is telling me about Ethan pretty much tracks with his overall attitude. That darkness I see within him—it makes sense now. The man carries deep shadows with him everywhere. Yes, he's handsome as hell, but he's also demonstrably deadly. Something must've changed in my brain chemistry at one point in the past three years because I now I find that combination downright enticing: a man who makes my body sizzle who is also capable of obliterating anybody who tries to hurt me.

I was never a fan of such extremes before, but after everything I've seen and lived through, I don't know…

"Ethan is a good man," Darla reiterates, as if she can somehow read my mind. "He just has a dark side that needs to be fed."

"How does he feed that dark side?"

"He's figured out healthier ways. The ranch keeps him busy: the company of animals, the clean air, the starry nights," Darla says. "Colton is a good influence on his brother as well. They stuck together from the moment they were born. Then Mitch came along, raggedy and covered in soot, crying his heart out… I'll never forget that night. They've been inseparable ever since, picking each other up all the time."

"Covered in soot?" I ask.

Darla's eyes widen, and she looks away. "Forget about it. It's personal. A slip of my tongue and not my story to tell," she says. "Point is, I think you should have a little more faith in yourself. You're entitled to real freedom and a clean record, especially since you didn't commit the crime you were imprisoned for. It's just a damn shame."

"I appreciate it, Darla. I really do."

"Just think about it. I can put you in touch with our lawyers. If they won't take the case pro bono, they'll gladly refer you to one of the charities who do," Darla replies, then leaves me to my lunch prep work.

She also leaves me with a hefty new thought to mull over.

4

COLTON

Melissa has been on the ranch for a week, and absolutely everybody is fawning over her, Darla included. And our auntie does not do that often. Nobody seems to remember or even care that Melissa is still an inmate of the Ridgeboro Correctional Facility.

I have so many questions about how she ended up there in the first place, but she doesn't like it when we delve into that topic. It doesn't stop me from getting to know her better, though, so one morning I decide to follow Mitch's advice.

After breakfast is served, my brothers and I go back into the kitchen to find her.

"What are you up to?" I ask.

She whirls around with a plate and a dry cloth over her chest, her eyes as round as saucers. "Oh. Hey. Um, drying the dishes…"

"Leave that stuff," I say. "You're coming with us."

"Where?"

Instantly, she goes into self-preservation mode. Her frame stiffens as she slowly sets the plate down. It would be cute if there wasn't a layer of trauma underneath her behavior. Three years in prison will do that to a person I'm told.

"We thought you might want to join us outside today," Mitch says. "If you're going to be a ranch girl, you might as well learn the ropes around here."

Melissa chuckles nervously. "I'm just the kitchen wench."

"Wench?" Ethan raises an eyebrow.

"I'm kidding… okay, I'll come," she says, her cheeks blushing in the prettiest shade of deep red.

An hour later, Mitch is out with her by the barn as she struggles to put the harness on one of the gentler horses from our stables. Ethan and I sit atop our mustangs clad in wool sweaters and thick jackets, the horses' hooves crunching in the snow, watching as Mitch teaches Melissa how to prep her horse for a ride.

"Remember, they can tell if you're nervous," Mitch tells her.

He's trying hard not to laugh, but I know he's as smitten with Melissa as the rest of us. He is also endearingly patient with her. We've been here for twenty minutes, trying not to intervene as he teaches her the basics.

"I *am* nervous," Melissa says. Her mare, Isabella, is a beautiful creature with a robust back and a soft white coat. She's almost as patient as Mitch, but she won't be for much longer, not if Melissa keeps fidgeting with the harness instead of putting in on.

"She's getting excited. She wants you to ride her," Mitch reassures Melissa. "Here... allow me."

"Finally," Ethan mutters. "A couple more tries, and the mare would've just gone back to the stables on her own."

I chuckle subtly, steam rolling from my mouth. It has gotten a lot colder in the past couple of days, but at least our cattle are safely sheltered for the winter, with Kyle and Jason handling their daily feeding while Sammy handles the overall maintenance with my brothers and me. We divided our duties efficiently for the winter, thanks to Melissa taking over the cooking. Darla's got the administration, along with the business, so we're able to enjoy moments such as this.

"She's such a city mouse," I tell my twin.

"The ranch will grow on her," he says, unable to take his eyes off her.

"Alright, I get it," Melissa says, the harness properly secured on Isabella's pretty head. The mare neighs excitedly as Mitch helps Melissa get in the saddle, then connects a long rope to the harness to guide the horse in a circle. "Oh, this is... weird..."

"What's weird?" Mitch asks.

"The saddle. I mean, I've never ridden a horse before."

Ethan shakes his head slowly. "We need to be careful with this girl."

"We're not going to break her," I reply, half-smiling.

"She's going to break us."

We're several yards away from Mitch and Melissa, therefore out of their earshot. I lean slightly forward and pat my horse on his strong, muscular neck. Apex has been a loyal friend over the past couple of years, though he's not as fast as Ethan's horse, Elias. He's stocky and resilient, however, and I can never get tired of his cappuccino-colored coat and white mane. Elias, on the other hand, is a black bolt, his coat so dark it swallows any light that hits it.

"What more have we learned about her?" Ethan asks.

"Darla says Melissa is innocent," I say. "She wouldn't go into detail, just that she believes her."

"For what it's worth, Aunt Darla is a good judge of character. It makes sense, though," my brother surmises. "There's nothing about Melissa whatsoever to make anybody think she's a seasoned drug dealer."

I nod slowly. "I know there's more to that story, but we need to get her to open up to us. She's constantly on edge. Darla said she's prone to panic attacks."

"I saw the signs, too. Whatever has happened to Melissa in the past few years… it's taken a toll."

"Look at her go," I exclaim once Melissa performs a complete first circle ride around Mitch. The mare seems comfortable with her, trotting delightedly in the snow, while Mitch holds on to the rope and keeps guiding her in a steady rhythm. "Well done!" I raise my voice so they can hear me.

Melissa laughs and waves at me. "Not too bad, eh?"

"Not bad at all," I reply.

"She's a new kind of trouble," Ethan says.

"And Mitch knows it, too," I reply. "We can either keep our distance, or we can act on what is clearly there. Her body doesn't lie."

My twin nods again. "I noticed."

We bring our horses slightly closer, taking advantage of Melissa's divided focus to kick-start a much-needed conversation. She's too busy paying attention to Isabella and her posture in the saddle to mind the topic we're about to delve into.

"So, you're from Lincoln, Melissa?" I ask.

Mitch gives me a wry smirk, fully aware of where I'm going. We talked about it long before we came downstairs for breakfast this morning. We always talk about what piques our interest, and Melissa has been an enticing topic for us since day one. I've yet to recover from that moment in my bathroom. I can still taste her on my lips.

"Born and raised," Melissa says.

Above us, a brighter shade of grey unravels. We're going to get more snowfall this evening. The sun is hidden behind a thin layer of clouds, but the existing snow gives us a clear view of the surrounding hills. It's a quiet day on the ranch today. I like it when it's quiet.

"Only child?" I inquire.

"Yeah."

"What about your parents?" Ethan asks, his gaze fixed on her.

Melissa's cheer fades for a few moments, but she doesn't miss a single beat while riding Isabella. Her posture is quickly improving, a sign that she's getting the hang of it. "My dad bailed when I was five years old. My mom died about four years ago."

"I'm so sorry," I say, almost regretting the questions.

"What were you doing before prison?" Mitch asks next.

Melissa gives him an amused glance. "You're really working me over here, aren't you?"

"The purpose is to teach you how to multitask," he shoots back. "Talking and riding, roping a calf and riding…"

"Wait, roping a calf? Why on earth would I need to do that?"

Mitch laughs lightly. "It's what ranch girls do."

"I think I'd rather stick to cooking," she mutters, but she doesn't get off the mare. Instead, she keeps riding and getting to know Isabella better with every completed circle.

I lose myself in the details for a long minute. The jeans hug her thighs tightly, while the dark blue parka with a furry collar hides her curvy figure—but I remember those full hips, the firm, plump breasts, the inviting wetness between her legs.

Dammit, Ethan might be right. Melissa could be the nail in our coffin in so many ways. It's been a while since we've been enthralled with the same woman. I like it, though. It says good things about Melissa. I dare hope she'll join us for the ride.

"You didn't answer my question," Ethan reminds her. A smile tests the corner of his mouth as soon as she looks at him again. "I'm curious."

"I was working as a sous chef at a restaurant in Lincoln," she says.

"What restaurant?" I ask. "I know Lincoln pretty well."

"The Sommelier," she replies.

We've been there a couple of times while visiting the city. It's a pretty high-end locale, with French cuisine and a discerning wine selection. "So, cooking is your calling," I conclude.

"Pretty much. I've always been good at it," Melissa says. "It keeps my mind quiet, and I love it when I get a dish right, from execution to aftertaste. The Sommelier was a wonderful experience. We had a French chef heading that kitchen. I learned a lot from the guy."

"I'm still trying to figure out how you went from sous chef at a fancy French restaurant to drug-running felon," Ethan says.

Melissa ignores him. Instead, she looks at Mitch. "How do I gently stop her?"

"Just pull on the reins. She knows," he replies.

Slowly, Isabella comes to a halt, and Mitch, ever the gentleman, goes over to assist her as she dismounts. His hands linger on her hips, and she briefly peers deep into his eyes. I see it then. The spark. The much-needed spark that makes me think she's anything but indifferent to the three of us. It makes Ethan's apparently intrusive probing all the more important, despite its unpleasantness.

"We all do stupid things," Melissa says to Ethan, her brow slightly furrowed. She doesn't look as angry with that brown wool cap on, but I know she's bubbling just beneath the surface. I reckon she'd make a fiery lover. "My stupidity was trusting the wrong man."

"Not here to judge," Ethan replies. "Just trying to get to know you better."

"I thought Darla told you everything," she sighs.

"Your conversations with Darla stay between the two of you. We respect each other's privacy on this ranch," I gently cut in.

Melissa stares at me. My guess is she's probably wondering if I kept the bathroom incident to myself. I kept the details to myself, but I couldn't hide the palpable chemistry from Ethan and Mitch, not when the three of us are drawn to her more and more each day.

"I appreciate that," she says. "Thank you. Now, if you don't mind, I'd like to go back to the house. I could ride Isabella again tomorrow, if you want me to."

"Do you want to ride Isabella again?" I ask, smiling broadly. She nods enthusiastically. "Then it's a date," I shoot back and get Apex into motion. "Come on, boy, let's go for a ride."

"Hold on, let me take Isabella back to the stable and I'll join you!" Mitch says.

"You can catch up," Ethan chuckles and gently heels Elias into a trotting rhythm beside me.

As the days go by and the winter establishes a firm hold on the land, my brothers and I find ourselves looking for work to do around the house more and more. With the field work we did over the summer, there isn't much left for us to do in the winter, except take care of the cattle and horses and patrol the fences every day. Both tasks are often left to Kyle and Jason, occasionally accompanied by Sammy, while Ethan, Mitch, and I focus more on any home improvement projects and ranch business affairs.

Melissa is part of the family already, though she hasn't realized it yet. I have a hard time staying away from her. Ethan and Mitch, too. We're not too subtle about it either, a fact that Darla hasn't failed to notice.

"You three are incorrigible," she whispers to me one afternoon.

The two of us are in the kitchen at the breakfast table, poring over recent paperwork that needs some untangling while Melissa is prepping the meat for tonight's dinner. There are two pots simmering on the stove—preserves for the upcoming Christmas holidays, their scent fills the room and makes my soul feel warmer with each deep breath.

Apples and cinnamon. Pears and nutmeg. And a dash of cloves in both, just enough to put a smile on my face as I admire Melissa, quietly slicing through the veal and dipping each strip in a soy-based marinade, her nimble fingers treating our food like it's something meant for the gods. Her reverence toward her craft makes me fall harder, and I fear I have no way of stopping this train. It left the station the minute I kissed her.

"Colton."

Darla's voice pulls me back to a list of bank transactions I'm supposed to double-check before she slips it into last month's archive folder.

"Sorry," I reply. "What were you saying?"

"That you three are incorrigible."

"We three?" I give her a skeptical look.

"Yeah. You. Ethan. Mitch. It's almost hilarious to observe," she chuckles dryly. "Smitten like teenage boys, yet not one of you has bothered to bring this girl a single flower."

"Darla, we're her bosses. It would be inappropriate."

"Spare me the BS, Colton. I've known you since you first came into this world, naked and screaming."

"That's a nice visual," I mutter.

Darla pours herself another glass of wine. "I'm just saying. If you want to do something, do it. If not, focus your attention somewhere else. Just don't bother her out of sheer curiosity. She's not some circus animal for you to gawk at all the time."

"Where is this coming from?" I ask, my voice low as I steal glances at Melissa. She can't hear us from across the kitchen, but I know she looks my way when she thinks I can't see her. It's driving me nuts.

"She's clearly different from the kind of women you and your brothers are used to. This one's dignified. And a convicted felon. Guilty or not, it doesn't matter. The stigma is there, and it's gonna follow her around forever."

"The last thing I want to do is disrespect her."

"Good. So, as I was saying. Either you three back off completely and keep things strictly professional—and that means y'all stop fawning over her like lovesick teenagers. Or you take the first step and woo the girl properly."

"Thank you for the input, Auntie. I will take it under advisement," I tell her. "Now, what's with the Christmas music? We're still three weeks away."

"We're *just* three weeks away, you mean," she scoffs, then raises her voice. "Melissa?"

"Yes?"

"After dinner, I'm gonna get a few boxes out of the attic for you. Feel free to look through them and see what you can put up around the house to make it a little more festive," Darla says.

For a moment, I'm not sure if Melissa registered the assignment, as she keeps staring at us. The silence is almost deafening, heavy enough to drown out even good ole' Frankie.

"Is everything okay?" I ask her.

"Yeah, sorry." She shakes her head. "I zoned out for a moment. I forgot about Christmas. I mean, it's been a while since I've actually celebrated it."

"Y'all didn't put up a tree in Ridgeboro?" Darla asks. I've learned to love my aunt from a young age, despite her occasional outbursts. They're part of her charm.

"Oh, no," Melissa replies. "Any part of the tree, natural or faux, could be used as a makeshift shiv. The warden didn't even put up Christmas lights. Those could be used as rope— for hanging."

"Good grief," Darla gasps, her eyes glistening with horror. "Sorry I asked."

"It's okay." Melissa laughs lightly. "I got used to it. Yeah, I'll unpack the boxes after dinner and see what I can do with the decorations. Sure."

"Thank you," Darla replies, then shifts her focus back to me while Melissa returns to her veal. "You can use this as an opportunity to assist the girl. She shouldn't be left to put the decorations up all by herself. Right?"

"You're absolutely right," I sigh deeply.

I thought Darla's cooking had become dangerous, but it's her matchmaking skills that I should've been more wary of. Then again, I'd be lying if I didn't agree that the home décor boxes do present me with a much-needed opportunity.

After dinner, the house becomes quiet.

Everyone's in their room, snuggling beneath the covers to watch a movie or read a book. It's snowing heavily outside, and frost flowers are quick to blossom across the windows. The smell of fruits and cloves and cinnamon lingers every- where, courtesy of the kitchen doors left wide open. The silence comforts me.

Winter is never easy, not because of the heavy labor, for there isn't much unless we have an emergency to deal with, but because it's a waiting game. It teaches us to settle down and give the season its time to restart the entire ecosystem. The creek often freezes. The temperatures are too low for us to take the cattle out every day. Hell, if the weather keeps up like this, it will be a while before we're able to safely let the animals out to stretch their legs.

Some of the decorations are already up—red, green, and gold ribbons adorning the staircase, white snowflakes hanging from the ceiling lamps, and the miniature Nativity scene on the side table in the hallway.

"I see you've been busy," I say to Melissa as I walk into the living room.

She's struggling with a tangled string of lights, her eyes tired as she looks up at me. "Huh?"

"Thought I'd lend a helping hand."

"Oh. Yeah. Thanks. I don't want to mess this up. These lights are so pretty."

I smile as I sit next to her on the soft carpet, then take over the untangling project. "I remember these," I mumble, the memories rushing back from a distant past. "Ethan and I found them at a shop near Fort Berry, where we were stationed before they sent us off our last tour. He liked the oil-lamp shape of the lightbulbs."

"They're cute. Retro," Melissa says with a smile.

"You're exhausted," I conclude, giving her another glance.

"I just want to finish this, and then I'll go to bed, I promise."

I look at the old grandfather clock in the corner. "It's close to midnight. You do realize Darla won't mind if you get the rest of it done at any point during the day tomorrow, right?"

"Yeah, but…" She pauses and takes a deep breath, lowering her gaze. "I can't sleep."

"Why not? What's troubling you?"

Melissa thinks about it for a few seconds while I visually retrace her hourglass figure beneath the velvety green jammies that are one size bigger than they should be. A woman like her would look glorious in anything tight. My cock jumps at the thought.

"I get anxiety attacks sometimes. They started in prison. Closed spaces make me jittery."

"The house is huge. Your room is the largest on the upper floor," I say. "The warden did mention that we should give you more space if we can. Is this why?"

She nods slowly. "I usually control them. Sometimes I get ahead of the whole thing and stop it from ruining my day. But tonight, I don't know what happened," Melissa says. "I finished putting the snowflakes up about an hour ago. I went up to my room thinking precisely what you suggested; that I'd do the rest tomorrow. I put my head down, and I couldn't breathe. The living room is bigger, so I figured I might as well finish the decorating."

"What starts the attacks?" I ask, scooting closer to her.

"I'm not sure. Sometimes a simple memory. An unpleasant event. I had a fit the other day after I accidentally locked myself in the pantry," Melissa scoffs. "All I had to do was jiggle the latch, but I had to freak out for a hot second first."

"While I'm not a medical professional, I would dare venture a guess and say it has something to do with the absence of freedom."

"Yeah, pretty much. I'm sorry," she says, giving me a kick in the guts with that pained look in her eyes.

It breaks whatever strength I had left, giving me no other choice but to intervene and pull her out of the darkness. I move closer, and she stills for a moment.

"Come here," I say and wrap my arms around her. She feels so soft and warm against my chest, her heart echoing furiously against mine. "Don't ever apologize for the way you feel, Melissa. Your emotions are yours and yours alone. Nobody can judge you for it."

"I know. It's just a force of habit, I guess."

"We need to teach you some new habits, then," I reply, a smile stretching my lips.

She melts in my embrace, her gaze almost golden under the rustic chandelier dangling above us. "What new habits?"

"First and foremost, a woman should kiss her man when he takes her in his arms. Here, I'll show you."

Melissa doesn't object. I kiss her. I take possession of her lips with mine and conquer her defenses with remarkable ease. She loses her breath as she welcomes me, her tongue eager to play with mine. I taste the apple spice and the slivers of pain in her soul, tightening my hold on her as I deepen the kiss.

A delicate moan escapes her throat, and I quickly understand that there is no turning back from this—whatever this is.

5

MELISSA

His hand slips down my back, exploring the hem of my velvety top.

I shiver in his hold, immediately sinking into an even wilder state of arousal. I'll soon lose what little self-control I have left.

Colton stops and looks at me, the tip of his nose against mine. "You are insanely sensitive to my touch," he concludes.

"I think it's because I had no physical contact for so long," I whisper.

"I think it's something else," he replies and proceeds to kiss me again.

He's hungry. I'm hungry. Desperate.

All hell breaks loose as we devour one another, tongues swirling, souls clashing and hands roaming everywhere. I don't even register when my top comes off or when his fingers unclasp my bra and release my breasts.

"Fucking hell," Colton growls as he trails wet kisses down the side of my neck.

I tilt my head back and abandon myself completely. His lips ignite little fires everywhere, my nipples perking as his fingers explore, touching and squeezing and pinching until I whimper from sizzling arousal.

Liquid heat pools between my legs as he beckons me to lay on the carpet.

Colton slips out of his sweater and pins me down with his whole body. I caress his shoulders, registering every muscle and recording every inch of smooth skin as he kisses my breasts.

"Oh, yes…" I whisper, my chest rising.

He takes a mouthful of my bosom, his tongue circling frenetically before he sucks my nipple harder and harder. "You taste like fucking heaven, Melissa," he growls and continues his exploration, kissing every bit of naked skin on his way down.

"It's been so long," I manage, his tongue finding my navel. "Fuck."

My pants come off. My panties are so wet; he peels them off me before he spreads my legs. I glance down and admire the fiercely ravenous look on his face as he gazes at my pussy.

"This must be what heaven looks like," he says.

I'd laugh, but he dives right in, his tongue sliding between my wet folds and setting me on fire. I moan, instead, harshly as he uses two fingers to test my entrance. Pressure gathers in my core, tightening into an electrifying ball that will wreak havoc upon its release.

Colton licks my pussy, reveling in the moment as his fingers go in and curl on the way out. The stimulation is too much to bear, and I clench furiously as he closes his lips around my swollen clit and sucks harder until I fall off the edge of the world.

"Oh, God," I cry out as I come gushing. He finger-fucks me and presses his tongue over the swollen nub, squeezing every drop of this magnificent orgasm. "Oh, God... Colton... OH..."

"That's it, baby, give me everything," he says, forcing me to ride the whole thing out until I'm shaking and spasming with pure delight. "That's it."

The sound of his belt buckle has me opening my eyes.

"I need you inside me," I tell him. "All of you. Please."

"Touch yourself for me," he says, smiling devilishly as he wrestles his way out of his jeans. I love the way his rippling pectorals bounce with each rushed motion.

"Okay."

He stops as his cock springs free. It's huge. It's thick and veiny and twitching, asking for me. I lick my lips as I bring a hand down between my legs. I'm so wet, my pussy still rippling in the aftershock of my climax.

"Yes, sir," Colton says.

"What?"

"That's what you say when I give you an order in the bedroom. Say it."

I can't help but offer a mischievous smile before I bite my lower lip and proceed to touch myself. "Yes, sir."

He strokes himself a couple of times, watching me as I flick my fingers over an insanely sensitive clit.

"Please, sir," I beg him with a pout. "I need you. Please."

"Keep touching yourself," he commands me. "I'm coming, baby, but I need you to come with me."

"Yes, sir."

Colton grins and plunges deep inside me. I hold my breath as he fills me to the brim, stretching me until it almost hurts. He's on top of me, his massive frame obscuring everything else. My fingers keep moving. Teasing. Working my body into a second round of raw pleasure.

Slowly, he begins to move.

One thrust and I whimper and lock my legs around his narrow waist. I keep one hand on my breast, kneading the flesh under his watchful eye while I bring myself closer to the peak of a maddening release.

"That's it, baby," Colton says, pumping harder and deeper into me.

He uses one elbow to support himself, while his other arm snakes around my hips, raising me to better receive him. "Holy fuck," I gasp as he goes all the way into the center of my soul. "Oh, wow. Oh, God, yes! Don't stop!"

"I need to feel you come all over my cock, Melissa."

"Yes, sir," I play along, eager to explode.

Our eyes are locked, our lips glistening and parted as he fucks me faster, harder, deeper. I love the sound of skin slapping skin, his hardened balls bumping with every intensifying thrust. He spears me, over and over, and I stroke my clit, harder and harder. The tension becomes unbearable. His breath is ragged and uneven.

"Fucking hell," he snarls and kisses me, then flicks his tongue over my lips before he bites into my breast, pounding into me like a wild beast.

I fall apart, feeling every inch of him inside me. My pussy clenches hard as I come apart. "OH, GOD!" I manage and bite his shoulder as I let loose. He goes wild and splits me in half, harder and faster until I glaze him with my juices, and he releases everything, and I feel the hot jet of cum streaming through me.

"Oh, Colton."

"Melissa," he whispers in my ear, beads of sweat trickling from his temple.

I taste it. I lick it off his cheek, then kiss him as he gives me the last few pumps.

My whole being is ablaze, an explosive supernova that expands into the great wide nothingness. My lips quiver as they meet his for the kiss that ultimately seals the deal. Tonight, I am his, and he is mine.

We're locked and fused together, having forgotten about everyone and everything else. We've given into a hunger that had been growing within us since the moment I got here.

I'll regret it in the morning, I tell myself again as we dissolve into the sparkling afterglow. He collapses on top of me, leaving soft kisses along my neckline as he takes his sweet time pulling out of me. Not that I mind. My core is still rippling, my pussy still squeezing him tightly.

As the minutes melt into the sweet silence that follows, Colton's body keeps me warm and motionless beneath him. I try to make the most of this moment and live in it fully, unapologetically, but something snaps, somewhere in the back of my head. A pressure builds up in my chest, and it is not pleasant.

Oh, no.

My eyes pop wide open.

I feel trapped under the full weight of the man I welcomed deep inside me. I can't breathe. Everything turns white as I suddenly fight to get him off me.

"Melissa, what's wrong?" he asks, quick to pull back.

"I can't... I can't breathe..."

I'm crying and wheezing, my chest too tight. My lungs hurt. My heart feels like it's about to explode. I have no control over any part of my body. Hot tears stream down my cheeks, and I try to look at Colton, but all I see is an impression of him through a curtain of steaming water. My skin is so tight. My bones so heavy.

"Melissa, try to breathe. You're having a panic attack," he says, gently caressing my bare back, my shoulders.

But nothing seems to work.

His presence alone should be enough to soothe me, yet all it does is push me farther down this spiral of pain and anguish, my inability to regain my senses crippling me beyond repair. I cry my heart out and feel my chest constricting even tighter with each attempt to breathe normally.

The room feels small.

Too hot.

"Outside," I manage. "I need to get outside."

My hands reach for my clothes, but they're nowhere to be found. I can't even feel the carpet's soft, plush fabric, though I know for sure I'm touching it. I do feel Colton's hands like fluttering butterfly wings traveling up and down my arms.

"Hold on," he says.

A second later, he wraps me in a thick blanket and scoops me up in his arms.

I take a short breath in, just enough for my vision to clear and for me to see where he's taking me. It's the middle of the night. There are red, green, and gold ribbons decorating the hallway staircase. White and gold snowflakes. Colton opens the front door. I catch a glimpse of the miniature Nativity scene on the side table.

The icy cold of the winter night hits my face.

Colton carries me outside onto the porch.

It's snowing, a biting wind snapping at my cheeks. But it's working. Somehow, it's working. I hold on to him, hold on for dear life as he shudders and sits in the nearest chair. It doesn't matter that he's cold, it doesn't matter that the snow falls heavier and thicker in the darkness of the night. What matters is that he's holding me close, snuggled in the blanket.

Holding me close and waiting for my panic attack to subside.

"It's okay," he says through clattering teeth. "You're going to be okay."

I can breathe again. The air feels so cold and sharp as it invades my lungs. Blood flow is quickly restored, and I become more and more aware of my surroundings. The ranch unravels at Colton's bare feet, toes mingling with the snow on the porch.

"Colton," I mumble. "Thank you."

"It's okay, baby," he says, kissing my cold cheek. "It's fine. Let it pass."

"I am… It's working. The freezing temperature is doing something right."

"I'll stay out here with you for as long as you need me to," he says, lips constantly pressed against my cheek. Oh, Lord, how can this man be so kind, so good to me?

I snuggle in his embrace, trembling as my body temperature catches up. Soon enough, it gets uncomfortable.

"Okay, please take me back in."

"Are you sure?" he asks.

"I'm freezing my ass off," I say with a laugh. "I'm sure, thank you."

He chuckles and carries me back in. But we don't stop in the living room. No, he takes me upstairs, straight to my room. I end up under the warm covers while he goes back downstairs to lock the front door, to collect our clothes from the living room, and to turn the lights off. A few minutes later, he's in bed with me, his naked body glued to mine as I regain my senses, one layer at a time.

"How are you feeling?" he asks, one arm draped around my shoulders as I rest my head on his hard chest, my fingers absently playing with the few curls of blonde hair just below the base of his neck.

"I'm okay. Breathing is back to normal. Tingling sensation is gone," I reply. "Again, I apologize. I don't know what started this."

"Melissa, I'm going to say it again, hopefully for the last time. Stop apologizing."

"Sorry. Oh, shoot," I huff, almost ready to punch myself. "I'll just keep my mouth shut."

He laughs lightly and kisses my forehead. "The episodes are relatively short, aren't they?"

"Most of the time, yeah."

"A few minutes, tops."

"This one was shorter because of the sudden cold exposure."

He sighs deeply and gives me a tender look. "I'm not really comfortable dumping you out into a snowy blizzard when you have an anxiety attack."

"I won't hold it against you. It works." I smile softly. "Thank you, Colton. I really don't want to get you or myself into any trouble. If this is too much, I'll—"

"There's something you should know," he says, prompting me to lift my head so I can properly look at him. "Before you express your concern about losing this job for the umpteenth time."

"I'm well within reason to—"

"No, you're not," he cuts me off. "I asked my lawyers to file for your permanent employment after you finish your Path to Freedom Initiative program with our ranch. It'll be a smooth transition. You won't have to go anywhere. You are more than welcome to keep living and working here after your sentence is completed."

"Oh…" I'm speechless. My mind has gone blank, yet my heart has grown a few sizes as I stare at this man, this gorgeous man with deep blue eyes and a sandy-blond mustache that tickles me when we kiss. This gorgeous man with a gigantic soul and the touch of a god. "Colton, are you for real?"

"I am, yeah," he chuckles, then pulls me into a deep kiss. "I told you, Melissa. You're safe here. You're home."

"But why?" I ask. "I'm just a cook. An inmate."

"We both know you're infinitely more," he replies. "And if you don't want to see it, well, then, I guess I'll just have to prove it to you."

His lips catch mine.

The taste of him has me drunk and softening beneath the covers. A different kind of heat takes over. The good kind as my muscles melt against his, as my soul begs for his. Soon, we're tangled and making love again. Losing ourselves again, with no care for what tomorrow might bring.

6

MELISSA

Isabella shudders as I brush her mane with gentle strokes. "Oh, I know you love it," I giggle as I enjoy every second I get to spend with this beautiful mare. "Pretty girl."

Growing up in Lincoln, I didn't get to see many horses. I've been around a few, but never close enough to feel their silky coat tickling my fingertips, to feel their skin twitch under my touch the way Isabella's does when I stroke her. She's a gorgeous creature. Downright majestic.

"When Mitch gets back from town, he'll help me with the saddle, and we'll take you and Cosmos out for a ride in the fresh snow. How does that sound?" I ask her.

By now, Isabella has learned that I groom her before and after a ride. And since she hasn't been out today, she can anticipate what comes next. Checking my watch, I know Mitch should arrive in about thirty minutes. It gives us an hour or two for a proper ride before I have to get back into the kitchen and prepare the ranchers' supper.

"I think I'm getting used to this place," I tell Isabella.

I know the mare doesn't understand me, but it does me good to let these words out from the bottom of my heart.

"I'm glad to hear that," Ethan says, startling me.

Isabella stirs beside me, but I quickly and gently tug on her harness for reassurance. She's incredibly responsive to my commands. I'm permanently in awe of her—though I'm even more in awe of Ethan's ability to virtually sneak up on me at any given moment.

"You scared the crap out of me," I gasp.

He smiles as he comes into the barn, the spurs on his boots jingling subtly with every step. That winter jacket hugs his torso and gives him an air of authority, making me feel vulnerable in comparison.

"You should be used to that by now," he says, moving closer.

Elias, his horse, hears him from the stalls and lets out a welcoming neigh.

"He's happy to see you," I mutter, unable to take my eyes off this clean-shaven and slightly stocky Avery man.

"And you're not?" Ethan asks.

The distance between us is shrinking with every step he takes, and I cannot find the will to move away. The pull is magnetic or like a flame, and I'm a foolish moth. My brain goes haywire when I look at his lips.

His icy blue gaze scans me from head to toe.

"I'm always happy to see you," I politely reply. "How can I help you, Ethan?"

"I was just popping in to say hello. Darla said I'd find you here, grooming Isabella. You two seem quite at home with each other."

"Yeah, she's a sweetheart," I say with a smile as I stroke the mare's strong neck.

"She can tell you're a good person, otherwise, she'd never give you the time of day," Ethan replies.

I can't help but blush a little. "Oh, that's sweet. So, I've got the Isabella seal of approval, huh?"

"You've got mine, too," he says.

The air between us thickens and Ethan keeps coming closer. I should do something. Step aside. Get behind Isabella. Anything. But I can't. I don't think I want to because Ethan is nearing, and my heart is throbbing with anticipation and my curiosity is getting the best of me. I shouldn't, but I want to see where this is going.

He is mere inches away now, and my mind's a blank as I look up and lose myself in a pair of cold, blue eyes.

"You're not afraid of me?" he asks.

"Should I be?" I reply with a raised eyebrow.

"My brothers say I can be intimidating, and I gotta admit, I lean into that pretty hard."

"Well, you can lean into that all you want for all I care," I shoot back.

"You don't strike me as the bold type," he says, visibly amused. "What changed?"

"Nothing's changed," I reply. "I'm just not easily intimidated."

"To be fair, intimidating you is not what I planned."

"You just want to see how far you can go with me, right?" I laugh lightly.

"I just want to figure out why I can't stop thinking about you, Melissa."

The words hit me hard, knocking the wind out of me. He takes another step, and I quiver in my boots as I feel his hot breath tickling my lips. I can't move, nor do I want to, and it's an alarming thought, given what I've started with his brother. Whatever this is, it is perilously exciting, and I can't seem to back away from it.

"Ethan…"

"You're clearly not indifferent to this either," he says.

"Well, no, but—"

He shuts me up with a kiss. It is quick and intense, and all of my defenses crumble like a house of cards. One by one, my senses unravel as I feel his tongue spearing mine. A moment later he pulls back, his breathing heavy.

The blue in his eyes is almost black, desire burning beneath those long eyelashes while I struggle to regain my composure. I'm flustered and turned on and definitely losing my mind here because all I can do in response is throw my arms around his strong neck and kiss him again.

His scent—leather and sea salt—fills me. His taste—coffee and maple syrup—makes my core tingle. His body is hard, unyielding as his arms snake around my waist. He pulls me in and deepens the kiss. I devour him, and he responds in kind as liquid heat seeps through my panties. Beneath layers of winter clothing, there are two beings made of flesh and bone, burning for one another.

"No," I manage and finally find the sense to pull back. I step away from him, panting and panicking as I nervously look around. "No, this is… oh, this is so wrong. What did you do to me?"

"I didn't do anything," Ethan quips. "You're the one who asked for seconds."

He runs his thumb over his lower lip, and I damn near come from just looking at him. I shake my head in fear of hyperventilating if I don't put a reasonable distance between us. Ethan doesn't seem angry or offended. If I didn't know any better, I'd say he's actually enjoying this. Maybe a little too much.

"Dammit, this is not okay," I snap. "I can't do that again."

"Melissa, it's alright," he says, slowly raising a hand to touch my face.

I jump back, and for a brief moment, Ethan seems offended. "It's not. Oh, God, if Colton finds out…"

"Melissa, hold on."

I run blindly out of the stables as a steady snow begins to fall. The skies are grey, draped in thick clouds and the cold air pierces my lungs with every frantic breath. My cheeks burn, my lips tingle from the memory of his kiss. I wanted it. That's why I feel so damn guilty.

I wanted it.

And just like Ethan said, I went in for seconds, too.

What was I thinking?

I forget all about my ride with Isabella.

I barely notice the winter cold and the twinkling Christmas lights hung around the ranch house windows as I rush back inside. I head straight upstairs and decide to hide in my room until it's time to start prepping for dinner. I'm staying put, between these four walls, and taking deep, controlled breaths until the panic passes.

7

MELISSA

To my relief, dinner is mostly quiet.

The guys are too tired after a day of hard work in the snow, prepping the livestock for a full winter. I focus on cooking and the cleaning that follows the meal, avoiding eye contact as much as I can. Darla leaves me be, probably because she's also exhausted from driving back and forth to the doctor in Long Pine.

By midnight, I'm showered and tucked in bed, trying to sleep.

I toss and turn, restless as my own past comes back to haunt me. I mull over the bad decisions that landed me in jail. So many regrets. So many things I cannot take back. The future is straight ahead, yet I keep looking over my shoulder and wondering what I could've done differently.

"Dammit, Melissa," I whisper to myself and turn over, dragging the covers with me.

Then, there's a knock on the door and I sit up, my heart suddenly racing. A second knock pulls me out of bed and I tiptoe toward the door. My pulse races as I turn the knob and pull the door open. I think my heart stops beating altogether at the sight of Colton, Ethan, and Mitch standing in the doorway, the dim hallway lighting throwing dark shadows across their handsome faces.

"We need to talk," Colton says.

I stare at him with a mixture of disbelief and confusion. "It's midnight," I whisper.

"It can't wait," he replies.

Panic is quick to set in. "What's wrong?"

"There's nothing wrong," he says. "We just need to talk."

"Can we come in?" Ethan asks.

I nod slowly before I even register my body's own motion. Stepping back, I let the three men walk into my room. Ethan carefully and quietly closes the door behind them while I look at them, wondering what is going on.

Mitch is quiet, but his eyes never leave my face. They say so much in the absence of words—they say things I dare not even think, let alone say aloud. On the other hand, Ethan begins to slowly move around me, one cautious step at a time, while Colton takes a deep breath and gives me a warm, reassuring smile.

"I want you to stop worrying about what happened at the stables today," Colton said.

"You know?" I gasp, then give Ethan a stunned look. "You told him?"

"We don't keep secrets from one another," Colton says. "Don't be mad at him, Melissa. Ethan did the right thing."

I nod at Mitch. "So, I'm guessing Mitch knows, too. That's why the three of you are here at this ungodly hour?"

"We just need you to listen to what we have to say," Colton insists.

My blood is boiling. I don't know what to do. Can a person die of shame? Because that's what it feels like. I'd welcome death if it would ease my embarrassment and guilt.

"Deep breath," Mitch gently says. "You're going to be okay. I promise."

"We're brothers," Colton says. "We don't keep secrets from one another, and we share everything. It's how we've remained close over the years, through school, boot camp, the Rangers, and hell itself. It's how we survived and ultimately thrived. We share *everything*."

Outside, an icy wind howls, making the windows rattle ever so slightly.

"We've shared women over the years," Colton adds. "It's how we function, Melissa. So, I don't care that you and Ethan kissed. If anything, I welcome it. I'm glad you're drawn to him as you are to me. I can tell you're into Mitch, too."

My gaze shoots up and I feel my face burring.

Mitch chuckles softly. "There it is... the adorable indignation."

"You share women?" I mumble.

"Intimately. Emotionally. Yes," Ethan says. "It's not your usual menage. It's on a much deeper level."

91

"A level I know you're capable of reaching with us, if you want to," Colton says. "Look at me, Melissa."

I look at him, my heart thudding viciously and toying with my resolve. It shatters my dignity, and I find myself imagining what it would be like to put all these desires I've been experiencing into practice.

They share their women. What would that be like for me?

"I'm looking," I whisper.

My resistance snaps like a twig.

"What do you see?" Colton asks, the depth of his voice causing the heat to penetrate my spine as he comes closer.

"A man I've already given myself to."

"Would you do it again?"

"Without hesitation," I manage, my lower lip trembling slightly.

Ethan joins him in this slow but steady siege of my senses. "Would you let me join you?" he asks, and my head moves in a nodding motion before I can stop it.

"Will you let us share you tonight?" Colton inquires, desire blazing in the blue diamonds of his beautiful eyes.

"I will."

Mitch offers a soft smile. "Just so you don't feel overwhelmed, I'd like to watch."

"You'd like to… watch?" I mumble, my core clenching with savage anticipation.

"You're one hell of a woman, Melissa. But if we're going to do this right, we have to take it one step at a time," Mitch replies, hands in his pockets. The hard bulge in the front of his pants makes my throat dry. An image of him ramming into me flashes before my eyes.

And I nod again. "Okay."

"Come here," Colton says and pulls me into his arms.

His kiss blows my mind. Our tongues entwine. Our lips crush together as I breathe him in and taste him. Ethan moves to get behind me, and I'm sandwiched between their hard, exquisite bodies. Our hands roam everywhere, finger-tips registering every line, every curve, every layer of fabric left between us.

"Put your hands up," Ethan whispers in my ear, his lips brushing against my lobe.

I do as I'm told, shivering with desire as he takes my top off. My breasts are naked, basking in Colton's full attention. He brings his hands up and fondles them, squeezing and kneading the flesh while I rest my hands on his sculpted shoulders. Ethan peels my pants off, and I'm naked. Vulnerable. Theirs for the taking.

Colton trails kisses down the side of my neck, while Ethan explores my shoulders, one at a time. My skin burns, a fire expanding from within as Colton's lips close around my nipple, as Ethan bites into my neck.

"Oh, damn," I hear myself gasp, stealing a glance at Mitch.

He sits in the chair by the window, his legs comfortably spread, while one hand rests on that ginormous bulge in his jeans. Hunger radiates from under those long, black lashes, his lips slightly parted as he watches the Avery twins pull me apart, piece by piece.

93

"Help me," Colton says.

I smile as I help him out of his sweater, my fingers fumbling with the buttons on his jeans before he chuckles slowly and handles the rest. Ethan's clothes join mine and Colton's on the floor, and all I can do is give him a look over the shoulder as he comes to hug me from behind.

His cock slides between my buttocks to find me wet and wanting. "There's nothing I love more than that sweet, sweet glaze," he says as he brings a hand around my hips.

"Melissa, this is happening," Colton adds and pulls me into a dark, dangerously delicious kiss while his fingers find my nipples and start pinching, tighter, tighter, until the wonderful sting makes me quiver and push my ass back into Ethan.

"Spread your legs for me, darlin'," he says to me.

Again, I obey, eager for what tonight has in store for me. It has already exceeded my expectations. I can't even remember what I was worried and outraged about earlier. I can barely remember my name at this point, but it doesn't matter. Nothing matters except the release my body so desperately needs.

I reach behind me and dig my fingers into Ethan's side, hard muscles greeting me while he slips a hand between my parted legs. He finds my clit swollen, primed and ready, desperate for a good tease.

Colton bends down and showers my breasts with suckling kisses, riddling my skin with delicate red petals, traces of his affection.

"Bend forward," he says.

He takes a couple of steps back, and I bend forward. Ethan's right hand grabs my hip. The left one is busy flicking my clit. At the same time, Colton offers me his gargantuan cock—all stiff and veiny, a drop of precum glistening on the engorged tip.

I look at Mitch. He gives me a slight nod. Oh, God, this is so fucking hot. I let loose, abandoning all common sense as I take Colton in my mouth. Simultaneously, I feel Ethan's hard cock testing my entrance. A split second later, he slips right into me. I scream a muffled scream, unwilling to pull away from Colton while I'm left breathless by Ethan's sheer girth.

He's significantly thicker than his brother, and just as long.

I feel the veins along his shaft twitching as he inches back, then plunges into me.

I hold on to Colton's chiseled hips, looking up to find him smiling lovingly down at me. He bites his lower lip as he tucks a lock of hair behind my ear. I loosen my jaw, moaning with raw pleasure as Ethan starts fucking me harder, deeper, faster. His fingers circle my tender nub, causing my juices to flow and pressure to thicken in my core.

Every stroke of my clit matches his pounding.

Mitch is enjoying every goddamn second of this, his jeans unzipped as he grabs his equally majestic cock and pleasures himself. I'm taut and ablaze, relaxing the back of my throat as I let Colton slide deeper and deeper.

"Take it all, baby," he groans, and I taste his saltiness on my tongue as he pulls back for just a moment, just long enough to caress my face. "You're such a good girl."

"Oh, fuck, FUCK!" I cry out as Ethan's finger savagely massages my clit while fucking me harder. My legs are weak, but I don't want him to stop. He holds me up, splitting me in half as Colton slides his cock back into my mouth.

I come, gushing like a fountain, my pussy contracting with every thrust. Ethan growls and smacks my ass with his bare hand, causing a new round of ripples to explode within me. This has to be some kind of madness. Some kind of miracle, a double orgasm blowing through me as Ethan fucks me into extinction.

"Switch places," Ethan tells his brother.

In the span of a few seconds, my whole world is turned upside down as Colton takes me from behind, and I end up sucking Ethan's cock until he can't take it anymore. I'm fucked out of my mind, shared between two men, filled to the brim and stretched until it hurts so good... I come again, my pussy clenching around Colton's cock tighter and tighter until I feel him explode inside me.

"Fucking hell, Melissa!" he roars as he gives me everything he's got.

Ethan holds my head still. Colton's hand comes down to slap my ass. The sting travels upward as Ethan looks into my eyes. I close my fingers around the base of his cock. I can feel him, so close to the edge. I want to see this. I squeeze tightly and suckle the head, tasting myself as Colton drills the last of himself into me.

"Yes..." Ethan grunts and hisses.

I feel the liquid heat shooting into my mouth, his cock twitching in elation. His salty cum slides down my throat. I swallow every drop, beads of sweat blooming on my temples as Colton lovingly bends forward and cups my full breasts.

He takes good care of me while I take good care of his brother.

Mitch smiles and comes as well, his eyes closing for only a moment as the Avery twins gently guide me to the bed. I'm panting, still high up in the clouds, every fiber in my body shaking in the aftermath of my tumultuous climax. A grin slits across my face.

"We're just getting started, darling," Colton says as I lay on the bed.

"I'll leave the three of you to it," Mitch says after a while. His voice is so smooth and calm. His zipper is back up as he heads for the door. "But I will join you soon enough."

"I want that," I tell him.

He gives me a hungry smile. "Good."

The door closes behind him, and I abandon myself in the arms of my twins. Colton and Ethan revel in the afterglow in honey-like silence

Before long, they're taking turns fucking me again.

Harder.

Deeper.

Faster.

Until I let go, until I fall apart at the seams and hold on to their bodies.

Tomorrow is another story. Tonight is ours, and every damned second counts.

8

MITCH

Melissa is an early Christmas gift.

I see it now. After years spent hoping and praying for the kind of woman who would want the three of us in equal measure, I'd almost given up. I was ready to go back on the market for myself, as were Colton and Ethan. Then Melissa came along. What a beautiful surprise she's been...

And what a mystery for me to unravel.

I'm dying to know everything there is to know about her.

It still doesn't make sense. The woman doesn't even smoke. She gets tipsy after a single shot of whiskey. I simply cannot imagine her driving around with kilos of cocaine with the intention of dealing. I just can't. I'm not the only one either.

Colton and Ethan have agreed to look into it. A sensible question here, a phone call there—discretely, of course, until we find out what the real story is.

She looked so beautiful, being taken by my brothers. Smiling as she let herself go, completely trusting us with her most intimate layers. That's the purest form of trust, and I'm obliged to reciprocate in any way I can. The next time I set foot in her bedroom, however, I'll be the first to claim her.

"What's up with you?" Darla asks, snapping me back into the present.

"What?" I mutter, remembering where I am and what I'm supposed to be doing.

The weather outside is grey and cold. The kitchen, however, is warm and cozy with Christmas decorations hanging all over the walls and cinnamon spice candles burning by the frosted window. The breakfast table is loaded with a second round of fried eggs and bacon, and Melissa is kind enough to bring over a second bowl of fresh fruit salad for Darla, Sammy, and me.

I give her a soft smile as she sets the bowl on the table. "Thank you."

"You're welcome," she says, her gaze warm and her voice as sweet as powdered sugar.

"Something's up with you," Darla insists as Melissa goes back behind the counter and gets busy tidying up. "What is it?"

"Nothing's up," I chuckle dryly.

Sammy refills my coffee from a hot pot. "Don't mind her. She sees trouble everywhere."

"I do not," Darla snaps. "I just know my boys well enough to be able to tell when there's something off."

"Well, is it off or is it up?" I shoot back with a cool grin, then take a long sip from my coffee before I obliterate the eggs and bacon on my plate.

Darla gives me a confused frown. "What do you mean?"

"This something of mine. Is it off or is it up? 'Cause they're two different things."

Sammy holds back a hard laugh and tries to focus on what's left of his plate before he goes out with the ranch hands to patrol the eastern side of the fence. Colton and Ethan are in Long Pine for most of the day, handling some of our family's legal affairs before the year's end. It'll be Christmas soon, and our lawyers won't be back in their offices until after the new year.

"I will knock you so far off that chair, Google won't be able to find you," she replies. Her hand shoots out in a playful attack, but I catch her by the wrist and pull her in, planting a kiss on her soft cheek. "You devil child!"

"I love you, too, Auntie," I chuckle and continue eating my eggs while she and Sammy start bickering again.

"Did you handle those patches on the northwestern fence?" Darla asks, her fork and knife surgically slicing through a slice of bacon.

"Of course. I wasn't dilly-dallying, darlin'. I know my stuff," Sammy grumbles. He tears a slice of sourdough bread apart to gather some of the runny yolks and bacon grease from his plate.

"Yeah, you know your stuff, but those holes have been in the fence for weeks now," Darla mutters. "It wasn't until Kyle got closer during their patrol the other day that they even noticed them. We're sleepin' on this ranch, ain't we?"

"My gosh, woman, you are hell-bent on nipping away at my liver today, aren't ya?"

"Someone's gotta keep you honest."

"And someone's gotta keep you smiling, 'cause I don't like this cranky version of you at all. Let's go to a honky-tonk this weekend," Sammy says, leaning close to her.

Darla rolls her eyes and quickly finishes the rest of her plate. "I'd rather gouge my eyes out with a hot spoon. Make sure you check the entire length of that south fence, too," she says. "The last time we lost a few cows, they were grazing on that side of the pasture."

"You're no fun," Sammy pouts.

"When was I ever fun?"

"You used to be fun."

"Before we had to take over the farm," Darla reminds him. "We're grown-ups now. Remember?"

Sammy nods once. "I remember a lot of things, sweetheart. Even the things you claim to have forgotten. But it's alright. One of these days, I'm gonna remind you."

"Just fix the damned fence, you old dog," Darla chides and leaves the table, stopping by the kitchen sink to deposit her empty plate into the water basin. "There you go, honey," she says to Melissa. "Excellent meal, as always. Thank you."

"You're most welcome," Melissa replies, the shadow of a smile lingering on her lips.

She's heard the entire conversation, and I can't blame her for not being able to keep a straight face around Sammy and Darla.

Speaking of the devil, my favorite auntie points an accusatory finger at me. "As for you, Mitch... I'll find out what's up *and* what's off with you since you thought semantics was gonna throw me off your scent."

Melissa can't handle it and bursts out laughing as do Sammy and I.

Darla tries to keep a serious demeanor as she walks out of the kitchen, yet her mask does crack eventually, and I hear her giggling all the way down the hall.

"You two need to sort things out," I tell Sammy once I hear the front door shut behind Darla.

"I don't know what you're talking about," he replies, now also rushing to finish his plate.

"Right. You don't," I laugh. "Come on, Sammy, you've been doing this back-and-forth with Darla for too long. You both deserve a second chance. We're all rooting for you."

"Spare me the trip down memory lane," Sammy scoffs. "I've known Darla longer than you, boy. We grew up together."

"Yeah. You and Darla and Tammy. I know. And I also know the love between you and Darla is the once-in-a-lifetime kind of thing, and marrying Tammy didn't change that. Not one bit."

"I loved Tammy."

"No one's saying you didn't. But she's gone. And you fumbled Darla."

"Nothing I can do about it anymore."

I smile gently. He's been through so much over the years. I want what's best for him, though, and I know that no other woman would give him the moon the way Darla would. "All isn't lost. Did you see how she keeps bustin' your balls? She expects better of you. If she didn't care, she wouldn't be on you like that. Besides, a little bird told me Darla still hopes you'll try again."

"What little bird? What?" His interest is suddenly piqued, proving a theory of mine.

"Doesn't matter. What matters is you should try again."

"Didn't you just hear me earlier? I did say we should go to a honky-tonk together."

"You don't take your future wife to a honky-tonk, Sammy. Dinner and a movie. Or dinner and drinks. Somewhere nice and fancy. There's a new place on 7th Street in Long Pine. An Italian restaurant. Why don't you try that?"

Sammy shakes his head. "It's not my style."

"It's Darla's," Melissa gently chimes in. "She loves Italian food. She actually said she'd love to try that place…"

"My Lord, my relationship with Darla is the talk of the entire ranch, ain't it?" Sammy gasps, giving Melissa a troubled frown.

"What relationship?" I say and laugh again.

He curses under his breath and gets up from the table. "I'll take care of that fence today," he says, then looks at Melissa. "Save me a lunch plate, will ya', darlin'? I'm not sure when I'll be back, but I saw that turkey in the fridge, and I know you make a mean cranberry sauce."

"Sure thing, Sammy," Melissa promises with a little smile.

Minutes pass in a sweet but awkward kind of silence while she finishes cleaning the worktable in the kitchen and I scarf down the rest of my plate before she clears the table and brews her coffee. I watch her, quietly admiring her curves beneath those jeans—high-waisted and held up with a wide leather belt. She looks good in green plaid. She's starting to look more and more like one of us with each passing day, although her Latin American heritage gives her a particular charm. It makes her more of a rare gem in these parts.

"Their story goes way back, huh?" Melissa asks, joining me at the breakfast table with her steaming mug.

Again, I'm mesmerized as she lifts the mug to her lips and takes a long, cautious sip, her facial muscles instantly relaxing as the drink works its magic on her taste buds.

"For as long as I can remember," I reply, half-smiling. Memories of those earlier days are mostly faded, but I can clearly remember some moments.

"You came here when you were a little boy, right?" Melissa asks.

"Yeah. I'd just turned six," I tell her. "The circumstances of my coming here may have been tragic, but the life I built here... I don't regret a single thing."

"Sammy and Darla were on the ranch, though."

"Yeah, stealing glances at each other. Tamara was still healthy. They were the three musketeers, as old man Avery called them. In their late twenties and still causing trouble here and there. Getting into fights with the neighbors, mostly."

"What for?"

"The fence. That same old fence they're still patching up today," I laugh. "All it takes is one section being compromised, and the neighbors take advantage of it. They sneak in and steal our cattle."

"Oh, wow, that's totally disrespectful," Melissa exclaims.

I shrug, used to the reality of running a ranch in these parts of Nebraska. "Oh, it's better now. Back then, they used to settle these issues with rifles or sugar in the gas tanks. Darla was a fan of the sugar method."

"She was a piece of work, huh?"

"Still is. She just targets it elsewhere," I say. "Thing is, Sammy and Tamara were married when I came here. They seemed to be in love and were trying—and failing—to have kids. Darla was always rooting for them. As I grew up, I could see there were things left unspoken between them."

"Between Darla and Sammy?"

I nod slowly. "Stolen glances. They'd spend too much time together, especially after Sammy and Tamara would have an argument. Darla tried to broker peace between them every time, but she never got involved, never made a pass at Sammy... you know, she's a good and righteous woman. She would never settle for someone else's crumbs."

"I like Darla," Melissa says, admiration twinkling in her eyes.

"Yeah. She's one of those rare birds. Too beautiful, too smart, too strong for most men. Tammy had more of a soft side, I guess. It drew Sammy in, but I know... I don't usually say it, and I never said it to Sammy anyway, but I've always thought, deep down, he regretted marrying Tamara. But I know he loved her."

"There are different kinds of love," Melissa replies. "I get it. But I agree, it would be nice if the two of them could resolve their differences. It's a shame to spend the sunset of your life alone when there's close by, hoping and waiting for another chance."

"Oh, Sammy isn't a saint either," I say. "They tried. About three years back, Darla and Sammy were a couple and it was great for a while."

Melissa gives me a curious look. "You told Sammy you'd warned him…"

"I didn't think he was ready."

"Tamara had been gone for two years, right?"

I nod again. "Yeah, but Sammy was still healing. He was just looking for company, somebody to warm his bed. He'd go into town and get himself a new gal every week. Some younger, some his age. Some paid, some charmed. It didn't really matter to him. I felt that Sammy got with Darla more because he couldn't stand being alone. Darla could sense it."

"Oh, I'm sure she did," Melissa confirms. "Most women can."

"I told Sammy to cool it with Darla for a few months at least. He shot me down. Said I didn't know what I was talking about. A year later, Darla broke it off with him. He was restless and she didn't have patience to nurse wounds he should've taken care of by himself. We were all sorry when they broke up. Hell, I walked on eggshells for months after that."

Melissa smiles. "Let me guess. Darla was a powder keg."

"And then some. Sammy actively avoided being in the same room with her. The fact that they can talk to each other now is a minor miracle."

"Maybe we'll get another miracle this Christmas," she says, her gaze softening as she glances out the window. "You never know."

Giant snowflakes drift loosely across the backyard. At least the latest blizzard's over and we can work around the ranch without going snow blind. It's eerily peaceful out there, as if the land is quietly preparing for Christmas. I suddenly decide I want to do something special for Melissa for the holiday.

"I think we already got our Christmas miracle with you," I say to Melissa, then lean in and plant a kiss on her lips.

She stills, then responds, letting my tongue slip through.

I taste coffee and brown sugar and a hint of the berries she nibbled on while making our breakfast. I smell the jasmine in her hair and the roses from the shower gel she uses every morning.

"That's the nicest thing anyone has ever said to me," Melissa replies as I slowly pull back.

"It's the truth," I say. "And I'll prove it."

I get up from the table and gulp down the rest of my coffee, then head out. But before I leave the kitchen, I stop in the doorway and give her one last look. "By the way, I loved what I saw last night," I tell her. "I look forward to what comes next."

She's speechless, flustered. And judging by the darkness in her eyes, she's also turned on. Nothing adds a kick to my heels better than the thought that I'm able to turn her on with such ease. Her lips stretch into a smile, and I give her a playful wink.

Once I'm outside, I zip up my coat and take a deep breath, spending a few moments on the porch before I head over to the stables. The cold air fills my lungs. The mornings are rough but beautiful out here. I wouldn't trade them for anything, especially knowing I'll be coming back to Melissa and a nice tall cup of mulled wine this evening. I can almost smell the red wine bubbling and the spices as they melt into the pot.

I imagine that gorgeous woman simmering in my arms, naked and wanting. I want her full surrender. Her complete abandonment of self. I want to protect her and make her smile, and should the weather turn stormy, I want to be her safe haven.

9

MELISSA

"I've never seen ranchers take their cattle out in the winter," I say, riding my darling Isabella next to Colton's Apex.

Ethan and Mitch circle the herd with their horses, dogs running around to keep the cattle in check. We're in the southern pasture, with the partially frozen creek acting as fence of sorts, keeping the animals from wandering off.

"Some ranchers leave them out to pasture all winter, but we like to keep ours sheltered so the grass can have a chance to grow back. Luckily, we're blessed with a bit of good weather today. Temperatures just a smidge above freezing," Colton says, smiling as he watches his brothers wrangling and laughing when one of the calves tries to explore the snow away from the herd. "We figured we'd get the big girls moving a bit before they're mostly confined for the next few months."

"You keep your animals happy."

He nods once. "It's the right thing to do. I know most people don't agree with our approach, but we're able to up the prices within a reasonable range and nobody ever bats an eye. Hell, if anything, our orders double in the spring."

"Was it always like this?" I ask.

"Nah, my brothers and I implemented this practice when we took over. Our father ran the ranch the old-fashioned way. There wasn't anything wrong with it, but the competition was slowly crushing us. Ethan's the one who suggested we figure out ways to keep our cows happy. It sounded silly at first."

"But then it started to make sense."

"Mmm." He gives me a long, curious look. "You like it here, don't you?"

"I love it," I quickly reply. "It's beautiful. The air is fresh and clean. I'm surrounded by good people. What's not to like?"

Colton flashes a cool smile. "Would you go back to Lincoln after you finish your sentence?"

That's a good question.

I have an answer, but I don't think I'm ready to say it out loud. I don't think I'm ready to admit it either. For as long as I can remember, I've had an aversion to drastic changes in my life. Yet coming here was precisely that.

"I think I'll answer that another day, if you don't mind," I tell Colton.

"That's alright. There's no rush. We'd like to have you here for as long as possible, though. I figured you should know."

"You would, huh?" I ask, thinking about the permanent position here when my time is served.

He steers Apex closer to Isabella. Our horses get along great, occasionally nudging one another in a playful manner. Isabella isn't as fast as Apex, so when we're racing across the pasture, I noticed Colton's horse doesn't dart ahead like he normally would when he's up against Cosmos or Elias. Apex actually slows down a little so my mare can keep up, and it's the sweetest thing.

"I know the paperwork has been put in for you to work here after your sentence is over, but you could always choose another path," Colton says, his gaze softening as it searches my face. "But wouldn't you agree that there's something between us? I don't want it to have an expiration date."

"Neither do I, but isn't it complicated? I mean, how would it work in the long run?"

"You've thought about it," he smiles broadly.

My face burns pink. "Well, yeah."

"That's sweet. Thing is… if you want something to work, you figure out a way to make it work, right?"

"I'm sure that applies to a car engine or a pie recipe, but not a relationship between four people, for Pete's sake," I shoot back, almost laughing as I shake my head. "This is crazy, Colton. I never imagined I'd be involved in something like this."

"Neither did I. Yet here we are," he says.

"Yeah. Here we are," I sigh deeply.

I can see the southern gate about a hundred yards away. Beyond it, a road stretches, connecting the ranch to the outside world, above it is an endless stretch of blue sky.

But a truck that pulls up to the gate is what catches my attention. The uniformed man who gets out of the truck is unfamiliar to me, but I can't see much from this position. He's steady in his movements, looking over the entire southern pasture as he gets closer to the gate.

"Colton follows my gaze. "Probably a prospector."

"A prospector?"

"Yeah, everybody wants to buy this land from us," he says with a heavy sigh. "Once a week, sometimes even twice during the summer months, people stop by. A few of them keep coming back, surveying the land. It's almost ridiculous. Though I get it."

"Prime real estate, right?"

Colton nods once. "For developers, for industrial farming, yeah. But it would destroy the ecosystem here. It would throw the other ranchers in the pit, as well. One of the reasons why the big industries haven't breached these parts of Nebraska is because we, the ranchers, have stuck together."

"Passing the lands down through generations?"

"Yeah. We'll do the same, you know," he replies, and I look at him. The hint of a smile stretching across his lips fills me with a peculiar, sweet warmth. A promise that has yet to find words. "Our children will inherit this land. And these plains and these hills will remain clean. Green. Like nature intended."

"You're brave, I'll give you that," I say, glancing back at the man by the gate.

"Why brave?"

"Most people would take the money. I suppose you've been offered well above the market value. Or am I wrong?"

"You're not wrong," Colton chuckles.

Somewhere behind us, I hear Ethan and Mitch are shouting, laughing. The cattle moo as their hooves thunder and crunch in the hardening snow. The dogs are yipping and barking.

"But the money is worthless when you've got all of this laid out at your feet," Colton adds, a beam of pride emanating from his blue eyes and his voice at the same time. "Money can't beat this view nor the bounty the land offers."

I nod in agreement. "I'm no rancher myself but know enough to recognize the value of this place. You've got rolling hills and strips of plains in between, you've got woodlands and the creek running through... I'll bet it's as green as emeralds in the summer."

"We have a small lake, too," Colton replies.

"Oh. I didn't see it. I thought you gave me the full tour."

"You'll see it in the spring. It's far on the north side and surrounded by thick woods. You haven't seen the whole thing because it's about 1,500 acres."

"Whoa, that's a lot."

"It is. But you have plenty of time to explore the entire property, that I can promise you."

And I believe the promise as much as I believe the kindness with which it's intended. If there's one thing I'm able to say for sure, it's that Colton and his brothers really do want me here.

The intimacy of our relationship could either boost the whole thing or jeopardize it, though. I don't know what to make of it. I want it to work. The way I feel about them demands it. But life has a way of kicking me in the gut when I least expect it.

"He's leaving," I mumble, watching the man by the gate return to his truck.

"May he have a blessed day," Colton chuckles, then gently nudges his horse with his heels to get him moving. "Come on, I'll teach you how to use Isabella to keep the cattle close to one another."

Come evening, my thighs hurt.

The muscles are sore, and the inner sides are slightly chafed even though I had on the thickest pair of jeans I own. Then again, we were out riding for hours, and I'm not used to being in the saddle for that long. Isabella loved it almost as much as she loved the bucketful of apples she got as a reward. And speaking of rewards, the guys were spoiled rotten with a veritable feast, as well.

"That was the biggest roast I've ever laid eyes on," Darla says after dinner, her dessert plate almost licked clean.

I join the table with a plate of my own. "Honestly, I outdid myself with the meat," I say, my fork slicing through the apple pie I made for dessert as though it's made of butter. "Oh, this is insanely tender. I'm loving that oven more and more."

"You used Marty's butter for the dough, didn't you?" Darla asks, half-smiling.

"How'd you know?"

"His is the best butter in the county. That's why the pie came out the way it did," she says. "Beats any store-bought butter by a mile. I asked him to send us a few boxes last week, and I'm glad to see you're putting it to good use."

Sammy is already upstairs, probably dozing off in his chair by the window while trying to finish a Cormac McCarthy novel. The boys have also signed out for the evening, so I'm left with Colton, Ethan, Mitch, and Darla for the remainder of this dinner—not that I mind. Sometimes it's nice to serve fast and then get a moment for myself to enjoy what I cooked.

Colton's thigh brushes against mine under the table.

I give him a shy smile. "Darla's right. The butter from Marty is exceptional."

"It's why his ranch is going so well. We call it the Butter Ranch," Colton says.

"The Butter Ranch," I laugh lightly.

"He supplies the entire county," Darla chimes in. "The man feeds his cows with some kind of magic. I don't know what it is, but that butter, dang it. Ours come close, but not like his."

"Happy cows, I'm guessing," I say.

Ethan scoffs. "I'm not going to serenade the cattle with my guitar, if that's what y'all were thinking."

"You'd make their ears bleed. Relax. Karaoke Keegan," Mitch chuckles.

"You play the guitar?" I ask Ethan, while the others laugh.

He offers a timid shrug. "A little. I'm no Elvis Presley, if that's what you're wondering."

"He's tone deaf, but we support him," Mitch is relentless, but Ethan doesn't mind. This is their usual banter, and it is drenched in brotherly love. There are moments when I think I never would've gotten in trouble with Jake if I'd had a sibling to keep me on the straight and narrow. A pang of regret lingers in the pit of my stomach.

"So, Melissa, tell us," Darla says after a while, pouring herself a glass of scotch. "Cooking's your thing, right? Your calling?"

"Yeah, pretty much. It's what I've always wanted to do," I reply, savoring the pie filling's ensemble of tastes and spices. That nutmeg kicks in right when it's supposed to, and the cloves are subtle enough to give it its own personality. "I've always dreamed of having my own restaurant."

That gets everyone's attention. All eyes are on me, and I can feel my cheeks warming under the amber-tinted ceiling light. Outside, it's frosted and quiet. All around us, sparkling shades of red, green, and gold decorate almost every surface —Darla decided to buy more Christmas-themed decorations, putting them up herself last night while everyone else was asleep. She's either restless about her medical tests or she's really getting into the holiday spirit.

"Your own restaurant," Mitch says. "That's ambitious."

"It's not impossible," I reply with a slight shudder.

"Oh, no, not at all. It's impressive," Mitch replies. "If you aim high, you have better chances of getting there or at least as close to that goal as possible."

"As opposed to settling for scraps," Ethan adds.

Colton gives me a curious smile. "What kind of cuisine would your dream restaurant have, Melissa? Italian? American?"

"Actually, a fusion between French and Italian," I reply with a smile. "It's like the best of both worlds for me. The buttery French sophistication mingled with the Mediterranean simplicity of the Italians. And I'd have a separate menu just for the desserts."

"Let me guess. Butter everywhere," Darla shoots back. "I know a guy for that."

"I'll definitely want to meet Marty at some point," I say. "I really am curious about how he makes that incredible butter happen." I pause to finish my pie, my mouth experiencing a culinary orgasm in the span of a few moments.

"I think it has something to do with the churning process," Colton says. "The last time I went over to Marty's a few years back, he was thrilled about some new churning machinery he'd gotten straight from an up-and-coming manufacturer. The guy was from California, but he was trying to break into the Midwestern market."

"Now that you mention it, I'm pretty sure that's when Marty's butter really started picking up," Mitch nods in agreement. "We should pay him another visit and take Melissa with us."

"Wouldn't that qualify as industrial espionage?" I ask.

"Do you plan on making a better butter than Marty's?" Colton raises a skeptical brow.

I shake my head. "Nope."

"Then it's not industrial espionage."

"I'm glad that's settled," Darla grumbles and gets up to clear the table. "If you'll excuse me, I need a couple of hours to sit down and let this dinner work its way through me before I hit the sack."

"Oh, don't worry about this, I'll do it," I try to intervene, but she gently nudges me back into my seat.

"You will not. For all the goodness you've filled our stomachs with, the least I can do is throw some dishes in the dishwasher. Relax and pour yourself a glass of scotch, honey. Rest."

"Thank you."

The guys rise and help Darla as she stacks the plates on top of one another, then they carry them over to the dishwasher. Darla methodically slides everything into the bottom rack before she adds the cutlery and a detergent capsule.

"All clear. I'll see y'all tomorrow," she says, one foot already out of the kitchen.

"Darla, hold on," Colton says, stopping her in her tracks. "You didn't tell us how your doctor visits went this week? Any closer to a diagnosis?"

Darla lets a heavy sigh roll from her chest. "Not really. They suspect a combination of causes now. Hormonal, a viral infection. I got a new treatment to try for the next couple of weeks. Let's hope this one doesn't make me break out in hives. Last month was hell."

"You'll tell us if you need anything, right?" Mitch asks.

"I sure will, kiddo," she smiles and walks out.

A minute pours by in a thick, pressing kind of silence. We're alone, now. The four of us, burning for one another, desire secretly sizzling between us. It's been such a busy and tiring day that this is literally the first moment I've actually gotten to simply sit down and enjoy the dessert I made.

"Darla's right," I mutter and pour myself a shot of scotch. I down it in one gulp, neat and fiery as it burns my throat, instantly spreading the sweetest, most comforting heat through my whole body. "Actually, let me get a second one."

I manage to even pour a third before Colton chuckles and takes the bottle away.

"That's enough for you, young lady," he says.

"I'm nervous."

Mitch smiles, leaning close enough for me to catch a whiff of his enticing cologne. "What are you nervous about?"

"Being alone with us," Ethan says, leaning back in his seat. Meanwhile, his boot nudges mine under the table.

"Well, yeah," I mumble. "I think I'm allowed to feel that way."

"Just as we're allowed to help you unwind so you stop feeling that way," Colton says, then pulls me into a kiss.

My defenses are immediately obliterated. Hell, I never stood a chance. I receive him with nothing but delight and raw hunger. Mitch's voice tickles my ear, his lips brushing my cheek. My body temperature spikes as I slowly turn to focus on him. His dark eyes drill holes into my soul, and I surrender without so much as a modicum of protest. I don't want to resist.

"Let's take this upstairs."

We go to my bedroom. Tonight, however, the anticipation of what is to come makes me shake with excitement before my clothes find the floor. Colton takes me in his arms while Ethan and Mitch casually remove their sweaters and jeans. Candles burn by the window, but only the pitch black of night awaits beyond the frosted glass. Ice flowers creep around the corners, while the central heating system makes my room feel cozy and warm.

"You're still nervous," Colton says, planting soft kisses all over my face.

Mitch comes closer, and I find myself staring at his magnificent, naked body. Ropes of toned muscle stretch across his torso, his shoulders broad and his hips narrow, perfectly sculpted, pulling my gaze farther down to his insanely strong thighs and twitching erection. Oh, Lord, he's just as big and just as hard and just as eager to take me, and all I can do is lick my lips as I look up at him.

"I've never done this before," I whisper. "All three of you?"

"It's alright," he says, gently cupping my face. "You don't have to do anything you don't want to."

He and Ethan undress me, one button at a time, while Colton gets rid of his clothes and watches as his brothers peel away at my layers until I'm left naked and wanting, quivering as liquid heat trickles down the insides of my thighs.

I reach up and put my arms around Mitch's neck. We kiss and let our hands roam everywhere while Colton and Ethan take their sweet time touching me, exploring me with their lips and their fingertips. I melt against Mitch's rock-hard pecks, his cock throbbing against my womb as Colton spreads my legs and lets his tongue slide through my wet folds, fingers digging into my butt cheeks at the same time.

"Oh!" I gasp, and Mitch suckles on my lower lip while Colton licks me into a trembling frenzy. Ethan's hands slip around the front, kneading my breasts as my head falls back, and Mitch brings his hand between us until he finds my clit.

Colton licks my entrance with burning enthusiasm.

Mitch flicks my swollen nub, teasing and adding tension to my core.

Ethan pinches my nipples, tighter and tighter until I squirm.

I lose myself and disappear somewhere in the dark pools of Mitch's eyes as he pushes me over the edge. I come shaking, arousal flowing freely as my pussy clenches in its tempestuous release. Mitch keeps flicking my clit, pressing and rubbing and destroying my senses altogether.

"That's it, baby, come for me," he says, his voice hot and harsh.

Colton's fingers slide in, pumping in and out of me until I come a second time, quickly after the first. I cry out, gushing like a fountain and holding on to Mitch for dear life while Colton bites my ass cheek and Ethan kisses me. Hungry. Desperate. Needing so much more.

"Oh, God," I manage, unable to stand.

They guide me to the bed, and as soon as I lie on my back, Mitch is on top of me, pinning me into the mattress with his full body weight. Colton and Ethan climb up, kneeling to my left and right, their sturdy, veiny, delicious-looking cocks mere inches from my lips. I surrender to my instincts, my most primal desire, and I reach for them. My fingers lock tightly around the base of their thick shafts.

"That's a good girl," Colton hisses as I take him in my mouth first. I lick and suckle on the bulging head, tasting the precum before I do the same to Ethan.

"Fucking hell," Ethan groans, and I feel a vein pulsating along his length and against my tongue. A twitch of longing travels through my body and makes my hips rise as Mitch spreads my legs.

With a mouthful of Ethan, tears of joy stream down my cheeks as Mitch enters me, stretching my pussy into the wildest madness of passion and complete surrender. Slowly but surely, a rhythm is established. The pace heightens with every thrust.

"You're the most beautiful woman I've ever had the honor to share," Mitch says, watching me suck Colton's cock while simultaneously stroking Ethan's.

I'm so wet, so primed for this.

It's insane, but I don't want it to end.

Mitch fucks me harder and deeper, my moans reverberating across the room. He spears me with his full, thick length, over and over, thumb teasing my tender clit again.

"Oh, fuck, this is perfect!" I cry out as a third orgasm blows through me. "Harder, baby, please... HARDER!"

I've lost my mind.

Mitch happily obliges, ramming into me until he, too, comes. His heat fills me, and I feel his essence melting into my body, his thrusts downright savage as my breasts bounce under his lustful eyes.

"My turn," Ethan says.

Mitch smiles like a lazy tomcat and lies on the bed beside me, watching as Ethan takes his turn and starts pounding me into oblivion. I keep one hand on Mitch's face, lovingly caressing him while my other hand is firmly fondling Colton's hard balls while he slides down my throat.

"Fuck," Ethan growls as he, too, comes inside me.

My pussy is overly sensitive with every thrust, and I feel his climax rippling through me. Mitch nibbles on the side of my neck as Ethan pulls out and Colton takes his place.

Colton throws my knees over his shoulders and slaps my ass, pounding me into the mattress until I'm close to passing out.

"Don't stop," I gasp, my hand instinctively nestled between my legs.

I coax myself into a fourth climax, losing complete touch with reality as I clench Colton's cock tightly with my pussy. I feel the stream of his cum shooting deeply into me, I hear the sound of skin slapping skin as he lets go of himself.

Colton grunts in pure ecstasy, loose and out of his mind as he pumps me full of his seed.

"I don't want this to end," I hear myself whisper.

A thin, silky layer of sweat covers my naked body. I'm tender and blushing. Sparkling and glowing, naked and surrounded by three of the most incredible, most dashing men I've ever had the fortune of crossing paths with. And tonight, they're mine.

The power is in my hands.

"It won't end until you end it," Mitch says.

And I carry his words with me into the milky shimmer of a most wonderful afterglow. Christmas may only be a few weeks away, but I already feel like I've been shot straight to the top of the nice list, because this is the best gift I could've hoped for.

10

ETHAN

"What do we know about her so far?" Mitch asks.

It's been three days since the three of us shared her. Three days since we claimed Melissa and made her a part of us, whether we're ready to admit it or not. It's a dangerous move, I know. We should've done the digging first, but our instincts made the decision for us.

I don't regret a single moment.

Hell, I relive it every night, every time I close my eyes.

"Born and raised in Lincoln, Nebraska," Colton says, going over the notes in his phone.

We're in the stables, out of anyone's earshot except for the horses. Elias is giddy and eager to be ridden. He's itching for a run across the snowy plain, but he knows I have to brush his coat first. It's part of our morning ritual.

"Melissa is an orphan. She was placed in the foster system when she was two years old," he says, his brow furrowed with empathetic grief.

"She must've slipped through the cracks, bounced from one foster home to another, from one group home to another."

"That's precisely what happened," Colton says. "She did try to stay out of trouble, but the other kids she used to live with kept roping her in. To her credit, she doesn't have a juvie record, nor was she arrested until the big one, so either she's smart and slippery or just—"

"Lucky as hell," I say.

"She was living in Ainsworth with a Jake Miller when she was arrested for driving that cocaine van," Colton continues, his thumb scrolling through lines of text on his screen. "She was working in the kitchen of a local watering hole. Diner-slash-pub, they called it."

"Flipping burgers and tossing fries," Mitch sighs. "She never really stood a chance, huh?"

"The system doesn't help these kids," I say. "Most of them end up in prison or dead in a ditch. A few join the military…"

Colton gives me a sad look. "Do you think she gave up on trying to keep her nose clean and just leaned into the drug distribution gig?"

"No," I say with a firm shake of the head. "Not buying that."

"Me either," Mitch replies.

Colton frowns. "Her boyfriend testified against her."

And now my interest is beyond piqued. I can almost feel a quiet kind of fury taking over as I begin to piece the whole picture together long before Colton finishes reading some of the details he picked up from his calls.

"What did he say in his testimony?" I ask, bracing myself for the worst.

"That it was his van, but Melissa had been using it for her late-night errands," Colton says, sounding as doubtful as Mitch and I clearly are. "He didn't know she was moving cocaine with it."

"Does the guy have a record?" Mitch replies.

Colton sighs. "Not that I could find and none of Melissa's past friends who I reached out to could tell me much about him. Just that they seemed deeply in love. He moved in with her about a month after they met, and then she pretty much fell out of touch with everyone."

"Something stinks here," I say.

"We need law enforcement help," Colton says. "I don't have access to any more information, especially where this Miller guy is concerned."

Sammy's boots alert us to his presence just before he speaks. "What are you three sneaking around for?"

"Who's sneaking around?" Colton replies but, at the same time, slips his phone into his coat pocket, looking like a kid who just got caught stealing candy. "We're not sneaking around."

"I would've agreed until I saw that look on your face," Sammy croaks and bursts into laughter. "What are y'all up to? We're supposed to revisit the south gate today."

"We're getting the horses ready," I tell him.

Mitch gets busy putting the saddle on Cosmos while Colton does the same for Apex. Elias loves an extra brush on his hind first, so I oblige, then grab his saddle and carefully set it on his strong, muscular back. It's sunny out there, despite the biting cold.

"Where's Darla?" Mitch asks Sammy.

"Heck if I know. Somewhere around the house, probably yelling at a supplier over the phone," he grumbles. "Gotta make everybody miserable just before Christmas."

"Oh, shove it, you love her when she's snapping at suppliers," Mitch shoots back, laughing. "It's how she gets the deliveries done on time. If it weren't for Darla, we'd all be eating canned beans and stale bread for Christmas. Let the woman work her magic."

"I'm not gettin' in her way," Sammy replies, then goes over to the stalls.

His horse, Murdock, neighs with anticipation. He's stockier than our mustangs, but he's got plenty of strength in his legs. That horse has seen some of the harshest winters in recent years, and he has yet to bat an eye when Sammy takes him out. Then again, today's going to be mild compared to the incoming blizzard announced for this weekend.

We let the old fella lead the way on horseback, and we follow.

It's going to be a long and loaded day since the southern gate needs some serious repairs. The damage occurred overnight, but it didn't exactly come as a shock. We knew the pillars might need replacing, and it took a hefty load of snow to prove us right. That gate needs to be back in full form before the weekend, otherwise we're going to have trouble.

Of course, said trouble is nothing compared to the mess we're going to embroil ourselves in if we don't cover our bases with Melissa. I want to know everything about her, including the things she doesn't want to share. I want to know her secrets, her darkest most sinful side, if only to find myself somewhere in there.

Colton and Mitch are the only people who truly know me.

They've seen me at my worst, deep in the bloody battlefield. They know what I'm capable of if I let loose. Secretly, I hope Melissa does have a dark and dirty side, just so I can better resonate with her. Just so she won't be appalled when she gets to see mine.

That's real love in my book.

And it's the most dangerous kind.

11

MELISSA

Thursday evening, the guys take me into Long Pine for drinks.

Darla and Sammy are manning the ranch in our absence, with Sammy doing the cooking. It left room for plenty of jokes regarding his ability to whip up a decent dinner, but since Darla's been having her taste issues, Sammy is the second best qualified to feed the ranch folks without killing them, so to speak.

"It feels weird not being in the kitchen at this hour," I tell Colton as we take a seat at one of the corner booths of the Cavalier, Long Pine's surprisingly not-too-shabby pub and diner.

"That's just force of habit," he replies, handing me the drinks menu. "Get yourself a drink, and the weirdness will slip away."

"Word of advice. The tequila makes everything slip away," Mitch quips.

"Including my consciousness," I laugh. "No, thanks. I think I'll stick to mulled wine tonight."

Ethan nods in agreement. "That actually sounds pretty good."

"This is nice," I say, casually leaning back as my fingers splay across the seating to enjoy the velvety feel of the burgundy red fabric. "Really nice."

"It used to be a local dive. A shady watering hole until about eight years ago, when the owners sold it to Marty," Colton says.

"Marty, the butter guy?" I ask.

"Yup."

"The man does get around," Mitch chuckles softly. "Lots of butter cash to spend."

Looking around, I see some familiar faces—mostly people I've met running with Darla. A few I met at the farmers' market here in Long Pine. It's nice to see them unwinding in the evening, laughing and drinking as the juke box takes everyone on a trip down '80s memory lane.

"Thank you," I tell the guys with a soft smile.

"For what?" Mitch asks me with a curious glimmer in his dark eyes.

"For taking me out on a date, I guess," I shrug shyly.

Mitch covers my hand with his. "Honestly, we can do a whole lot better than this for a first date. How about we consider this a night out for drinks and chatter instead?"

"Well, to be fair, we did agree we're going to keep things fun and simple," I say, reminding myself that I shouldn't bite more off than I can chew.

"I don't know about you, but I could eat," Ethan intervenes. "They make a mean pizza here at the Cavalier."

"Pizza sounds great," I reply, and he waves one of the waitresses over.

As soon as she sees us, she lights up like a star. Spry-looking and in her early twenties, the girl has a familiar shape to her face, her eyes, her smile, and overall demeanor. I can't put my finger on it, but I feel as though I've seen her before.

"Ah crap," Mitch mutters as soon as he sees her.

"Ah crap, what?" I ask him.

"That's Daisy," he says, nodding at the bubbly waitress practically gliding toward our table. "Sammy's niece. Bit of a Velcro chick."

Sammy's niece. Hence the familiarity. I recognize some of her features now.

"A Velcro chick?" I mumble, then give Mitch an even more confused look.

"Sticks to you like Velcro," Ethan says. "That is, if you're a guy and you seem rich."

Mitch looks at Colton. "You know the drill, Colt."

"What? What's going on here?" I ask, but nobody seems to want to answer.

All I can do is take a deep breath and put on a pleasant smile as Daisy reaches our table. A bubble gum blonde with bright blue eyes and brownish freckles spattered across her round face, she measures me from head to toe before she puts on a contemptuous smirk and whips out her pen and pad.

"Welcome to the Cavalier, fellas, it's been a while," she says.

"It's good to see you, Daisy," Colton replies with a soft nod. "Hope you're well."

"Oh, I'm much better now that you're here," she quips.

I glance around at each of the men and take a cautious deep breath. They don't seem interested in her, but she sure is interested in them. Her eyes are sparkling, and she keeps pushing her chest out under the guise of keeping a straight back.

"How've you boys been?" Daisy asks, her gaze glued to Colton.

"Great, thank you," he says. "Just work on the ranch keeping us busy. You know how it gets in the winter."

"There's ways to keep warm in the winter," she replies. "I remember giving you my number."

"Sammy would hang me by my balls," Colton laughs, a nervous tension hardening his voice as he gives me a brief but wary look.

I don't like the way she is deliberately acting in front of me. I've dealt with her kind before in prison, inmates who thought they could bat their eyelashes at the guards for special favors, employing every trick in the flirty female's book. It's disrespectful in my presence since I could be Colton's woman. I kind of am. I'm also Ethan's and Mitch's, but Daisy doesn't need to know the details.

"I'm ready to order," I cut in with the same polite smile. "I think I'll have some of that mulled wine I smelled when we first came in, and—"

"How's Uncle Sammy?" Daisy chooses to completely ignore me, laser focused on Colton the whole time. "He hasn't been around either."

Doesn't she have his phone number, too?

"Like I said, the ranch is keeping everybody busy," Colton replies.

"You could always sell a part of it. I hear Mr. Haynes is still looking to get about 500 acres off you if you'll consider it," Daisy says.

Ethan gives her a hard look. "Are you a broker for Mr. Haynes now?"

"Nah," she laughs. "Just sharing some of the gossip. He's always in here, moaning about how you don't wanna sell."

"Some mulled wine would do great," Ethan says. "The lady is ready for you to take her order."

Daisy looks a tad surprised, even offended. But she smiles and starts writing things down without ever looking my way. "Alright, then. Mulled wine, you said. For the four of you?"

"Yes, ma'am," Mitch says.

"Make that for the three of them. I'll just take a lemonade. And we're gonna order a couple of pizzas, too," Colton adds. "A carnivore and the Cavalier special."

"You're the designated driver, huh?" Daisy asks with a giggle.

"Yes, ma'am."

"I like my men sober," she says.

I could kick her.

Ethan senses my muted hostility and squeezes my thigh under the table. I feel his firm touch through the thick fabric of my jeans. It's enough to soothe me as I exhale deeply and give the girl one final glance.

"I'll have dessert, too, after the pizza," I say.

"Sure thing. A fruit salad? Something light to keep the figure in check?" she asks, eyeing me.

"I'll have the pecan pie with two scoops of vanilla ice cream," I reply, my tone sharper.

Daisy rolls her eyes, and the atmosphere around the table changes subtly. She doesn't immediately notice it, but Mitch and Ethan are completely put off. Colton isn't her biggest fan either, yet he remains polite. I'm guessing they don't want any issues with Sammy in the future.

By the end of our dinner and drinks, Daisy has made enough trips to our table to make it clear to me that she plans on trying to get into Colton's pants sooner or later. He keeps politely diverting every flirty attempt she throws at him, yet she keeps coming back for more. Once the check is paid, I can feel my heels on fire.

"Thank you for the generous tip," Daisy says and places a hand on Colton's shoulder. "I'll buy you a drink sometime, handsome."

"That's nice of you, Daisy, but that's not going to happen," Colton replies.

"Oh, you'll change your mind. Have a wonderful evening, gentlemen!" she giggles and sashays away with the bill and the cash in one hand.

I shake my head slowly. "Some people have a nerve."

"She's twenty years old." Mitch says, chuckling softly, "and prettier than most girls in town. She thinks it opens every door. But Daisy is harmless, Melissa. Trust me."

"I trust you. I don't trust her."

"Come on, let's get you home," Colton suggests and gets up.

"Yeah, let's," I respond crisply.

"There's nothing to be jealous about," he says, stifling a smile. "It's cute how she riles you up, though. She's just a kid. Harmless."

"You keep throwing the word around," I say and roll my eyes at them, "as if you've never dealt with a determined woman before. Young or not, she knows what gets a man's blood pumping; that much is obvious."

Ethan steps closer, his hand resting on the small of my back, while Mitch gets our coats, and Colton looks for his car keys. "Melissa, you're the only woman who gets our blood pumping," Ethan whispers. "Besides, nobody in our family wants to mess with Daisy. Not even Sammy. Her own uncle. We're all just being nice."

As soon as we step into the thick snow, and the cold air hits my lungs, I shudder under my coat and hurry to Colton's black pickup truck. The night is a harsh mistress during Nebraskan winters, and I can't wait to get home and cuddle under the blankets, wrapped in the arms of my three men. It certainly beats what I had anticipated what this Christmas would look like back in Ridgeboro.

"What do you mean you're all just being nice?" I ask the guys once we're all in the truck.

Colton smiles as he starts the engine with the turn of his key. "Daisy has a penchant for trouble, the legal kind," he says. "She's been a troublemaker since she was thirteen and doesn't seem like she's going to change anytime soon."

"She hangs out with the wrong crowd," Mitch adds. "Sammy's had to bail her out of jail a couple of times. Perry, the bar owner, is good friends with Sammy, otherwise he never would've let Daisy anywhere near the cash register."

"Oh," I mumble, "and her parents?"

"Just as reckless," Colton says. "Sammy practically grew up on our ranch with our father because of the nasty situation at home. His whole family was trouble, and it got passed down to Daisy. Sammy had our father to steer him away from them. He checks in on the girl once in a while, but he's come to realize there's only so much he can do."

"Can't protect her from herself," Ethan scoffs.

I nod slowly, watching the world go by in the darkness as Colton drives us out of Long Pine and onto the main road leading back to the ranch. There's not much to see at this hour, except for the twinkling lights of houses up on the hills and a full moon rising above, a fat pearl that seems to see and know everything its soft light touches.

Once we're home, I make my way upstairs.

Colton, Ethan, and Mitch follow. I give them a look as I turn around and get out of my boots first. Not a word is said while Ethan closes the door to my room and dims the overhead light, then proceeds to also undress. Mitch and Colton do the same, and the tension between us thickens to the point where I can barely breathe.

"You guys are determined, aren't you?"

"Do you want us to leave?" Mitch asks.

"No," I take a deep breath. "I guess I've just never been pursued so thoroughly before."

Colton steps toward me and slips his hand between my legs. "We will always pursue you. You're our woman, Melissa. Ours. Don't ever doubt that."

My resistance crumbles altogether. I throw my arms around Colton's neck and kiss him, breathe him in, taste the hint of lemon on his lips. It becomes a swirling chaos of hot bodies and sizzling hearts as they take me to bed and claim me over and over until I'm completely exhausted.

"I could get used to this," I whisper, half asleep as I rest in Ethan's arms.

Colton sits on the edge of the bed, while Mitch plays with my hair, his head on the pillow next to mine.

"You could," Ethan says.

Basking in the sweetest afterglow, I know they're not done with me yet. I can feel Ethan getting hard again. His pulse racing. His heart thudding against my ribcage.

"It's not a good idea," I mumble, closing my eyes for a moment.

"I think it's the best idea you've had so far," he insists.

1 2

COLTON

Come morning, as the sky gives us a grey nod of what's to come, I let Melissa rest in my arms for a few more minutes before we start the day. Ethan and Mitch are already downstairs, getting ahead of the breakfast situation. We can hear the pots and pans clanking, and it makes Melissa giggle as she hides her face against my chest.

I love this feeling.

It's a tricky situation. I'm letting myself fall before I get a full picture, and it could be a recipe for disaster. I know it, and so do my brothers. Yet none of us are hitting the brakes either. Regardless of her past, Melissa came to us for a fresh start.

"You know they're going to serve burnt bacon and charred eggs if I don't go down there soon, right?" Melissa says, raising her head so she can look at me.

I love the way her rich, dark hair falls over one shoulder, a splendid mess framing her beautiful face and soft, hazel eyes that sparkle when she smiles.

"Give them some credit. They *can* cook."

"Are you sure?" she says just as something made of glass breaks downstairs.

"We're not entirely helpless, you know," I say to her. "We can always whip up some PB&J if push comes to shove."

"Darla will wring my neck like a chicken."

"Nah, she barks a lot, but she doesn't bite."

"That doesn't sound as reassuring as you think it might since the prison expects a monthly review of my performance," Melissa replies.

I kiss her softly on the lips, welcoming the warmth she covers me with beneath the thick blanket. "You'll always get glowing reviews from us. Besides, I'm the one writing them, not Darla."

"Oh, so you're the one I need to keep happy."

"You most certainly excel in that aspect," I say, then decide to take advantage of this private, peaceful moment between us. The clock is still ticking, and my brothers and Sammy are counting on me to join them later so we can finish the southern gate repairs today. Judging by the wind I can already hear rising outside, the blizzard will land at some point tonight.

"Melissa, I need to ask you something."

"What is it?"

"What happened with Jake?"

Slowly but calmly, she sits up, the sight of her gorgeous, bare breasts making my throat feel dry. It's hard to focus with her naked, but I do need answers. I need the whole truth if we're to turn this into something more—Melissa deserves a real, fresh start, too. No secrets. Nothing between us.

"What do you want to know?" she replies, a slight tremor in her voice.

"How did you two meet?"

Melissa glances over to the window, her gaze hazy as she takes a trip down memory lane. "I was working at a diner in Lincoln. My last shot at a decent job in that city, to be honest. I'd gotten in trouble at my previous workplace. The manager was a handsy type of sleaze, I punched him in the nuts... anyway, that's a story for another time. The diner was okay. Relatively safe. Jake kept coming in, working on his laptop, drinking way too much coffee. He was always nice to me, you know? He made me feel like I was worth something."

"I suppose you loved him," I say, unable to ignore the aching pang in my heart. It's a selfish thing to feel, so I keep it to myself. Of course, Melissa had a life before us.

"I thought I did," she replies with a heavy sigh, a bitter smile blooming on her lips. "Thing is, most of the time, we think the person we love is amazing, but we just project onto them what we want, you know? It's our love that makes them special."

"So, Jake wasn't that special?"

"He lied. From the moment he struck up a conversation, he lied through his teeth about pretty much everything. About what he did for a living, about where he lived, the people he knew, where he came from. For almost a year, I thought I'd finally found the one. He played the part well; I'll give him that."

"What do you mean?"

Melissa chuckles nervously as she gets out of bed. "He bought me flowers, took me out on dates. He made just enough of an effort to make me go all the way with him, to stop guarding my heart around him. He said all the right things, but at one point, I stopped minding his actions and only fed on his words. I was blind."

"So, what happened?"

"He moved in with me. I was renting a studio apartment on the nicer side of town. His apartment was being fumigated, he said. It was only supposed to be for a week. Then he said the building was raided by inspectors. It was condemned. The city would reimburse him—"

"I smell BS."

"If only I'd smelled it, too," she scoffs. "Actually, I think I did smell it. I just didn't want to face it. Anyway, weeks turned into months. His income dramatically fluctuated. There were days when he splurged on food and even bought me expensive chocolates, the Belgian ones. Then there were days when I had to fill up his gas tank so he could get around. He said his delivery business had ups and downs, that it was normal."

I nod slowly and get out of bed. "I'm sorry you had to deal with that kind of man."

"Hey, it was a lesson learned, a very expensive and life-altering lesson," she chuckles, "but the best lessons are like that, huh?"

I sense the sadness in her voice, the emotional exhaustion. I don't know what it was like for her in prison, but I can imagine that three years is a long time—long enough to reflect, to go over every chapter from her past and to draw the wisdom she carries with her today. Most women her age are looking for a husband or are eager to grow their careers, to travel and have fun, to live every day to the fullest.

Melissa, on the other hand… she's tempered, calm and tranquil. Surprisingly positive considering the shitty hand fate dealt her. And despite the panic attacks and her softness, she is incredibly strong and resilient. I like that about her. I admire that.

At breakfast, it's just the two of us. Ethan and Mitch are getting the horses and the tools ready with Sammy, while Kyle and Jason are in charge of patrol. They've been tasked with checking the eastern gate pillars for similar defects. We may not be able to fix them before the blizzard hits, but we'll know what to watch out for when the snow settles.

I can hear Darla upstairs, vacuuming the hell out of each room.

"The drugs were Jake's, weren't they?" I ask Melissa, practically out of the blue.

"Like I told Darla when she first asked me," Melissa replies, holding my gaze with firm conviction, "that crap wasn't mine. Everything Jake said in court was about him, not me. He's the one with a secret life. He's the one who made money from moving drugs for various dealers and cartels. I never touched the stuff."

"And the night you were arrested?"

"Ainsworth is a small town. The delivery business Jake claimed he was building couldn't grow much without expanding into neighboring towns or so he said. Point is, that night, he called and asked me to move the van for him."

She goes on to tell me how it all went down from the moment she got behind the wheel to her arraignment. And every step of the process convinces me that Melissa is, in fact, innocent. "He had access to my laptop, my phone, my things. We were living together after all. It was ridiculously easy for him to plant the evidence the DA needed to nail my ass to the wall."

"Nobody believed you."

She shakes her head. "They kept offering me deals, telling me that if I gave up my dealers and my suppliers, the judge would go easy on me, that I'd get probation. It's not like I could pull names out of my ass for the sake of a deal. I didn't know any of Jake's dealers. And then we went to trial."

"And Jake testified against you."

Melissa's lips twist with disgust. Even so, I'm tempted to kiss her, if only to make everything go away. I want to see her smiling and laughing. Damn, how did she burrow so deep into my heart?

"He sure did. He matched his story to every piece of evidence the cops found. I don't know how much he paid them, but he supplied the DA with a couple of witnesses who confirmed that they'd seen me moving product with his van before."

"Who were the witnesses?"

"Laurel something and Bruce whatever," she sighs deeply. "I didn't even know them, but they said they knew me. Honestly, I don't think the DA ever bothered to check their stories, to see if those so-called witnesses were in any way connected to Jake."

Well, I have some new information to work with now. New names to look up and track down. Whoever Laurel and Bruce are, they knew Jake Miller. It's time for me to reach into the past and start talking to old friends of ours from the

Rangers—fellas I know moved into law enforcement after they were discharged. Generally, I don't like calling in favors, but this situation demands that I tap into every possible resource.

"You will be vindicated," I tell Melissa at one point.

She gives me a bitter smile. "I doubt it. What's done is done. There's no point in dredging up the past. I just want to start over and forget Jake Miller ever existed."

"I think we both know that's never going to happen," I say. "That man had a lasting impact on your life. You loved him, you were close to him, you trusted him, and he destroyed you, took away five years of your life."

"Just three, actually," she says. "If I spend the next two out here with you, I'll be more than happy. They certainly won't be wasted years."

She has a way of softening me when I least expect it. Mindful of Darla's footsteps upstairs, I chuckle and pull Melissa into a long, ardent kiss. I'd like nothing more than to brag to the whole world about her, about what a fine woman she is. But the world is shallow. Most people wouldn't understand. And in these parts of Nebraska, they wouldn't understand how my brothers and I operate either.

13

MELISSA

Darla is out until the evening running the last of the errands before the weekend while the guys are handling the southern gate issue. I thought I'd feel weird being in the house all by myself, but it's nice. The halls are decked, the air is loaded with a soft hint of apple and cinnamon, the candles burn gently in their brushed bronze trays, and I'm almost done decorating the Christmas tree.

My heart is so full, overflowing with a warm kind of sweetness. And I'm honored and humbled that they asked me to do this. When Kyle brought the Douglas fir in earlier this afternoon, I was beside myself. Heck, I almost cried when he told me Colton and his brothers were "kindly asking" me to decorate it. Of course, the guys knew it would make me so happy.

Once Kyle supplied me with the ornament boxes, I was ready to get to work.

"Lord, you look so pretty," I tell the tree, now mounted in the living room by the eastern window.

Mug in hand, I freeze when someone knocks on the door. I know to keep the doors locked when I'm alone, and there are motion sensors and cameras everywhere, so the guys know if somebody comes through the gates. Whoever is on the porch right now, the Averys or their ranch hands can't be too far behind.

"Who is it?" I call out.

But there's no answer, just a second knock.

I set the mug down and cautiously walk to the door. One look through the peephole, and I can feel my insides burning. An unpleasant heat washes over me as I break into a cold sweat—an odd sensation I'd hoped never to feel again.

"Jake," I say with a trembling voice as I open the door. "What the hell are you doing here? How'd you find me?"

He looks different, meeker. He hasn't gotten much sleep lately judging by the dark circles under his eyes. His over-sized black woolen coat makes him appear thin. His legs look like two sticks coming out of a barrel. He's clearly had a rough few years.

Good.

"Hey, Melissa," he says, his voice soft, his smile friendly. "I wasn't sure I'd found the right ranch, but I saw you with the cattle the other day and—"

"That was you," I gasp, "by the gate?"

"Yeah," he chuckles. "Sorry, I didn't mean to come by unannounced. I just wanted to see you." He looks me up and down. "You look wonderful."

Once the initial shock wears off, the anger I thought I'd bottled up and hidden somewhere in the recesses of my consciousness, somewhere deep and dark enough that it would never see the light of day again comes back with a vengeance.

Every muscle in my body tenses, fury loading my fists with an itch to hit him, to throw things at his head, to pummel him into a bloody, lifeless mess who I once thought I'd raise a family with. Unbelievable.

"What the fuck do you want?" I ask, my tone clipped.

"You're angry; I get it," he says. "But if you'll just let me explain—"

"Explain what? You framed me!" I shout, my rage at a maximum level. "I went to prison because of you, you asshole!"

Jake takes a deep breath and nods with an infuriating sort of piety. "I did you wrong and dirty, Melissa. And I need to apologize first and foremost."

"I was sentenced to five years in prison. My record is forever blemished. There's no apology in this world that will ever fix what you did to me. Those were your drugs!"

"And we're in trouble, Melissa," he interrupts. "That's why I'm here."

"What the fuck are you talking about?" I manage.

It's cold outside. A rising wind blows through the house, bringing some of the snow in with it.

Jake notices me shivering in the doorway. "Can I come in? We need to talk. I swear I come in peace," he says.

"Fine," I reply with clattering teeth.

The guys should be on their way back anyway. But just to be sure, I take the phone Colton gave me out of my jeans pocket and briefly text him while Jake steps into the hallway and politely shuts the door behind him. My instincts are on fire, but I'm not sure what the danger is—Jake was never violent, nor did he ever threaten me in any way. For as long as I can remember, he was soft and well mannered, and that doesn't seem to have changed. It's just his shitty character that I've become aware of.

"Okay, I am sorry," he says. "I am so sorry for what I had to do. But I didn't have a choice, I swear, Melissa."

"You didn't have a choice but to lie about me in a court of law?" I shoot back. "It's perjury in case you didn't know."

"It's in the past either way. I can't change any of it. I'm sorry for that, too."

"Oh, good, you're sorry. All is well and right with the world again. Whoop-dee-doo."

"All isn't well and right with the world because the cartel knows you're out."

Again, I find myself dumbfounded and staring at him, unable to keep up with what's coming out of his mouth. "The cartel?"

"Those drugs you were moving—"

"The drugs I was unknowingly moving for *you*."

"Yeah, they belonged to the Esparza cartel," Jake says, "Colombians who've spent the past decade setting up quite the market out here in Nebraska. You don't want to mess with them. They're bad, Melissa. Really bad."

"Not my fucking problem. I'm still serving my sentence."

Jake smiles. Part of him is enjoying this. He's trying to be apologetic, but the true side of him is slowly but surely rearing its ugly head as he speaks. "Melissa, those drugs were worth about two million dollars. The cartel wants their money."

"Oh, my God," I gasp, finally realizing what he's saying. "You didn't just pin this on me with the law. You sold me out to the cartel, too. You fucking bastard!"

I take a few deep breaths to regain my self-control as Jake keeps talking. I can feel a panic attack coming, and I certainly can't afford to be in any way impaired or vulnerable in his presence. The more I hear, however, the deeper I sink into despair, making it harder and harder for me to breathe.

"Oh, Jesus," I mumble, holding on to the edge of the Nativity side table to stop myself from crumbling to the floor.

"They were going to kill me," Jake says. "I had to tell them something that night. It's how I got the idea to testify against you, in fact. And I know it sounds awful. I get it, but I didn't have a choice. The Esparza cartel… Melissa, they slit throats and hang the bodies out for everyone to see in order to send a message. I didn't want to end up with a Colombian necktie over a goddamn mistake."

"A mistake?"

"You weren't supposed to take that route. I specifically told you, remember? Take Maverick Avenue. Stay away from Circle Street. And you went right down Circle Street… there were cops there, screening traffic for a van."

"They were tipped off," I say, remembering my crappy defense attorney's notes during our prep sessions prior to the trial. "They were tipped off about *your* van."

"Well, I made enemies in that business," Jake says and sighs. "It was only a matter of time before they got the cops involved just to mess with my operation."

"Why did you ask me to move the van for you?" I ask.

Jake shakes his head. "Believe me when I tell you that none of that matters anymore unless we find a solution."

"Unless *we* find a solution?"

"Your ass is on the line, too," he says.

"My ass belongs to Ridgeboro Correctional Facility for the next two years," I reply harshly.

"Melissa, the Esparza cartel wants their drugs back. Or two million, cash," Jake sighs again. "I tried to get my hands on the stuff, but the cops have it. They put it in evidence, and it will be destroyed sometime this year, which leaves us both short by about two million bucks to stay alive."

"Jake, you've lost your damned mind. This is *your* responsibility."

"They think you were stealing the drugs from me that night."

My stomach drops. All I can do is lean back against the wall, my vision gradually losing focus.

"They... oh, God," I mumble, tears pricking my eyes.

"I know, I know..."

"You know," I repeat his senseless words, wishing I had some strength left to beat him bloody because that's what he deserves. "I finally had some peace. I was okay with going through the rest of my sentence... and then you... you show up—"

"I didn't want to, believe me," Jake says. "But I had to tell you… Melissa, it doesn't look good. I can't exactly walk back on everything I said either. I'm just here to warn you as a favor."

"To warn me?"

"The Esparza cartel. I found you here, and so will they. So you need to figure out a way to get them that money before they do. I can hold them back for as long as I can, throw them off your trail, but that's it."

The blows just keep coming.

"You want me to get two million dollars so the Esparza cartel, whose drugs *you* lost by putting me in *your* van, so they won't kill *me* for your fuck up? Am I getting this right?"

"That's correct. It is what it is, Melissa. There's no other way around it."

"And what if I get a better lawyer and appeal my sentence? A good defense would probably poke holes in every lie you declared on the stand."

Jake's expression darkens. His once-bright brown eyes take on a feral glow, and he moves toward me. For the first time, I see the real Jake, the monster hiding behind good manners and soft-spoken words. The bastard who put me away, who destroyed my life. And I'm afraid. I am genuinely afraid, paralyzed, barely able to breathe.

"If you so much as think about screwing me, Melissa, I'll release the hounds of hell. I'll let the cartel come for you. They won't even bother squeezing that money out of you. They'll just torture you until you beg them to kill you. And then, the cops will find your body in pieces scattered all over Nebraska," he says, his voice cold, his glare deadly.

"You fucking prick," I snarl. "Where am I supposed to find two million dollars?"

"You're a resourceful girl."

"I'll go public—" I say but he slams a fist into the wall right next to my head, and I yelp, the blood rushing up to my head with lightning speed.

"I'll tear you to fucking shreds!" Jake snaps.

A split-second later, he's yanked away and thrown out the door like a sack of potatoes. I hear his grunt as he lands on the porch, the thuds accompanying the rolling motion down the steps.

In his stead, I see Ethan.

"Ethan," I whisper, though I still can't move.

"Are you okay?" he asks, panting with raw anger.

I nod slowly, though we both know I'm lying.

"Who's that?" he asks, pointing at Jake, who's done tumbling in the snow and is now struggling to get back on his feet.

"Jake," I manage.

Ethan pauses, his gaze darting between Jake and me. The look on his face is impossible to decipher, but I feel the deadly intention in each of his moves. He's like a tiger on the prowl, the blue of his eyes are pitch black as he walks back out. With automatic movements, I follow him to the edge of the porch just in time to see Jake get up.

"What the fuck, man?" Jake shouts.

"You punched my wall and threatened a lady," Ethan replies bluntly. "A lady I'm very fond of. So, at this point, you have two options."

"Whoa, buddy. Melissa and I go way back—"

"I know who you are, you piece of shit. Your options remain the same. You stay here, and I kill you slowly or you get the fuck out of here and never show your face around these parts again. I'm giving you five seconds."

Jake laughs nervously, but Ethan's hand is already reaching behind him where he keeps a gun holstered on his lower back.

"Hey, I'm not trying to start anything here. Let's chill," Jake says. But his gaze follows Ethan's hand as well, and he knows what's coming if he doesn't choose. "Buddy, come on."

"Five," Ethan says.

"Now, hold on—"

"Four."

"Get out of here, Jake," I tell him, shaking like a leaf beside Ethan. "We're done talking."

"Three."

"Come on, Melissa, I'm trying to help you…"

"Two," Ethan says.

And Jake finally takes a few steps back, raising his hands in a defensive gesture. "Alright, alright, I'm going. I'm going."

"One."

"I said I'm going!" Jake replies and starts running to his pickup truck. The snow is thick and treacherous under his boots. He slips a few times, stumbling and falling and crying out in pain from the tumble he took down the porch.

Ethan watches him like a hawk, hand fixed on his gun, ready to whip it out.

I hold my breath until Jake gets in his truck and fumbles around with the key. A second or two later, I hear the old engine roar to life, and Jake swerves around and back up the driveway leading to the gates.

"Melissa," Ethan turns to me with the same dark look on his face.

Nausea wraps me in a bitter blanket, a horrible taste invading my mouth as I realize I'm going to puke all over him unless I get to the bathroom. "I'm so sorry," I reply and bolt into the house.

Ethan doesn't follow me.

I spend the next half hour hunched over the toilet, crying and losing my lunch down the drain. My chest hurts, my throat burns. Droplets of cold sweat cover my face, dripping down my temples until they seep into the collar of my plaid shirt.

Just when I thought I was out from under the dark cloud of my past, it descends on me once again.

14

MELISSA

The Avery brothers stay away for a few days, giving me room to breathe and process what happened with Jake. In the meantime, they've alerted the staff to keep an eye out on the security feeds on their phones. Jake can never be allowed to get that close to the house again.

I can't bring myself to tell them the truth: The reason Jake was here in the first place. If what he said is true, then it's only a matter of time before the cartel tracks me down at the Avery Ranch. I can't put these good people in such terrible danger.

"Oh, fuck," I mutter as I stare at the plus sign on the pregnancy test I bought secretly when I went to town with Darla. The sickness wasn't just from my past catching up to me.

My synapses are rapidly firing as I toss the stick into the bin and come out of my ensuite bathroom. What do I do?

It takes a while, but I manage to make my way back into the kitchen and prepare lunch for the crew as a blizzard rages outside.

Sammy, Kyle, and Jason take their seats at the table, where I've already laid out the bowls, the drinks, and the bread baskets. The stew is just about ready, though it needs another minute to cool down.

I'm so hungry, I could eat the whole pot.

"Melissa, are you alright?" Sammy asks, while Kyle pours water in his and Jason's glasses. "You don't look well."

"Oh, sorry. I'm just tired. This weather is making me feel groggier than usual."

"Tell me about it," Sammy says. "I hate being cooped up inside like this."

"Yeah, he needs to be out there, roaming the wild plains with the other mustangs," Colton says as he and his brothers come in.

Suddenly, the atmosphere in the kitchen and the dining area changes. The ranch hands can't really tell, but I certainly can feel it. The stench of secrets and fear engulfs me as I give Colton, Ethan, and Mitch a warm, welcoming smile. "Hey, guys," I mumble. "Lunch is almost ready. Have a seat."

"It smells fantastic," Mitch replies.

Sammy is nibbling on a slice of sourdough rye. "This is good bread, Mel. Did you bake this?"

"Yes, sir," I reply with a hint of pride. "Putting that stored grain of yours to good use."

"Someone had to grind this," Sammy says, frowning as he glances down at his bread. "Who'd you fool into grinding the flour?"

Kyle clears his throat. "Guilty. Did it yesterday before the blizzard landed," he says. "I almost froze my ass off in the barn, but clearly, it was worth it. Dang, this is good bread."

"I'm glad y'all like it. I baked it with love," I say with a chuckle, trying my best to ignore Colton, Ethan, and Mitch's quiet yet persistent gazes. "Darla isn't joining us. Is she okay?"

Colton nods once. "The meds the docs have her on are making her extra sleepy. She'll find her way to the fridge if she gets hungry."

"As long as she doesn't touch my sausage," Sammy cuts in. "Only got one left, and it cost me a fortune."

Mitch gives him a wry grin. "Oh, Sammy. Pretty sure Darla doesn't want to go anywhere near your sausage, you dirty old man."

"I meant a real sausage!" Sammy croaks, his face red with indignation.

The whole room bursts into laughter before Ethan focuses on me. I almost scrape my knuckles on the cheese grater when he calls out my name.

"So, Melissa."

"Um, yes?"

"Are we going to talk about the other day or are you planning to keep us in the dark?"

"Sorry. Yes," I reply with an awkward smile, my heart beating a million miles per minute. I'm dangerously close to hyperventilating, but I chew on a piece of parmesan instead while stirring the rest of the grated cheese into the veal stew. "Like I said before, I'm really sorry about all that."

"What did Jake want?" Colton asks.

"He was trying to reconnect, I guess." God, I hate lying.

Mitch raises a skeptical eyebrow. "Reconnect? After he threw you under the bus and sent you to prison?"

"If I were him, I'd have moved to Mexico by now," Sammy adds.

"He heard about my position with the Path to Freedom Initiative. I don't know how, though," I say with a heavy sigh, then carry the pot over to the table and place it on a sturdy wooden board for the guys to help themselves. "My guess is he had somebody in Ridgeboro keeping an eye on me."

"An inmate or a prison guard," Mitch surmises.

"Yeah, that's my guess. But honestly, I don't care about his endgame, I just don't ever want to see him again. I regret opening the door. I guess I was curious about what he had to say," I reply, filling my bowl with more food than usual.

Colton notices, half-smiling. "The cold's upped your appetite, huh?"

"It's a really good stew," I respond, hoping the conversation about Jake will end here.

But Ethan's not having it. "What did Jake say specifically?"

"He's sorry he did this to me, but he can't change it. He had no choice or whatever. Really, it's not worth anybody's time or attention."

Ethan clears his throat, elbows resting on the table as I sense his anger bubbling just beneath the surface. "Melissa, he had you cornered and shaking. I heard him say he was going to rip you to fucking shreds before he punched the

159

wall. That wasn't an attempt at reconnection. That was intimidation."

"Yeah, I guess. He didn't like it when I told him to screw off," I blurt and get up, unable to sit still for another second. My skin is crawling, my sweater too tight, my palms all clammy, my appetite scrambled. "I... Listen, I'll let you guys have lunch. I'm not that hungry after all."

"Melissa, hold on, we need to talk about what happened," Colton takes my hand, but I yank it away as though I touched a hot stove.

"No! We don't need to talk about it. I'm really sorry it happened, but there's nothing to address here," I snap. "Ethan was clear when he told Jake never to show his face around here again, and I'm sure Jake will keep his distance."

"You're not telling us something," Ethan announces.

Mitch gives him a stern nudge. "Stop. She'll tell us when she's ready."

"I'm sorry for the trouble," I say, trembling again. "Things got out of hand, but it will never happen again. I just want to do my job and serve out my sentence."

"We want the same thing," Colton replies.

Sammy frowns. "Mel, if that fucker is giving you trouble, all you gotta do is tell us. The law in Nebraska is pretty clear about trespassers and a man's right to self-defense."

"Oh, God, no, it's okay," I laugh anxiously. "Thank you, though. You are the sweetest man ever, Sammy."

With that, I bolt out of the kitchen and up the stairs to my room. Thankfully, none of them follow me.

* * *

THE GUILT IS TOO much to bear. My thoughts are scrambled. My resolve is in the gutter.

It's Christmas Eve.

We're supposed to gather around the tree, drinking eggnog or hot chocolate in my case, unwrapping presents and watching a movie on TV. We're snowed in again, and it's beautiful outside. I gaze out the window of my room, wishing my heart could be as silent and as still as this night.

I hear them downstairs.

Talking. Joking. Laughing.

It's been a week since Jake's visit, since my world was turned upside down, and I have yet to figure out a way to tell Colton and his brothers the whole story. How can I? How can I tell them the Esparza cartel is coming after me because of something I didn't even do? That the ranch and the people who live here might be in danger.

I can't tell them any of that.

And I can't stay here either. It's bad enough that Jake ruined everything—again. I couldn't live with myself if something were to happen to any of these wonderful people.

I've put everyone in danger simply by being here, and it's not fair.

"Melissa," Colton's voice startles me. He's at my door, waiting for me to let him in.

I take a deep breath, putting on a sour face. I've been faking a headache all day. Gotta play my part and keep my distance, no matter how horrible it feels. It's killing me. But the more I think about it, the clearer my decision becomes.

"Hey," I mumble as I open the door.

"How are you feeling?" he asks, holding up a cup of hot chocolate with tiny marshmallows on top. It smells of honey and cocoa, and it makes my mouth water. "Figured you'd like some."

"Thank you." I take the cup and hold it with both hands for a while, letting its warmth flow through me like some kind of newfound peace. "I'm still not feeling all that great. I think I just need some time alone."

"You take all the time and space you need," Colton replies softly. "I'm not happy about it, but if it's what you want, I can't force you to be where you don't want to be."

I give him a long, curious look. "How are you so kind and understanding, Colton? I don't get it. I brought that bastard here, and—"

"That wasn't on you, Melissa. It was all him. He's the one who decided to show up uninvited. But rest assured, it's not going to happen again," he says. "I look forward to talking about what happened that day, and I know you'll tell us when you're ready. In the meantime, I'm content with just knowing that you're okay, that you feel safe here, 'cause we love having you here."

His gaze lingers on my lips for a sweet moment.

"I don't deserve you," I tell him with a heavy sigh.

"Oh, but you deserve so much more." He laughs lightly. "And let's get one thing straight: You have to fight back, Melissa. You have to clear your name."

"That'll do more harm than good," I mutter, but even I can hear the doubt in my voice.

Clearing my name would certainly get the Esparza cartel off my back. Who would believe me, though? Jake worked closely with the prosecution to nail me. He fabricated witnesses and planted evidence. He played his part so well that I didn't stand a chance.

"When it became clear to me that the only way to avoid a much longer sentence was to give a false confession, I understood that the system wasn't on my side. Jake played his cards right. Shed a tear here, planted some fake proof there, and wham. I was done for," I say with a trembling voice. "I would like nothing more than another shot at a trial, but I don't have any evidence. No witnesses. It's just my word against his. I was so shocked, so stunned by Jake's presence here that it didn't even cross my mind to use the recording app on the phone you gave me. I could've gotten something for a defense attorney. But I didn't think of that."

"Melissa, it's okay. No one expects you to know everything and to think of everything when the unexpected happens. I just need you to understand that you're not alone in this, not anymore. You have to learn to let us in."

"Ethan was so quick to protect me. And how did I repay him? By not telling him the whole truth. He must be so mad. We've barely spoken this week."

"My brother isn't good at expressing his emotions," he says. "Granted, I'm not a model of emotional health and neither is Mitch, but among the three of us, Ethan is the worst."

"I've seen worse." I chuckle.

"He wants you to be safe and happy. And he wants you to open up, much like Mitch and I. We all want the same thing, Melissa. We just need you to want it, too."

"I need a bit of time is all. A little more time to figure some things out," I reply, my heart breaking as I plant a kiss on his lips and take a couple of steps back.

He smiles and nods slowly. "You've got it. But you should still join us downstairs."

"I can't. I'm sorry."

"Santa left you a little something under the tree."

"Oh, no, he didn't."

"He sure did. You've been a very good girl."

The way he says the words arouses me on a whole new level. I'd rather tear that sweater off him and have him fill me, stretch me, claim and consume me, instead of sulking up here in my room. But the distance I've put between us is more for their protection than mine.

"I'll see you in the morning," I say, my voice barely audible, my throat closing up as I force myself to smile.

"We'll have coffee."

"Mmm."

Colton closes the door, and I listen to the sound of his receding footsteps before I burst into tears and start rummaging through the drawers. I grab only the essentials and shove them in a duffel bag—just enough to get me out of Long Pine. I saved all the change from every errand they sent me on, and I've got about fifty bucks in cash. It should cover me for a day or two before I land a diner gig somewhere far away from here.

I'm leaving tonight.

It's snowing again. It's past midnight, and as I sneak down the flight of stairs, I can hear the winds raging outside. I hear the snow pummeling the house as well as ice flowers bloom over the windows. One candle remains burning in the living room on a solitary sill, its amber light dancing against the treachery awaiting outside.

It's insane. It's senseless. Yet I can't think of a better way to keep the Avery brothers out of this new, terrifying chapter of an old mess that has cost me too much already. I don't want my baby to be born in prison. I don't care what I do with myself as long as I find a way to stay safe, healthy, and out of Jake's and the cartel's reach.

Looking around, I make sure no one sees or hears me as I carefully tiptoe toward the front door. I find Mitch's car keys in a catchall bowl and fish them out. I'll leave his truck somewhere easy to find and pray for his forgiveness. I'll drive until I'm far enough from the ranch and close enough to a Greyhound station. Lord, have mercy on my soul for what I'm about to do.

The house is dark and quiet but for that little candle, so I unlock the door and sneak out into the crippling cold night. "Oh, shit," I hiss as the icy wind smacks me right in the face.

I can't see more than a few feet ahead. The winds rise thicker and louder, throwing heaps of snow everywhere. I remember where the trucks are, covered in thick tarps and secured to a sturdy grounded log.

I reach the bottom of the porch steps before the first doubt hits me. What if I can't find Mitch's truck in this nightmarish blizzard? What if I can't start it? No, it's a hybrid. It's got enough electrical juice to get me out of here.

"What the fuck do you think you're doing?" Darla's voice startles me.

She's on the edge of the porch, holding a rifle. It's pointed right at me, and I don't know what to do with myself.

I follow Darla back into the house where she directs me to drop my bag and sit in a chair by the fire. There's a look of disappointment in her eyes as she calls the guys down.

"She was running away," Darla says, her tone as biting as the blizzard wind still pummeling the house. "In the middle of that," she adds, pointing at the window, She grabs the car keys from my hand and tosses them to Mitch. "She was gonna steal your truck apparently."

"I can explain," I whisper, barely able to look any of them in the eyes.

15

MITCH

"**W**hat's happening here?" I ask.

My brothers are just as confused, each taking a seat on the sofa next to Melissa's chair. Darla stays by the window, arms crossed and foot tapping furiously on the floor—reminding me of all the times she caught me stealing from the pantry. Same look. Same body language.

"If you thought I was just gonna sit back and let you hurt my boys, missy, you got another think coming," Darla says to Melissa.

"Darla, if I may?" I politely intervene, searching for Colton and Ethan's approval. I get it in the form of a slight nod and move closer to Melissa's chair. She can't even look at me. "What happened, Melissa? Were you really running away?"

She doesn't answer at first, but a scoff from an understandably disgruntled Ethan gets her talking. "I'm sorry. I didn't have a choice," she says.

"You're not getting away with an 'I'm sorry' this time," I tell her. "It's time you tell us what's going on."

"Just send me back to Ridgeboro. It doesn't matter anymore," she says, defeated.

Colton curses under his breath. "Dammit, woman, just talk."

"She's a proud and stubborn one for a thief in the night," Darla grumbles.

"I'm not a thief."

"You were going to take Mitch's truck," Auntie Fearless says. "That's theft."

"I was going to leave it at the Greyhound station."

"Melissa, look at me," I insist, and finally, she does precisely that. I see the pain in her beautiful eyes. The tears welling up. The shame that makes her lips quiver. Roses bloom crimson on her cheeks, and the snow is quickly melting into her hair, tightening the curls and darkening it.

"I'm sorry," she says it again, close to breaking down.

I shake my head slowly and give her another reassuring smile. "Talk to us. Come on. It's time. We deserve that much."

Once Melissa starts talking, she has a hard time stopping.

"Apparently the courts weren't the only ones Jake lied to about the drugs. He also talked to the people the drugs belonged to. They know I'm out of prison and they want their money. They told Jake to find m, so he did. He said I need to come up with two million dollars, which is the street value of those narcotics," Melissa continues, "or the cartel will kill me. I need to get the money or I'm dead."

"The cartel?" Colton asks.

Melissa nods. "Yes. The Esparza cartel."

My blood runs cold.

"I know that name," Ethan mumbles, his eyes widening as he starts going through his phone. "I've got buddies in the DEA who've been trying to take those fuckers down for a long time."

"Mexican?" Colton asks.

"Colombian," Melissa clarifies. "Jake was moving product for them. He said he tried to get the drugs out of evidence lockup, but—"

"How would he be able to pull something like that off?" Darla frowns.

I shudder at the thought. "He'd have somebody on the inside: a cop, a security guard. It's not impossible, but he didn't get it, did he?" I ask Melissa.

"No. And the only reason the cartel didn't kill Jake is because he pinned the blame on me and thought he might get me to cough up the money." Her laugh is humorless as she adds, "Which is fucking insane. I don't have two million dollars."

"Why didn't you tell us about this?"

"I was ashamed. I knew being here put you all in danger and I needed to figure a way out. That's why I was leaving tonight, to protect you all."

"Jesus, Melissa," Colton cuts in.

"I threatened to appeal my sentence, to tell the truth to anybody who would listen," Melissa replies. "It made him really angry. Violent, even. That's when Ethan stepped in and threw him out."

169

I look at Ethan. "He was scared. Imagine if Melissa went public with her story. A Ridgeboro inmate or not, she could still get the press's attention if she plays her cards right. She gets her story to the media, and soon, Reddit will be over-flowing with conspiracy theories. All it takes is one member of the Esparza cartel to lean into her story, and poof... there goes Jake Miller's safety. If they suspect him of framing Melissa in the first place—"

"They would absolutely kill him," Ethan concludes.

Melissa shakes her head. "Nobody is going to listen to what I have to say. Public exposure aside, and the risks it would entail... the court didn't believe me. The tabloids won't either. It'll only take one statement from the DA's office to shoot my claims down before I even make it into an appeals court." She frowns. "Besides, I could never forgive myself if Jake were killed. He might be a piece of shit, but I can't have that on my conscious."

"Melissa, you took the rap for a man who now expects you to cough up two million bucks so he can cover his ass," Colton harshly reminds her. "This is not the time for you to take the higher road or be the nice girl. Being the nice girl is what got you into this mess."

"I don't want the cartel to find me here." She starts crying. "I don't want them to know about you all, to hurt any of you because of me. I'm fucking radioactive, can't you see? I'm radioactive and anybody who gets close to me could end up dead."

It's tearing me up on the inside to see her like this. I lean in and wipe some of the tears from her warm face with my bare knuckles, wishing I could find the right words to soothe her frayed nerves. But I don't have the right words because I have yet to figure out a solution to this particular hot mess.

Melissa has every reason to be afraid.

We should be worried as well. If that piece of shit Jake Miller is right, then we're going to be dealing with the Esparza cartel soon enough. I'll be damned if I'll let any of them get anywhere near Melissa. And I know Colton and Ethan are on the same page.

"There's only one way I'll be able to survive this," Melissa adds after a long, heavy moment of silence. "I need to disappear for good."

Colton thinks about it. "There has to be another way. We'll figure something out."

16

MELISSA

"Tonight's no good for making any kinds of decisions," Colt decrees.

"I can't stay here," I insist, though I'm gradually melting into the armchair. I can't even use alcohol to numb my feelings. A baby is growing in my womb, and one of these men is the father. I should have a heart filled with joy right now, not spine-crushing dread. "They'll come after me."

"Nobody's coming after you yet," Colton says. "And until we do a little bit of digging, talk to the cops, get the lay of the land, so to speak, you're not going anywhere, Melissa. Your only destination is your room upstairs, which is still yours if you want it."

"Of course I want it."

"Then go upstairs and unpack that duffel bag."

"I'm sorry," I reply.

"Stop saying that," Ethan sighs. "We'll talk later."

"For now, the three of us need to talk," Mitch says.

Darla frowns and pours herself another scotch. "You're lucky I came downstairs for a midnight snack. Otherwise, we would've found you out there, frozen to death, you foolish girl."

I'm about to say I'm sorry again, but I swallow the words and get up instead. With my head down, I grab the duffel bag and make my way upstairs.

They wait until they hear the door to my room close, then get to talking. Their voices are muffled, but I can tell they're angry and rightly concerned. I've brought trouble to the ranch, and I've got a feeling they're debating what to do with me. Sending me back to Ridgeboro is still an option, whether they want to admit it or not, and it hangs over my head like a dark cloud.

"I don't want to disappoint them," I tell my reflection in the bathroom mirror as I take my clothes off and jump into the hot shower. The freezing cold has penetrated my bones, and I can't stop shaking, even as the heaters rage in my room.

An hour passes in dark warmth. I'm tucked in, but I can't sleep.

A subtle knock on my door pulls me out of my thoughts.

"Melissa," Colton's low voice breaches the night.

Outside, it's still snowing with a vengeance, the roof shuddering under the weight of it all. I get out of bed and open the door to find Colton, Ethan, and Mitch standing in the hallway, a wall sconce shines some light on their handsome, pensive faces.

Ethan is the first to come closer, cupping my face as he pulls me into a hard, possessive kiss. It's a different flavor, and it sends chills down my spine—the good kind that sets my core on fire. "Do you still want us?""

I nod. "Yes, I do."

"Good. Then undress for us," Ethan says, his voice low.

"Okay."

He kisses me again, even harder, his lips crushing mine. "That's not how you respond. How do you respond when I give you an order, Melissa?"

For a few seconds, all I can do is blink slowly as I try to catch my breath. Something is definitely different between us. The atmosphere feels loaded with a new kind of heat, flames blazing and licking at my senses as I peer deep into the darkened, tourmaline pools of his eyes. Colton and Mitch wait, thumbs hooked into their jeans pockets and hunger dripping from their gazes.

I welcome this thrill.

It takes every semblance of control away from me, which is, oddly enough, precisely what I seem to need in this moment.

"Yes, sir," I say, giddy with anticipation.

"Good girl," Ethan replies. "Now, undress."

"Yes, sir," I say it again, almost smiling.

Slowly, I unbutton my pajama shirt. My matching green pants join it on the floor, followed by my panties. I'm already wet and yearning, my hair falling freely over my shoulders. My breasts are tender, my nipples perked under their attention.

The guys undress as well, standing naked before me in mere seconds.

"Do you like what you see?" Mitch asks as my eyes slowly rake up and down each man.

"Yes, sir."

"Get on your knees then," Ethan commands me.

"Yes, sir." I sink to my knees, the three of them crowding around me.

I close one hand around Mitch and the other around Ethan while parting my lips so Colton can slide down my throat. I stroke them with deliberate precision, tightening my grip at the base, then slowly working my way up. Colton holds my head in place, and tears spring from my eyes as I let him deep-throat me at his leisure. I feel the veins twitching against my tongue. Tasting the precum as he pulls back, I can't help but smile.

"You're delicious," I tell him as I pull back for a moment.

"I'm not done with you yet," he says.

Ethan hisses as I stroke him faster, while Mitch runs his fingers through my hair. I take turns with each of them, relaxing the back of my throat to let each of them in, reveling in their heady, deliciously manly flavors. Mitch takes a step back with a sharp gasp.

"I'm not going to last if you keep doing that," he says. "Stand up."

"Yes, sir," I smile as I do as I'm told.

My whole body is ablaze, but they don't touch me. It's what I long for the most, and they're not giving me any of it. They're tormenting me on purpose.

"Walk over to the bed and bend over," Mitch says.

"Yes, sir!" I exclaim, positively delighted.

I'm about to get filled to the brim, and it's a sensation I missed over the past few days. Gladly, I obey and spread my legs wide for them as I hold on to the edge of the bed. I'm horny as hell, my juices dripping down the insides of my thighs as I shudder and moan softly.

Ethan's hand comes down with a hard smack, and the sting makes me cry out.

"Have you really been a good girl, Melissa?" he asks, his voice low and raspy.

He slaps my ass again.

"Oh!" I whimper. It's a sweet kind of sting. It's doing quite the number on my senses, my pussy clenching tightly with every contact between my buttock and his heavy hand.

"Have you been a good girl?" he asks again.

"No, sir, I haven't."

"And what do we do to bad girls?"

"Whatever you want, sir," I reply, unable to stop the grin from stretching across my face. "Whatever you want."

His fingers probe my entrance, and I turn my head to look at them.

"Eyes forward."

I jerk my head around and moan loudly as he uses three fingers to penetrate me, curling them with every retreat. "Oh, fuck, I'm so fucking wet."

"Good."

"Permission to touch myself, sir?" I manage.

"Why?" he asks.

"I really want to come."

"Not yet," Ethan replies.

My vision is blurry, my climax so close, I can almost feel it, but it won't arrive unless my clit is taken care of. The little nub is swollen and tender, in desperate need of attention while Ethan finger-fucks me out of this world. I moan and gasp with every stroke, my core stiffening.

So close... oh, God, so fucking close.

Ethan withdraws his hand, and I'm left feeling naked and alone.

Colton pulls me back. I arch my spine in response, catching a glimpse of Ethan as he comes around and climbs onto the bed, his arms long enough for him to hold on to the posts while Mitch sits on the edge.

"Relax," Colton whispers as he gently lifts me off the ground and positions me on top of Mitch. I'm as light as a feather in his grip.

"Deep breath," Mitch says. He digs his fingers into my hips and beckons me to slide onto him. My pussy clenches with desire as he fills me and stretches me.

Ethan jerks his hips forward, and I lean over and take him in my mouth, practically unhinging my jaw to let all of him in.

At the same time, Colton holds me by the back of the neck and joins Mitch inside me.

"Easy, baby," he grunts and thrusts himself deep.

I hold on to Ethan's thighs while Mitch tilts his hips upward. Colton fucks me slow from behind. I feel them, both of them, sliding into me. Every thrust brings me closer to the much-needed edge, my clit pressed against Mitch's groin. It's all I need.

"That's it, Melissa. Take it," Ethan growls as he goes deep down my throat. My neck muscles tighten with each motion, the world around us dilating and expanding into a blurry nothingness.

Colton slaps my ass hard, and I come, gushing like a fountain, my pussy rippling around both of them while Ethan shoots his hot load down my throat. Mitch explodes next, filling me and consuming me at the same time.

"Fuck!" Colton manages as he brings his hand down again.

I ride the wave, drinking Ethan in as Colton comes inside me.

We come down from our highs together, and my men gather me in their arms. They surround me with their warmth and pull the covers over us. It doesn't take me long at all to drift into a contented and exhausted sleep.

Everything but this can wait until tomorrow.

17

MELISSA

Christmas morning finds us in the living room.

The blizzard has stopped, but the others are still sleeping, which gives us at least another hour of cuddling in front of the TV, drinking hot cinnamon tea, and devouring an entire platter of cookies while the fireplace is ablaze and filling the air with the generous scent of burnt wood.

"We should open the presents," Colton says, getting up from the armchair next to the couch. "Before the others come down. We got you something."

"Oh, you didn't have to," I mumble. "I certainly don't deserve it after the stunt I pulled yesterday."

"You more than made up for it," Ethan replies, his index and thumb clasping my chin as he lifts my head and kisses me softly on the lips.

Colton carries over the pink box with a pale blue bow. "And you've certainly earned this."

I sit up, blushing as I receive my present, then give him a smile. "I left each of you a little something under the tree as well."

"You did?" Mitch sounds surprised.

"It's nothing fancy. I snuck them in with the others when I first came down. The brown boxes with the gold ribbon."

Colton and his brothers exchange excited glances, then he goes back to the tree and fetches their presents, making sure Ethan and Mitch get theirs according to the labels I added on the top of each box. "Now I'm curious," he mutters.

"We'll open them at the same time," I say. "On the count of three?"

"Okay, three," Mitch shoots back and proceeds to untie the ribbon first.

My gift steals my breath. As I open the box and pull the wrapping paper aside, I discover a beautiful cowboy hat. It's made with a gorgeous shade of caramel hide, the brim expertly sewn with gold thread and a beautifully ornate hatband that reminds me of a charm bracelet. Different gold-brushed miniatures hang from a delicate chain attached to the band, and they jingle with every movement.

"Oh, God, it's beautiful," I manage, tearing up.

"Can't be a cowgirl without a proper cowgirl hat," Colton chuckles as he unwraps his gift. He stills at the sight of a hunting knife with an ornate ivory handle, manually carved and dressed in fine silk thread. It comes with a leather holster. "Melissa, this is really something."

I offer a shy shrug. "Darla and I went out before the blizzard struck and stopped at a small holiday fair. I thought you might like it."

"It's incredibly thoughtful," Colton says and leans in for a loving kiss. "Thank you."

Ethan laughs lightly as he opens his present. It's a leather belt in smooth black with a perfect finish and silver-thread embroidery, and the belt-buckle is a silver-coated stainless-steel reproduction of a bull with black enamel eyes. "This is so cool!"

"I figured it would look really good on you," I say, "especially when I get to take it off you."

He gives me a dark, but equally amused and aroused look. "You naughty minx."

"I am what you made me," I giggle and welcome his thankful kiss.

"My turn," Mitch chuckles as he untangles the ribbon and removes the lid from his labeled box. His eyes widen with delighted surprise as he takes out a leather-bound journal with antique-looking pages. It comes with a beautiful fountain-pen made with onyx and swirls of gold paint, making it capture every glimmer of light it meets. "This looks like something out of a Western movie."

I smile softly. "It's a reproduction of a mid-nineteenth-century journal and pen, made with pretty much the same materials and in the same fashion. You can actually tell from the paper texture."

"Oh, yeah," he says as he opens the journal and admires the blank pages.

"You love writing down your thoughts, so I hope you like it."

"Like it? I love it." He kisses me, and I melt a little on the inside, my heart growing too many sizes with pure joy. I'm so glad I nailed the gifts.

"You're remarkably good at gift shopping," Mitch adds. "We might ask you to do our Christmas shopping for us for next year."

"You got Sammy another pair of funny socks again, didn't you?" Ethan asks him.

Mitch shrugs. "He loved the last pair. Wore them all winter."

"It's settled, then," Colton laughs. "Melissa's in charge of gift shopping from now on. It'll make for less awkward Christmases to come."

The declaration is sweet enough to bring a smile to my lips, yet bitter enough to add a pang of anguish to my heart. Somewhere deep down, I think we all know there's a chance I won't be here next year. I want to be. I really do. But if the cartel threat looms closer, I might still have to leave—whether back to Ridgeboro or not remains to be seen.

"Melissa," Colton notices my discomfort. "What's wrong?"

"Nothing. Just hoping I'll make it to next Christmas. I'm not trying to sound dramatic or anything, but—"

"We won't let anything happen to you," Ethan interjects. "I thought I made that clear last night."

"You did," I say.

"Then put it out of your mind," he replies. "Whatever happens next, we're going to face it together. There's no way in hell I'm going to let some fucking cartel make your life any harder than it's already been. And the next time I see Jake Miller, I will pound him into a pile of mush."

Colton clears his throat. "We might need him alive. Or maybe you can pound a confession out of him first."

"As long as I get to pound him," Ethan grumbles.

 I don't know what kind of plan it's supposed to be, and I certainly don't know what my odds are against the Esparza cartel at this point. There's a lot I don't know in the short term, let alone as far as next year. I do know there's a child growing in my womb, and one of these incredible men is the father. I know I should tell them about this sooner rather than later.

But the unknown, the fear…

They take up too much space in my head, hijacking my decision-making process. Today, I choose to take another sip of my cinnamon tea and devour another cookie as I admire my present.

Outside, the snow is so high it nearly reaches the windows.

"Somebody's going to have to shovel all of that," I mutter.

Colton follows my gaze and smiles. "Yeah, Kyle and Jason are not going to be too happy about it."

"That's mean," I giggle. "We should at least help."

"We're going to handle breakfast," Mitch suggests. "They'll handle the snow shoveling."

"Well, hold on, if you're handling breakfast, what will I do? Pretty sure you hired me for that," I reply.

Colton shrugs. "You can assist us if you want. Today is Christmas Day. It's your day off."

Of course. Once again proving how kind and generous they are. It only makes me fall harder for them. I know it's wrong, but I can't help it.

18

COLTON

"There's two ways we can go about this," Mitch says.

We're three days away from New Year's Eve, and while the blizzard has stopped, most of our work revolves around keeping security tight on the ranch while shoveling snow into piles along the more traveled routes.

"About what?" I ask. I've been so lost in thought regarding Melissa that I may have tuned out of the current conversation.

"About Jake Miller," Mitch replies.

Ethan snarls. "I could just handle it."

"We both know that's not an option," I tell my twin. "Just as we know you left that version of yourself back in Bosnia."

"Well, he's not that far off from what I was going to suggest," Mitch says, half-smiling as he shovels another pile of snow out of the way. "Option number one is we take this to the sheriff's office. We exhaust every possible legal channel before anything else. If the Esparza cartel is operating in the region, the sheriff will want to know about it."

"Kavanaugh might want to know about it, but I doubt he can actually do something about it, especially in the middle of a rabid Nebraskan winter," Ethan says.

I agree with Mitch. "He needs to know what's going on in his county."

"Should the first option fail, however, option two is that we use our resources, our people, our network, and put together a strategy to get those assholes in a RICO bust."

Ethan gives him a hard look. "You're giving us solutions for the cartel but not for Jake fucking Miller. He's going to keep hounding Melissa for that money. I roughed him up a bit, but I doubt it was much of a deterrent, not for his desperate ass."

"If the cartel falls, they'll take Jake down with them," Mitch says.

* * *

ABOUT FIFTY YARDS east of our position, the northern gates of our ranch rise proudly from the snow, their steel pillars glistening under the sharp-toothed sun. The skies are clear, and there's plenty of sunlight to enjoy, though the snow is a blinding white.

Movement by the gate itself catches my eye, and I zero in on it.

"Fellas," I say, drawing their attention. I lift my chin in the direction of the gates and say, "Truck."

Immediately, they follow my gaze. Ethan opens the CCTV app on his phone and pulls up a closer view of the gate. "Motherf…" he mumbles. "It's him."

"Ethan, wait," I manage to say before he bolts to his truck, parked about twenty yards away and closer to the northern gate.

"We can't let him go off on his own," Mitch warns.

"No shit," I shoot back as I run after Ethan.

Before he can turn the key in the ignition, we're in the truck with him, fully aware there are at least two rifles at our feet, locked and loaded. He's never unprepared, and I need to make sure he doesn't go for option number three today, even though he's clearly itching for it.

"Don't be stupid," I tell him.

The truck engine roars to life.

"I'm not stupid. He obviously needs a reminder," he replies, his voice annoyingly calm.

"Let's see what he wants," Mitch suggests. "I'm going to text Sammy and tell him to stay at the house with Melissa or get Kyle or Jason to stay with her. Either way, while this fucker's prowling around, she shouldn't be alone."

"If she knows he came back, she might try to run off again," I mutter.

I think that's what the three of us fear the most.

"Ethan, stay calm," I remind my brother as he pulls up in front of the gate.

Beyond it, Jake Miller stands next to his truck, huddled under a thick brown parka.

We climb out of the truck and walk toward the gate.

"What are you doing here?" I ask.

"We need to talk," Jake replies with a subtle smile, stealing watchful glances at Ethan. "I would appreciate it if you kept your gorilla at bay, though."

"You might want to choose your words better," I warn him. "There's three of us here."

"Well, he started it," Jake replies, nodding at Ethan.

To my brother's credit, he is remarkably self-restrained. I thought I'd have to wrangle him off this bastard even though my blood is boiling, too.

"You came after and threatened Melissa," I say. "You're lucky my brother didn't do worse. Now, what are you doing here? I thought you were told to keep your distance."

"You clearly don't know everything about Melissa, otherwise, you wouldn't think of me as the bad guy in this picture because I'm not," Jake says.

"Oh? What are we missing?" Mitch shoots back, sarcasm dripping from his voice.

"She's not the saint you think she is. First of all, she got caught moving a hell of a lot of drugs and went to prison for it, right?"

"We all know those were your drugs," I cut in.

"Those weren't… Ugh, okay, so, here's the thing," Jake stutters, realizing we're not buying whatever he's so eager to sell us. "I didn't know the cops would be there that night, okay? She was supposed to take a different route."

"All I'm hearing is more excuses," I say.

"She knew exactly what I did for a living!" he snaps. "She knew, and she looked away. And when she agreed to drive that van, she knew what kind of product she was moving."

"I find that real hard to believe."

"Just more bullshit," Mitch scoffs. "We seem to know her better than you, buddy. How long were the two of you together?"

"A year. We shared a home. We shared a life," Jake insists. "I may not have been specific about what I did for a living, but Melissa was aware. She loved me anyway. She stuck by my side."

Ethan interjects. "None of us is buying any of this. It just doesn't track. You got any more bullshit up your sleeve, or are you just about done?"

"Hey, I'm not the bad guy here," Jake says. "I came to the ranch to warn Melissa."

"No, you came to tell her she needs to cough up the money *you* owe the Esparza cartel," I say. "And now, you're trying to do what, exactly? Win us over? Lie to us in order to put a wedge between us and Melissa?"

"I'm actually hoping one of you might do the right thing and give her the money," he replies.

Mitch stifles a chuckle. "And then what?"

"She gives it to me, and I broker a peace agreement between her and the cartel. They'll listen to me, especially if I have their money."

"Hold on. Let me see if I've got this straight." I laugh, shaking my head. "You want us to fork over two million dollars in cash. You want us to give that money to Melissa, so Melissa can hand it over to you, so you can get the Esparza cartel off her back. Is that it? You're the one who's gonna save her?"

"I was always going to be the one who saves her," Jake sighs. "I don't know what your deal is with Melissa, but I love her, and I always will."

I would no longer blame Ethan if he decided to just blow this bastard's head off. In fact, I walk back to the truck and take one of his rifles out. Jake immediately freezes, his eyes wide with shock and horror.

"Whoa, what are you doing?" he mumbles, shaking like a leaf.

"I've had enough of this," I say, raising my weapon.

Mitch's and Ethan's focus shifts to me. My patience is about to run out, and everything my brothers and I discussed over the past few days is quickly fanning the flames of my anger. There's nothing I won't do to keep Melissa safe and here with us.

"Don't shoot," Jake says. "I'm only trying to save her."

"No, you're trying to profit from an ugly situation you created," I say. "The way I see it is you have two choices, and only two. You either get back in your truck and leave the state of Nebraska altogether, or I will pump you full of lead and thus remove one problem from Melissa's life."

Jake stills, narrowing his eyes at me. "You're fucking her."

"Careful," I warn, pointing the rifle at his head. "I've got an itchy trigger finger."

"Alright, alright!" Jake scoffs. "I'll leave. For now. But you have to talk to her. You have to help her. The Esparza cartel is not known for their patience or their mercy. They'll want to make an example out of Melissa if she doesn't pay them back for the cocaine she lost."

"Jake, they'll make an example out of her even if she does pay them back," I reply. "Now get the fuck out of here before I do what my brothers really want me to do."

"Just think about it," he says, then carefully backs away and gets back into his truck.

Ethan, Mitch, and I watch as he fumbles with the keys until he manages to get the engine rolling. He drives away, wheels slipping along the battered snowy road.

"He's not as slick as he thinks he is," Ethan concludes.

"Nope, but he is desperate. And there's nothing more dangerous than a cornered animal," I remind him, then look at Mitch. "Let's try option number one first."

I LEAVE Darla and Sammy with Melissa at the house, though we don't share the details of our encounter with Jake. Mitch and Ethan get Kyle and Jason to help them with what's left of today's snow shoveling duties, while I drive into Long Pine.

Jake Miller's return is a bad omen, a sign of worse to come. Despair can make men crazy, and if Ethan's physical aggression didn't teach him a lesson, nothing short of death at our hands will. In order to avoid unnecessary bloodshed, however, I need to talk to Sheriff Kavanaugh.

I find the sheriff in his office, comfortable in his chair and nursing a mug of black, unsweetened coffee, frowning as he checks the news reports. His bullpen is almost empty, except for his secretary, Rhonda, who types away at her computer.

"Hey, there, Colt," Kavanaugh says as soon as I walk in. He doesn't set the coffee down, nor does he sit up straight in his chair. In fact, he doesn't move a muscle as I take a seat in the guest chair across from his desk. "What brings you around? The neighbors givin' you grief?"

"No, sir, everything's good in that sense," I reply, nodding at the many empty desks behind me. The phones ring, but every call is routed to Rhonda's desk. She answers each call with a nasal voice, asking people to stay calm and let the authorities do their jobs. "You're a little undermanned here, I see."

"Well, yeah," Kavanaugh sighs. "All my deputies are out on the road. You'd think the good folks of Long Pine would know to stay indoors after a blizzard like the one we just had."

"They're getting trapped in the snow, huh?"

He nods once. "Like flies on glue paper, I swear."

"People are going to do stupid shit no matter what you tell them. Hell, it keeps you and your deputies from getting bored."

He chuckles. "I'm glad you've got your trucks and your snow equipment. I never had to worry about the Avery boys in that sense," Kavanaugh says. "What brings you out here, Colt? Thought you boys would be busy shoveling your ranch roads."

"We're doing that, but I needed to talk to you about something else."

"Okay. How can I help?"

"I got a bit of a situation, and I was hoping you might be able to provide me with some information. Off the record, for now," I say.

Kavanaugh sits up. I've got his full attention. He takes another sip of coffee and sets the mug down, his gaze fixed on mine. "What's going on?"

"You know we're working with Ridgeboro prison, right? The whole Path to Freedom Initiative, the woman we've got working in our kitchen."

"Yeah, yeah, Melissa Carson. I've got her file here somewhere. Did she do something?"

"No, sir, she's been a saint. But her past is catching up with her, and I'm hoping I might be able to get ahead of it."

He frowns, his silvery brows furrow above his grey eyes. "Why don't you just send her back to Ridgeboro and get another inmate who won't bring trouble to your doorstep? I'm sure you have options."

The mere thought makes my stomach churn.

"No, sir. Melissa is a great woman, and frankly, I think she was wrongfully convicted," I say, shaking my head slowly. "It's one of the things I'm eager to look into, actually, but before that... I've just gotten word that we might have some people from the Esparza cartel hanging out around Long Pine."

"Jesus Christ. What can you tell me about them?"

"They're a Colombian cartel active across Nebraska. The drugs the cops seized from Melissa's van belonged to them." I frown. "Well, not her van, her boyfriend's."

"Didn't he testify against her?"

"He was the one moving drugs for the cartel," I tell Kavanaugh, but he gives me a sour smile.

"Careful with assumptions, Colt."

"Sheriff, my issue isn't with Melissa's innocence right now. I'm trying to paint the whole picture for you," I insist.

"Go on."

"They're ruthless and bloodthirsty bastards, and they might be coming after Melissa," I tell him. "So I need as much information about them as you can possibly provide me with as a civilian."

"As a civilian," Kavanaugh asks, "or as a former Ranger?"

"I'd prefer the latter if you'd extend me such a courtesy."

"Let's see…"

He pauses and logs into his computer. I watch his chubby fingers dance across the old keyboard, clacking until he inputs a few words into the database. His eyes scan the screened results, then his hand takes over the wireless mouse and prints a handful of documents.

"All yours," he says.

I retrieve the printed paper and glance at it. "This isn't enough," I tell him. "I could get this from a search engine, Sheriff, or the newspapers. I need details about their lieutenants, about their recent movements, their modus operandi. I need to know what we're dealing with."

"Colton, I'm getting the feeling the girl would be safer back at Ridgeboro, and you would be, too."

"That is not an option," I say sharply. "Sheriff, we've done this office a whole lot of favors over the years. I'm not the type to call them in, but I guess I have to. I need real, accurate, and recent intel on these people and on Jake Miller."

"Jake Miller."

"Melissa's ex."

"Dang it, Colt, what have you gotten yourself into, boy?"

"Nothing I can't handle provided I have accurate information," I reply with a cool grin. "Come on, Sheriff. Do me this solid. I just want to know who I'm dealing with. I came to you for help. You know I've got former Rangers up at the DEA as well. But I came to you first because I respect you."

And because calling in a favor with the DEA might end up with that agency telling us to back off because they've already got who knows how many RICO investigations open for the Esparza cartel. They might make matters worse, in fact. If the cartel senses the DEA breathing down their necks, they could accelerate whatever it is they're looking to do to Melissa.

I'm in love with this woman, and I intend to keep her safe.

Kavanaugh gives it a second thought, then takes a deep breath while his mouse clicks through a series of folders and links on his computer screen. "Alright. I don't have much in here, just what the Feds shared with us the last time they put a BOLO out on one of the cartel's people in the area."

"When was that?"

"Less than two months ago."

"Around the time Melissa came to us," I conclude. "Whatever you have, please, Sheriff."

"It's for your eyes only," he warns.

I offer a reassuring nod. "Yes, sir."

Five minutes later, I'm flipping through several pages with photocopies of criminal records and state trooper's notes on the margins, as well as a few interdepartmental memos from one of the higher-ups in the DEA.

My blood runs cold as a picture comes into focus.

"They're active in this district," I say to Kavanaugh.

"Not dealing. Not that we know of anyway," he says. "My boys would've picked something up by now, but nothing has happened. Those are just movements. Lease agreements. CCTV footage of suspected lieutenants at various locations across Long Pine and the neighboring towns. I'll admit, it's odd, but it's not enough for us to open an investigation of our own."

"Do you have eyes on these people?"

He shakes his head. "So far, we haven't been able to identify anyone except that guy."

"This guy?" I ask, showing him the mugshot of a black-haired man with a bushy mustache and several face tattoos. "Yeah, I suppose he sticks out like a sore thumb in these parts."

"Luis Menendez," Kavanaugh says, "a suspected lieutenant of the cartel. Supposedly answers directly to Ramon Esparza, the cartel jefe. But he's keeping his nose clean. Renting an apartment in town. I checked with the IRS as well. The rental agreement is legit and fully declared. The man has a salary coming in from a small company from Ainsworth for consultancy services."

So he *was* holding back on me.

"I reckon the company will come up clean as well if you dig deeper," I mutter.

"Probably, yeah. Whatever they're doing here, it's legal," Kavanaugh replies. "Doesn't mean I have to like it, but unless I put a tail on that guy..."

"Can you?"

He leans forward and gives me a hard look. "My constituents will grill my ass when they find out I'm using department resources to chase down one of your hunches. That Menendez fella is clean. He checks in with his parole officer once a week. I have absolutely no reason to put a tail on him and not enough manpower to do it with having to rescue half the damn county from the ditches."

"I'll look into it," I tell him. "Discretely, of course. Just for my peace of mind. But if you get any more information about these people, will you let me know?"

"Stay out of trouble, Colt. I'm warning you."

"I'll do my best."

I can't guarantee it, but I give the sheriff the reassurance he clearly needs at this point. We all require peace of mind in one form or another. This is his. And the information in my hands is mine. I now know more now than I did five minutes ago.

Trouble is, there's no mention of Jake Miller anywhere in these documents.

The bastard is particularly good at hiding his tracks.

19

MELISSA

Two days until New Year's Eve, and I've been given the green light to go into town. Darla, of course, is the designated driver, but she gives me my space to run my errands—which is a godsend because I made an appointment with Dr. Hartman, the OB-GYN at the local clinic.

But first, I desperately need a haircut, so I stop by the hair salon, thankful that Long Pine isn't a densely populated town because there's no one waiting.

My morning sickness is causing me trouble, but I manage to keep it under control with lemon and jasmine tea.

"I'll stop by the post office while you get rid of your split ends," Darla says as she drops me off outside the hair salon. Her tone is snappy. She's not the type to easily forgive, and my transgression will take a lot more time than I had anticipated for her to get over.

"Thank you," I reply with a faint smile. "I'll let you know when I'm done. The doctor's office is just up the road. I want to pop by for a new prescription as well if you don't mind."

"A prescription for what?" she frowns.

"Just my allergies. Nothing fancy."

"You've got allergies?"

No, but I couldn't think of anything better to mask the truth. I need to get an ultrasound and make sure the baby is okay. If I'm in good health, then so is the little one, and I can plan ahead in a more constructive way, no matter what happens next.

"Yeah, I usually get a refill from the prison pharmacy, but I'm almost out, and if we get another blizzard, the last thing you need is me sniffing and blowing my nose all the time—"

"Fine, fine, do what you gotta do. Just call when you're done," Darla replies and drives off.

I stand on the edge of the pavement for a while, looking around. Long Pine is not as quiet at this hour as I assumed it would be. Then again, New Year's Eve is right around the corner and the blizzard likely kept people from shopping early.

Of course, I'll need a good excuse not to drink that night. I hate keeping secrets and lying, but given the circumstances, I can't add more fuel to a potentially catastrophic fire. I'm in love with them, and I want more out of this relationship, but realistically, how would that even work?

Until Jake and his stupid cartel are out of my life for good, I can't even see the week ahead clearly, let alone the months and the years to follow. Plus, I'm still technically an inmate of Ridgeboro.

 I go into the salon and fully enjoy the pampering. I walk out feeling refreshed in a way I haven't in a long time. Prison hairdressers are just not the same as civilians.

The foot traffic has thinned in the hour I was inside, but the stores are still open, as are the cafes on both sides of the street. I can smell the cinnamon and the apple spice, the freshly brewed coffee, and the French pastries. My mouth is watering, so I stop by one of the street service windows and get myself a frothy milk and a bear claw.

I don't see the man coming out of the café, though, and I bump into him. The milk jumps out of my takeaway cup, most of it missing the man's pristine wool coat.

"Oh, my God, I am so sorry!" I yelp, absolutely mortified.

I almost drop my bear claw, too, but he catches it and laughs lightly, offering it to me. "It's okay," the man says with a subtle Spanish inflection in his voice. "Don't worry about it."

"Thank you. So sorry…" I say as I reclaim my bear claw, mouth still watering.

"Hey, accidents happen," he says, offering a warm smile.

He seems nice. Tall and good-looking, with an olive complexion and short, black-as-ink hair. His dark brown eyes search my face, and all I can do is smile back.

"Are you okay?" I ask him.

He takes the paper cup off the ground and tosses it into the nearest bin. "All is well. No harm, no foul."

"But my milk—"

"It's a white coat. We're cool." He laughs again. "How about you? You okay?"

"Yes, just mortified," I answer.

"You're not from around here," he says, studying me closely.

"You're not from around here either," I reply with a wry smile.

"No, I am not," he laughs and offers me a hand. "I'm Ramon."

"It's nice to meet you, Ramon," I reply and shake his hand. He holds it for a second longer than I'm used to, firmly as his eyes narrow with twinkling curiosity. "Well, if you're sure you're okay, I should be going."

"I promise you, I'm fine," he says again with a smile.

I offer a little awkward wave and head in the direction of the doctor's office, happily munching my bear claw along the way.

I arrive at the doctor's office and sign in, waiting for my name to be called, thankful there was a cancellation for today so I could get an appointment.

The tech calls me back and goes through the basics before squeezing warm jelly on my stomach and moving the wand over. Suddenly, the room is filled with the sound of a rapid thumping.

"Should it be that fast?" I ask, immediately concerned.

The ultrasound tech smiles and turns the screen so I can see the tiny little bean in the middle. "Yes. Babies' heartbeats are very fast and yours sounds perfectly healthy. Congratulations, Mama."

I stare at the little image on the screen, no more than a blip at this point, but I feel an instant connection, an instant knowledge that I will do whatever I can to protect that little life.

After the exam is over, I head into a room and wait for the doctor to come in.

"I'm pleased to give you a clean bill of health," Dr. Hartman says with a warm smile as he enters. "You're right where we'd expect you to be in your first trimester and your vitals are good. Tell me, how are you feeling overall?"

"Well, the morning sickness lasts well into the afternoon some days," I admit.

Dr. Hartman laughs lightly. "Yes, it's not an aptly named affliction. Have you found anything that works to help ease the symptoms?"

"Yes, so far lemon and ginger tea have been lifesavers."

"Both great options. How are you feeling emotionally? Pregnancy is a major step and can make you feel anxious."

I nod. "I've suffered from panic attacks over the last few years, though, thankfully, they haven't seemed to have gotten any worse so far. Usually, I use breathing techniques to calm down."

"Sometimes you need a little extra help if they get bad enough. Pregnancy can increase symptoms of anxiety. I can prescribe medication you can take if needed, or you can try a natural route first to see if that helps," Dr. Hartman offers.

"I think I'd like a natural route," I tell him.

He starts writing options down on a piece of paper. "Chamomile is your friend. Valerian root as well. Lavender. I'm adding a few supplements you can pick up from the drug store's holistic section as well as your prenatal vitamins. I want you to start them right away. Charlie, the pharmacist, will help you with this."

"Thank you so much, Doctor."

"You are most welcome, Miss Carson. I will see you again next month, and don't forget, you have my number in case you need anything. Let's just hope the weather won't keep you isolated up there on the ranch."

"I certainly hope not. Thank you again, Dr. Hartman." I collect my paperwork and head out the door. I hurry to the pharmacy before calling Darla to pick me up.

As soon as I step out of the clinic, the cold air smacks me in the face. My lower back hurts, and my legs feel heavier than usual. I just got a clean bill of health yet I still feel so damn sluggish and worn out? I head to the pharmacy and get the supplements and prenatal vitamins I need. I shove them all deep into the bottom of my bag before I pull out my phone to call Darla.

20

MELISSA

An hour later, I'm sitting in the living room, having a cup of chamomile tea when Darla walks in. She was uncharacteristically quiet on the ride home, and the way she's looking at me now makes me nervous.

She sighs heavily as she collapses into the armchair by the fire. "Don't think for a second that I don't know what's going on here."

"What?" I feel the blood drain from my face.

Darla gives me a flat kind of look, her lips pressed into a thin line. "Seriously? I've lost my sense of taste, not my sight. I know Colton, Ethan, and Mitch. I've known them their whole lives, Melissa. I'm well aware of their lifestyle choice and their... let's call it their complicated way of loving a woman."

"Oh, dear," I mumble, positively mortified.

"It's the ranch's best-kept secret, so just relax," she groans and rolls her eyes at me. "We protect our own, remember? And you're one of us, for heaven's sake. Stop acting like you're on your own all the time, 'cause you're not."

"I'm not trying to shut anyone out. It's just that, in prison, you learn not to trust anyone. Even someone who seems like a friend won't hesitate to stab you in the back if it helps them in some way. I'm just not used to people caring."

"You are rare, I'll give you that," Darla says after a long and heavy silence.

"Rare?"

"My boys don't easily fall for a woman," she replies. "It speaks to your character more than you think. They're good men, Melissa. Really good men. And they went to hell and back to get the peace they've built here on the ranch. Did they ever tell you about their service with the Rangers?"

I nod slowly. "Bits and pieces, here and there."

"They've taken bullets for one another. They've pulled each other out of harm's way," Darla says. "Their bond is tighter than most."

"I can imagine."

"You live this life thinking you're fine, you know? You wake up early, you have breakfast, then you get out to the stables... it's pretty cut and dry out here. Sure, there are risks aplenty on a ranch, too. Mind you, this was basically the Wild West before the sheriff really started enforcing the new laws on land ownership," Darla adds. "But what my boys went through... it's part of the reason I never married or had children of my own. I couldn't bear the constant fear their mother and father had to live with every damn day."

"That must have been terrifying for all of you," I say sympathetically.

"Oh, it was. But my point is that those boys don't love easily, but when they do, they love hard and with everything they've got."

I bow my head, thinking of how I almost ran and how I'm still keeping secrets.

"It's not easy for me either," I admit.

Darla nods her head. "I bet not. Your parents abandoned you; the system abandoned you, and the man you thought loved you fed you to the wolves. But if you want love, Melissa, you can have it. You can have it here. You just have to open up and trust the boys. I know you're trying to protect them, but trouble is coming, and it might as well find you in the company of people who can actually do something about it, who can protect you. One Colombian cartel isn't going to make them quiver in their boots."

"The Colombians are extremely violent," I remind her.

Darla shakes her head. "This ain't Colombia. This is Nebraska. We still have law enforcement here. The ranch is well secured. And the boys... well, like I said, they're fearless. They've been up against the worst humanity has to offer. You're safer here with them than anywhere else, you understand?"

"Alright," I mumble, nodding slowly. "I understand. Thank you, Darla."

As I gaze out the living room window, I'm met with a sea of white. So much snow and cold beauty, it's almost breathtaking. The house still smells of cinnamon and other seasonal spices. I'd missed it. I didn't even realize it until I came here

—how much I had missed the comfort of a home, of safety, of Christmas and time spent around good people.

Darla has made plenty of sensible points here. I need to do better by my men. They deserve more.

"You keep surprising me," I tell Darla.

She gives me a curious look. "With what, exactly?"

"The care you show me. I'm not used to it. I'm also not used to getting my ass handed to me the way you keep handing it to me. But I do appreciate it. It keeps me honest."

She laughs lightly. "Just get it through your thick head, kid. You're not alone anymore. We've all grown fond of you here, and you have proven yourself more than once as a valuable member of this team, of this family. Don't make me regret putting my faith in you after all of this. Alright? It's all I ask."

"Okay. I promise."

21

MELISSA

I'm still reeling from the first real Christmas I've had in years and it's already New Year's Eve. The guys have not left my side, and neither have Darla or Sammy. Heck, even Kyle and Jason keep finding reasons to check on me once in a while. In the meantime, I'm still hiding my pregnancy, still trying to cope with the nausea and the sudden bouts of hunger without arousing suspicion.

"We're all set for tonight," Colton says as he walks into the kitchen.

Ethan and Mitch are already here, halfway done with their hearty breakfast. Since it's a special day, I decided to sneak out of bed and away from their strong arms about an hour earlier than usual so I could put this veritable feast together.

"You got the champagne," Ethan replies, half-smiling.

"Two cases. You know, in case we decide to go wild," Colton chuckles and joins them at the breakfast table, but not without dropping a kiss on my cheek first as I load his plate with a hefty serving of everything. "Morning, beautiful."

"Morning," I reply, feeling warm and golden on the inside.

His blue eyes search my face. "So, this is why you ran off before dawn."

"Figured you could use proper sustenance," I reply with a giggle. "We've got a big lunch before the New Year's Eve dinner as well. You boys better show up hungry."

Mitch chuckles. "Oh, you bet your gorgeous ass we're gonna show up hungry. We don't have much to do for the rest of the day. Darla's upstairs in her home office closing up the admin year for the ranch. Sammy's got Kyle and Jason patching up the last damaged section of the northeastern fence."

"All we have to do is handle the cattle feed, check on the rest of the livestock, and take the horses out for one last ride of the year," Ethan adds. "Oh, Colt, the fireworks."

"Already in the garage," Colton replies, clearly satisfied with himself.

My eyes pop wide with excitement. "Y'all do love a raucous New Year's Eve, huh?"

"Normally, we'd just go out to the Cavalier and celebrate with everyone else, but we figured we'd try something special this year," Colton says in between morsels of food. "My Lord, Melissa, this is one of the best omelets you've made so far."

As I watch my men work through their breakfast, I think of ways I could tell them about the baby. They should know. I'll start showing soon enough, and when that happens, I have no idea what will happen.

I'm suddenly struck by a terrible thought. What if the guys don't want anything to do with me or the baby once they find out? My baby will be born in prison and end up in the foster system like I did. The thought is enough to bring on another wave of nausea.

I'm biting my lower lip, and Colton is the first to notice. "Are you okay, Melissa?"

"Yeah, a few things on my mind, that's all."

Ruckus erupts outside. Engines roaring. Horns blaring.

Instantly, everything changes. Time speeds up. The guys jump from the table and head for the front door. Instinctively, despite my rapidly beating heart, I run after them.

I barely register the moment in which Colton, Ethan, and Mitch each grab one of the rifles mounted in the hallway cabinet before they step out onto the porch. I don't register the warnings they give each other either.

"Melissa, stay inside," Ethan tells me.

"What?" I'm just about to join them on the porch when I'm not-so-gently pushed back, the front door shutting abruptly in my face.

I need a few seconds to catch up, but as soon as my brain is back online, I rush into the living room and peek through the window. The view unraveling before my eyes fills me with a sudden wave of dread and horror.

Three black SUVs have pulled up outside, right in front of the house. How they got past the security gate, I have no idea.

The air feels thick and practically unbreathable as Colton, Ethan, and Mitch reach the porch steps, rifles locked and loaded in their hands.

Two men get out from the car in the middle. They're clad in black, their winter parkas thick and unzipped.

"Bring her out," one of them shouts, a hint of a Hispanic accent coloring the words.

My blood runs cold. I'm frozen on the spot, face practically glued to the frosted window.

"Who the fuck are you, and what are you doing on my property?" Colton replies, firmly gripping his rifle. Mitch and Ethan are already pointing theirs at the strangers.

"You know who we are. You were warned," the guy replies.

The other one whips out a weapon of his own, but—BAM!

"Oh, shit!" I yelp.

Ethan shoots him in the leg. The man falls to the ground with a scream as the first guy pulls a gun from the back of his pants. Mitch swings his gun toward him and fires inches in front of the man's toes.

"What the fuck!" the startled man yells as he takes a step back.

"That was a warning. Don't be stupid," Mitch warns. "You're on our turf."

Another man jumps out to help his injured comrade, pulling him into the SUV.

The first one speaks again. "Give us Melissa Carson, and we'll be on our way."

"You need to be on your way, period," Colton says. "Or we will fire again. And again. And again. I've already called the sheriff. He's on his way."

I doubt that. There was no time. But these cartel pricks don't need the truth. They just need to know someone's coming. That we're not alone out here in the middle of nowhere, theirs for the picking. Instinctively, I cradle my lower belly with both hands, terrified of what might happen if these men get past Colton, Mitch, and Ethan.

Ethan descends the first porch step. "You heard my brother," he shouts. "Get the fuck out of here, or I will shoot you."

"Give us Melissa Carson," the first guy insists.

"Apparently, you didn't get my message," Mitch says and fires a second round, even closer to the previous.

It makes the driver jump. "You fucker!"

"Not going to say it again." Colton stands his ground as well.

I'm pretty sure they're outnumbered and outgunned, but the cartel already has one injured man and the Averys aren't afraid to shoot.

"Oh, God," I whisper as Ethan points his rifle at the chatty driver.

"One last time. Are you pricks leaving on your own, or will we be burying bodies in the back pasture?"

"We'll be back," the driver says, backing toward the SUV. "Either deliver the girl or the money, or you won't like what happens."

To my relief, the men get back in their cars. The three black SUVs turn around and bolt up the driveway leading back to the gate, while Colton, Ethan, and Mitch stay right where they are.

Watching.

Waiting.

Ready to fire if needed.

"I can't believe it," I whisper, shaking like a leaf. The adrenaline courses through me like an endless, unstoppable surge of electricity, making my chest feel heavy and my knees weak.

Me or two million dollars.

Anything other than that will result in something much worse than what just happened.

Next time, there won't be three cars. Next time, I wager my guys won't have the precious few seconds they'll need to grab their rifles to defend me. Good grief, I almost believed there might be a way out of this hot mess.

22

COLTON

"Kyle and Jason are with the sheriff at the gate," Sammy says as he comes back into the house, snow falling from his boots. "They're checking the cameras and the motion sensors. Some of the wires were cut apparently."

"And that's how they got through without triggering the alert on my phone," I grumble while pacing the living room.

I stop by the fire for a few moments, welcoming the heat as I give Melissa a long, wondering glance. She's glued to the armchair, pale as a ghost and scared out of her mind. I wish I could hold her and kiss it all away, but clearly it wouldn't be enough.

"How are you holding up?" I ask her.

Darla scoffs. "Dumb question, son. She's terrified, and for good reason."

"Hey, I'm trying to help," I defend myself.

"Sorry. We're all on edge, I guess," Darla sighs. She gives Melissa a shot of whiskey, but the glass ends up on the table, untouched. "You need to unwind a little, honey."

"I'm fine," Melissa mumbles. "What do we do next?" she asks me. "They came all the way up here. Hell, they practically walked through the front door, Colton. God, I should have just left like I planned."

"You're not going anywhere," Ethan snaps. "We protected you, didn't we? They left."

"Doesn't mean they won't be back." Mitch sighs heavily, his head hanging in defeat.

I've never seen him like this before. "It's not over, but we know what we're dealing with now," I say. "We can handle them. We *will* handle them."

"How?" Melissa replies. "Mitch is right. They only left because they were supposed to give you a message if they couldn't get to me."

"And because we wounded one of them," Ethan grumbles.

"I've already spoken to Sheriff Kavanaugh," I say. "Deputies will be stationed at every gate, 24/7. He's bringing state troopers to assist as well. And I called in a favor with a buddy of ours from the security company. They're coming in tomorrow to install a couple of new features on the system, as well as to fix whatever wires were cut."

Melissa exhales sharply. "They got too close, too fast, Colton."

"I need you to have a little more faith in us," I insist, though I can't exactly blame her for being wary. They did take us by surprise, and it could've ended way worse than it actually did. Dammit, she's right. They got too close, too fast. It cannot happen again. "Stay here. Ethan, Mitch, with me."

Darla and Sammy stay with Melissa while my brothers and I head outside.

It's afternoon, but the temperature is quickly dropping. It'll be near freezing soon, and it's still New Year's Eve. The champagne won't go down as easily as I'd hoped, but I sure as shit am not letting the Esparza cartel ruin this for us. We survived fucking Bosnia and a whole lot of other fresh hells so we could live out here in peace.

We'll do whatever it takes to protect our ranch and our woman.

That much I know.

"Melissa's right," Mitch reminds me as we get in my truck.

I turn the key in the ignition, and the engine rumbles to life. "I know. I just couldn't let her sit with these thoughts, man. The last thing we need is to for her to try to run off again."

"The law can't do much," Ethan says. "They don't have the proper resources up here."

"But we do," Mitch replies.

"We need to cross the T's and dot the I's before anything else," I cut in, driving up the dirt road to meet with the sheriff at the front gate. "We secure support through every legal channel, and then we draw a plan for ourselves. Those Esparza fuckers are determined to make an example out of Melissa. Jake Miller needs to pay for this."

Mitch nods in agreement. "We need to handle the cartel before we take care of Miller."

Ethan snarls. "Miller is the one who ripped off the cartel. They should be after him, not our woman."

"We don't have any proof to support that yet," I say as I pull over by the gate.

Kyle and Jason give us slight nods as they continue to assess the damage done to our security systems while taking notes on their phones. Sheriff Kavanaugh keeps looking around, squinting at the great sea of snow surrounding us.

"Sorry you had to come out here today, Sheriff," I tell him. "We certainly didn't have angry cartel goons on our bingo cards for the end of the year."

"We sort of knew this was coming, didn't we?" he replies with a raised eyebrow, hands deep in his dark green jacket pockets. "They took you by surprise."

I point at the wires Kyle is currently photographing. "Only because of that."

"We'll need to secure the wiring," Ethan mutters. "To stop others from doing the same or worse."

"I put a BOLO out on the three SUVs," Kavanaugh says. "I wouldn't hold my breath, though. They probably dumped them already."

"Every bit helps," I tell the sheriff.

He gives me a curious look. "How's the girl holding up?"

"Scared out of her mind," I say. "But we were there. Let's just leave it at that."

"And are you always going to be there? All day? All night?"

I know where he's going with this, and while I don't want to call in any favors too soon, the situation demands it. I place a hand on his shoulder. "We're grateful for your men, Sheriff. Having them on patrol duty will surely help. I need more, though."

"Listen, as soon as you fellas called, I reached out to the DEA. They're sending somebody over tomorrow to assist us. We're opening an investigation into today's events," he says. "I'm not sure how else we can help."

Frankly, I'm not too sure either.

It's a small town and a small county. A whole lot of land, but only a few souls scattered across. My guess is they drew their courage precisely from this line of reasoning. Small town, small town folk... they could get away with a lot in these parts if they keep moving and stay out of sight.

"Colt," Ethan says, looking somewhere to the east.

I follow his gaze and hear the rumbling of snowmobiles. Three of them, to be specific, approaching the ranch gate at high speed. They slow down as they get closer until they reach the gate and stop altogether.

As soon as they get off and start walking toward us, I recognize them.

"Marty?" I call out.

"And my two strapping young lads," he replies with a broad grin as he removes his woolen scarf, lips instantly red upon contact with the cold air.

"Marty, what the hell are you fellas doing here?" I laugh lightly and shake his hand, then do the same with his sons, Joe and Marty Jr. "It is good to see you both. And damn, y'all are going to be taller than your daddy by the looks of it."

The twenty-something-year-olds give me a pair of crooked smiles.

"We heard you need help," Marty says.

"We were going to celebrate New Year's Eve at the pub, but Joe thinks riding those bad boy snowmobiles and chugging champagne would be more fun," Junior adds.

"What are you talking about?" Mitch asks, understandably confused.

Marty gives the sheriff a slight nod, then looks at me. "Colt, I've known you boys since you were in diapers. This is our land, too, in a way. If anybody comes for you or your loved ones, they're coming for us as well. As soon as the sheriff told me what happened, I had to do something."

"I'm not following," I say.

"I told you I'm bringing Staties in, but even they're limited," Kavanaugh replies. "Marty had an idea, and I figured you'd be alright with it."

More engines roaring. Trucks aplenty drive up the road and pull over just beyond our gate. I recognize all of them. The patriarchs—and in two cases, the surviving matriarchs and widows of ranchers revered across the county. Our neighbors, spanning as far as half a county over. People we only see once a year maybe at cattle auctions and seasonal fairs. Good people.

"I can't believe this," I mumble, humbled by the people who are willing to stick their necks out to help us.

"Well, I can't guarantee we're going to be able to protect the whole ranch twenty-four-seven," Marty says, "but we're going to do our best. We'll take turns patrolling; you'll have deputies and Staties at the gates. That way, you fellas can do your thing and get those cartel schmucks out before they hurt somebody."

"Marty, you're serious," Mitch exclaims. "Y'all did this for us?"

"You would do the same for us," Joe, Marty's eldest, says with a stern brow. "You served this country, fellas. Loud and proud. We thank you for your service. Consider this our way of expressing our gratitude."

My eyes sting. I could probably cry a little if there weren't so many people around.

"Colt, Mrs. Ramsay wants to know if she and her ranch hands can handle the western hills patrol," Kyle cuts in.

I look over to Mrs. Ramsay, in her late fifties but still rocking jeans and plaid shirts and a cocked rifle on her arm, beige coat making her seem bigger than she actually is. "Mrs. Ramsay, you're too kind," I tell her. "Of course, you can take the western hills. I just don't want to impose."

"Nonsense, you're not imposing," she says, smiling with deep crow's feet extending from her pale blue eyes. "It'll be easier for me and the boys to bolt back to the ranch if something comes up, since your western hills are closer to home."

"I cannot thank you enough for this."

"Don't you worry," she says. "Somebody needs to show those drug lords this ain't Miami."

"It'll certainly help," Ethan says. "Thank you. All of you."

Mitch and Ethan start dividing the patrol tasks among our fellow ranchers, fetching a map from my truck to show them which sections of the property fence may be more vulnerable to a breach than others. Marty and his sons join the gathering while I stay behind with Kavanaugh. In the meantime, Kyle and Jason finish assessing the security system damages and send me their notes.

"Fucking hell," I mutter as I gloss over their observations. "They were prepared and familiar with the system."

"Jake Miller was over here twice," Kavanaugh reminds me.

"He must've surveyed the gate and the security measures," I reply with a slow nod. "I really need to get that fucker out of the picture before he does something worse."

"It's safe to assume Jake's helping the cartel with the whole scheme," Kavanaugh says. "But without any proof against him, she does get the short end of the stick here."

"He lied to the cartel because he was the one delivering for them," I reply. "My guess is they squeezed the door on him. He has no choice but to hound Melissa, even though he is responsible. Speaks to his character aplenty."

I look forward to smashing his face. It should be me, anyway, because if Ethan gets first dibs on the guy, Jake won't survive.

"He saw the ranch, Colt," Kavanaugh says. "All these acres, all this land. He thinks you're loaded. Speaking of, would you be able to pay him off if push came to shove?"

"I could pay the cartel off, yes," I tell the sheriff. "But it won't stop them from killing Melissa the first chance they get. I spoke about this with my brothers as well. And they agree. The Esparzas will never let Melissa walk away from this, not while they consider her responsible for the bust. Our best way forward is to find evidence on Jake that would clear Melissa's name."

"And in the meantime, you gotta keep their goons at bay," Kavanaugh sighs. "You've got your work cut out for yourselves, huh? I wish we could do more."

"I get it, I really do. We're stretched thin enough as it is," I say.

"I'll keep trying them, Colt. We've got that DEA fella coming; maybe I'll get him to apply some pressure on his bosses, get us a few more boots on the ground. It's gonna be worse otherwise."

I nod slowly, fully aware of the implications. And he's right. Each and every one of these ranchers, Marty and his sons, Mrs. Ramsay, all of them, are putting their lives at risk to help keep us safe. I've lost so many friends already in my life; I don't want to see more fall, especially not while they're voluntarily protecting us.

"Let's just pray this will do until we find a way to bring Jake Miller to justice," I tell the sheriff.

He's inclined to pray with me, judging by the sour look on his face.

23

MELISSA

It's close to midnight and I hear rustling in the kitchen.

"Darla's getting us more champagne," Mitch says as he sits on the couch, closer to my chair, while I let the fireplace glaze me with its golden warmth. "You haven't touched yours, though."

"I don't really feel like drinking tonight," I say, offering a faint smile.

"We've got people guarding the ranch," Mitch replies. "They're not coming back tonight. They've sent their message. They're done for the day."

"Doesn't make me feel any better."

Ethan and Colton come downstairs, both smiling broadly.

I give them a curious look. "What's up?"

"It's almost midnight," Colton says. "We're gonna head out and get the fireworks ready," Colton adds. "I'll text you to come out when we're set."

"That sounds great," I mumble, but even I have a hard time believing my own words.

Nothing sounds great at this point. Nothing except anything along the lines of "we caught the cartel" or "we found evidence that'll put Jake in prison and vacate your sentence." Anything else falls short.

"Melissa." Colt sighs and kneels before me. "It's going to be okay. You're not alone in this. Hell, we're not on our own anymore either. You've seen the ranchers patrolling, right? Practically everybody is here tonight celebrating New Year's Eve with us, for us."

I nod my head. "I know and I'm grateful. Really. Now go do your fireworks thing."

"As you wish, milady," Colton quips and plants a quick kiss on my lips before he and his brooding twin brother head out. "I'll text you."

"I'll keep my phone close," I shoot back.

Once they're out of the house, Mitch resumes his mini-interrogation. His eyes are gentle, and a subtle smile graces his face. "There's something else."

"What do you mean?"

"I'm not doing this dance with you again. There's something else bothering you."

"You mean besides the dangerous drug lords who want me to cough up the kind of money I wouldn't even be able to make in a lifetime or they'll kill me?"

"Come here," he says, leaning toward me.

We kiss, and he grunts softly as he pulls me out of the armchair and onto his lap. I nestle in his embrace, finding warmth, comfort, and love in his presence. For a few seconds, the world around us simply disappears. I only hear the crackling of firewood and the clinking of bottles from the kitchen.

"I feel safe with you, with Colton and Ethan," I tell Mitch. "It's all I can say right now."

"Ah, so there is something else," he chuckles.

"Isn't that the way life goes?"

"Melissa, you missed out on a sparkling career as a politician, did anyone ever tell you that?"

"No," I reply, giving him a confused look.

Mitch narrows his eyes at me, albeit in a playful manner. "You've got quite the skill at deflecting, baby. Granted, if I were you, I wouldn't go around kissing all of your constituents when they try to hold you accountable. That's just bad PR."

I can't help but laugh, throwing my head back for good measure. Mitch takes advantage and nuzzles my neck, breathing me in deeply before we both hear Darla coming out of the kitchen.

"More booze is coming!" she calls out, probably knowing what we're up to.

Out of respect, Mitch and I go back to our original seats. By the time Darla comes in, we're both decompressing. Granted, the room feels a whole lot warmer than before. She stops to admire the Christmas tree, still standing by the window with its colorful lights and tastefully themed decorations.

"I swear, this is the prettiest tree we've ever had on this ranch," she says.

"It's the same decorative set from the past few years," Mitch replies, his brow furrowed.

Darla scoffs and sets the bottles on the coffee table, next to the champagne glasses and the hors d'oeuvres—I prepared a massive cheeseboard to accompany the pigs in a blanket, the mini quiches, and the crudité platter for tonight's first course.

"Mitch, you poor soul, you have yet to grasp the touch of a woman," Darla says, shaking her head in faux dismay. "The tree looks a lot better this year despite using the same decorations because Melissa touched it."

"Aw…" I giggle.

"No, I'm serious. You've got excellent taste," she says. "An eye for detail. I may be a cowgirl and a rancher's daughter, but I know a pretty tree when I see one."

Mitch sighs deeply. "I put the tree up last year. I'm guessing you didn't like it?"

"Mind you, with literally the same decorations, you made it look like Rudolph the Red-Nosed Reindeer puked all over that poor heritage balsam fir. By God, what a beautiful specimen that was," Darla replies. "You cut that one down from the northern woods, didn't you?"

"I did," Mitch mutters, while I'm doubling over with laughter.

It's what I need, and Darla can tell.

I need to laugh, to forget about the storm that has taken over my life and over the ranch. Hell, I think Darla needs this almost as badly as me, and Mitch seems to feel the brief relief as well. We have one another in this mess. We are, in fact, stronger together. A few months ago, I couldn't even imagine I'd come to a place like this, that I'd leave that wretched cell and rediscover everything I love about life on the Avery Ranch.

But Jake and the cartel threaten to ruin everything.

I can't have that.

I *won't* have it. I deserve better, and these people are determined to give me better because I've already proven myself.

My phone pings with a message to come outside quick, so I bundle up against the cold as Colton and Ethan get ready to light the fireworks.

"Five, four…" Darla counts the seconds to midnight on her watch.

We're out in the backyard, a safe distance away from the house. The snow twinkles underneath the full moon, the sky unraveling as the blackest backdrop overhead. It's so beautiful in this seemingly endless quiet, as if the rest of the world has gone away with the darkness of the night.

"Three," Darla keeps counting, while Colton sets the first tower of fireworks on fire, lighting multiple fuses, one after the other.

"Wow, y'all worked hard on these, huh?" I laugh as Ethan and Mitch light the other two towers, built after the same model.

"Two, one! HAPPY NEW YEAR!" Darla shouts.

We're cheering and clinking glasses. Hugging one another. Laughing and wishing each other well, better than the year we just left behind. I revel in the love and the affection they so freely give me, but I make sure to toss my champagne over one shoulder when nobody's looking.

"And here we go!" Colton exclaims as he motions for us to step back.

We follow his lead and move closer to the house. Just in time, too, as the first round of projectiles pops with a red flash before they all shoot upward into the night sky. I'm breathless, my eyes wide with wonder as I watch the fireworks bolt and explode in a dazzling display of colorful lights. Cascades of yellow sparks. Bursts of red and green and blue. Fiery swirls of orange and white. Poppers going off in the snow, too.

POP! POP! BANG!

For a moment, I'm reminded of earlier and Mitch's rifle firing. But I quickly put the thought away as my men flank me and hold me close.

Sammy and Darla stick to our side, arms tied around one another. I can't stop myself from smiling as I look at them. In this particular second, as we've just crossed into the new year, I see the brightness in their eyes, the hope for better days ahead, and the love they've yet to profess for each other.

"You're going to be okay," Mitch tells me. "I've said it before, and I'm going to say it until you see for yourself, babe."

"I'm with you," I reply. "And I believe you."

"At least for tonight, let everything go," he says. "It's a new year. In a few hours, the sun's going to rise. There are better days ahead."

* * *

A NEW DAY DOES COME.

Then another.

And a third.

Slowly but surely, Long Pine and its surrounding areas come back to life. It still snows heavily here and there, yet we haven't dealt with another blizzard. It doesn't look like the temperatures are going back up anytime soon, though, so we're constantly prepared for a new icy front to come through.

The guys spend their working hours split between the ranch and the whole issue with Jake and the cartel. I rarely see them during the day—they're always out, either patrolling the fence or driving around the district, liaising with the sheriff and the DEA to try and get a line on the goons who came to the ranch on New Year's Eve. I'm still reeling from that awful moment.

My nights have gotten harder.

I wake up in a cold sweat, and while the physical comfort of the men does put me back to sleep, it doesn't resolve the underlying issue. More than once, I dreamed of having a knife to my throat. I shudder from the memory of it as I go out on the back porch to drop a few pieces of cooked chicken for the barn cats. They're roaming somewhere around, but the smell will draw them soon enough.

"Oh, fuck," I gasp as soon as I step out.

The cold air hits me like a hammer, and the thousands of thoughts I've been trying to avoid come back with a vengeance. I don't know what happened, but I lose control of everything quickly. The plate falls on the porch with a devastating crash, pieces of chicken scattered everywhere.

My knees follow, and I hunch over, struggling to breathe.

"My baby," I whisper, terrified of what each of these panic attacks might do to my pregnancy.

I'm crying and wheezing, trying to take deep breaths.

"My baby," I say it again, cradling my belly underneath a thick, plush winter coat. I'm cold and I'm afraid, the truth of my reality haunting me from every damn angle. No matter how I look at it, the situation is dire, and this whole waiting game is doing one hell of a number on my psyche.

Deep breath in, slow breath out.

"Melissa!" Darla's voice cuts through the darkness that threatens to take me. "Melissa, hold on, I'm here."

I hear her falling to her knees with a grunt. She gets in front of me, her shadow instantly soothing me as she rushes to rub my hands with hers. "Deep breaths, honey," she says. "In and out. You know the drill, come on."

"Right, right."

Deep breath in.

Slow breath out.

"You've got this, Melissa. Keep breathing."

"I'm so tired," I sob when the worst passes and I'm able to inhale and exhale without a thousand nails poking through my lungs, my throat. "I'm so fucking tired of all of this."

"Oh, girl," Darla says and hugs me.

"I'm sorry," I manage as I pull back. "I... I broke a plate... All this chicken..."

"Leave it," Darla replies. "The cats will eat it. Relax."

"I can't relax…"

"You haven't had an episode in over a week. I thought these were getting scarcer," Darla says, her worried gaze scanning me from head to toe. For a moment, I worry she'll pick up on my secret, but I've managed to keep the symptoms mostly to myself—I blamed everything else on stress, and no one has batted an eye thus far. "What's going on? It's been quiet the last few days."

I give her a weary look. "That's the issue. They vanished. They're in hiding, biding their time, getting ready to deliver another blow. The cops can't find them. I've yet to hear Colton say anything about new evidence against them. We're in fucking limbo, every day the same while I'm barely allowed to leave the house."

"It's for your own safety."

"I know, and I should appreciate that more, but I… Dammit, Darla, I feel like a prisoner. Even here, surrounded by good people and with all this land at my feet, the fresh air… I feel trapped. The way I felt in my prison cell."

"I'm sorry," she sighs and pulls me into another hug.

This time, I give into it.

It's not like she can do much else about it. She is as helpless as I am. As dependent on the outcome as I am. It's the impotence that's killing us. The inability to fight back, to speak my truth and for people to believe me. In the eyes of the law, I'm guilty. I'm serving my sentence. In the eyes of the cartel, too.

"I'm so angry," I say, lowering my gaze. "I wish I could find Jake myself and rip his eyes out. Oh, the things I would do to him… Argh!"

"Let it out," Darla replies. "Cuss and scream and just let it out. Better out than in, I always say. Be loud. Be angry. Fuck 'em all."

"I wish they'd all just… die, and I feel awful for wishing such things."

"It's absolutely normal and perfectly okay to feel this way about people who wouldn't hesitate to kill you, Melissa. You're human. You're not a saint."

"I'm supposed to be a God-fearing woman."

"You still are. But with a lot of rage in your soul. And you're entitled to it. That man Jake Miller did you wrong; he did you dirty. Rest assured, if you don't gouge his eyes out with a spoon, I will. And don't even think that Ethan will hesitate to blow his brains out the next time they meet," Darla says. "You didn't deserve any of it. And you certainly didn't deserve part two, either. The audacity of that bastard… it boggles the mind."

"And the cartel… how'd they buy his bullshit so easily?"

"You pled guilty," Darla sighs deeply. "It didn't work in your favor where they're concerned. Either way, you have every reason and every right to feel the way you do. So don't fight it, just feel it."

"Oh, I'm feeling it." Hot tears stream down my cheeks. My lips quiver as I look up at her. For a moment, I'm met with the silence of her soft, blue eyes.

"I'm still a prisoner," I say. "And I've never felt more trapped than now."

24

MITCH

We finally caught a line on Jake Miller.

I take Ethan with me, while Colton sticks around the ranch with the rest of our people—about a dozen extra pairs of eyes, to be specific. We're on the southern edge of town, driving slowly in Sammy's truck. It's an older, dark brown model and has a better chance of not standing out while we follow this prick around.

"Someday, when all of this is over, we're going to throw a big barbecue party at the ranch," I tell Ethan. I'm driving while he keeps an eye on Jake's car.

"He ditched his truck, I see," he mutters, making a note of the license plates. "Arkansas plates. That's interesting."

"Why's that interesting?"

"I've got a feeling he's gonna skip there if things go south here. Otherwise, he'd have used a local car." He pauses and gives me a long look. "I'm down with a barbecue, by the way.

It sounds good. It's a nice way to repay these people for their support."

"I'm just glad to see everyone coming together like this. It gives me hope for the generations to come."

"Look at you, sounding like you're already in the sunset of your life," Ethan scoffs. "You're jumping over an important step here. Wife, kids to raise. We haven't done that yet."

I give him a surprised side-eye. "Of all the people in the world, I swear you're the last one I ever imagined I'd hear talking like this."

"Like what?"

"Getting married. Having children."

Ahead, Jake turns left, driving past a sprawling trailer park. Above, the sky is a dull grey—a sign of more snow to come. We've yet to hear about another cold front, but it doesn't mean the weather's going to tone down anytime soon. It's the first week of January.

On the right side, there's not much to look at, except for a string of storage facilities. Half of them are empty. To my surprise, Jake takes a sharp right turn through the open gates of one such facility—the emptiest, saddest looking of them all.

"What's he doing?" I mumble, keeping a safe distance as I pull over the side of the road.

"Not sure. This place is practically abandoned," Ethan replies.

I nod slowly. "Yeah. He's probably hiding something here."

"Or meeting someone."

"We should get closer," I say, quickly texting Colton to let him know where we are. We always keep tabs on each other, particularly during troubled times like these. My brother and I get out of the pickup truck and carefully approach the gate.

"Any sign of his car yet?" I ask Ethan as he takes the lead.

"No. He must've taken it all the way to the back of the building," he says, pausing to look up.

Both gate pillars are fitted with surveillance cameras. But they're not active, by the looks of it. In fact, I see the wires hanging out, cut off a while back.

"No CCTV," I say.

"Not a bad thing. Not a good thing either," he replies.

"We can go in," I suggest. "Light feet, mouths shut, eyes wide open."

"Yeah."

"Are you carrying?" I ask.

He gives me a quick but easy-to-read look. "Damn right."

"Good. Me, too."

"It's happened since Melissa came along," Ethan says in a low voice as we cautiously go through the open gates, our eyes constantly scanning everything around us.

"What?"

"This whole getting married and having kids thing."

"Yeah, I get that."

"Do you think it might work with us? The four of us, I mean, in the long term?"

I give my brother a soft smile. "There's nothing I want more, to be honest. She's it for us, isn't she? Colton certainly feels that way."

"Me, too," Ethan replies, his gaze warm as he looks back at me. "The last time he and I agreed on someone coming into our lives forever, it was with you. The night Sammy rescued you, remember?"

"Yeah, you two were weirdly close," I chuckle softly.

Movement on the right side of the storage building makes us veer off to the left and out of anyone's sight. We're still for a while, waiting and listening. We here footsteps receding, voices mumbling. Nothing close enough yet, but definitely something. I can't hear an engine running, so Jake must've switched his off.

"We're twins," Ethan reminds me. "Our bond—"

"It's unique. I know. I learned that pretty quickly," I reply. "But not a day goes by that I'm not grateful for the way your family took me in. You know that, right?"

Ethan nods slowly. "You were meant to be our brother."

I can barely remember my own family. I see their faces in a handful of photos that survived the fire, but they feel like strangers, distant memories of who they were and what they meant to me. I was a little boy, paralyzed with fear and covered in soot, my hair singed and my clothes half burned when they pulled me out of the house. I still remember the flames, though, with crystal clarity.

That giant orange monster destroyed my home and my entire family. I was too little to understand back then, too young to fully process the grief, the loss. But the Averys took such good care of me that the transition was almost natural. One chapter of my life ended, and another began in the blink of an eye.

"Hold on," Ethan whispers, ears twitching as he listens. He slowly leans around the corner. "Clear, let's go."

I follow him as we sneak along the wall, eyes darting everywhere. I'm getting wartime flashbacks aplenty, but this place is quiet, maybe a little too quiet for my taste. Something is going on here. Miller wouldn't have picked this spot unless he wanted to be out of sight.

"There he is," I mumble as both Ethan and I spot Miller at the same time as soon as we reach the next corner at the back of the building.

The parking lot is empty, with the exception of two cars: Jake Miller's Arkansas-registered sedan and a black Escalade. The latter looks familiar. The trunk is open, and there's movement at the back, but I can't see much from this angle and this distance.

"That's a cartel vehicle," Ethan confirms.

I snap a picture and text the intel to Colton in real time while we continue to survey the parking area.

"He's out by his car," Ethan says.

Indeed, Jake leans against the driver's seat, constantly checking his phone. A guy comes out from behind the Escalade, closing the trunk.

I recognize him from New Year's Eve.

Jake gives him a stack of cash, which the guy is quick to check and shove into his jacket pocket. At the same time, his other hand comes around and slips something into Jake's coat pocket.

"It's an exchange," I whisper.

"Yeah, but what are they exchanging?" Ethan mumbles. "You know what? Fuck this, let's find out."

"What? No—"

Too late.

Ethan takes his semiautomatic Glock out and steps forward. "Not one of you motherfuckers move," he barks.

"Shit, shit." I have no choice but to go with him. I take my gun out and point it at Jake and his cartel buddy. "You heard the man. Don't move."

"Oh, for f—" Jake groans and rolls his eyes.

"We're interrupting something," I reply, noticing how he keeps one hand on the coat pocket in question. "What do you have there?"

"It's none of your goddamn business," Jake says.

"I suggest the two of you get out of here and start putting that money together," the cartel goon says, nowhere near as impressed by our presence and weapons as I had hoped. This clearly isn't the first time he's been caught seemingly unprepared. "My boss is running out of patience."

Ethan scoffs. "Your boss needs to get his head out of his ass. How did he buy this asshole's story, anyway? His girlfriend tried to run off with two million dollars' worth of cocaine? Really?"

"You were told to put that money upfront," the goon replies. "Nobody's got time for finger pointing and explanations.

Jake knows what he's gotta do. You, on the other hand, seem to have a comprehension problem."

"What I also have is a fucking Glock pointed at you," Ethan says. "Back off Melissa Carson. She had nothing to do with your drugs."

"She pled guilty," Jake chimes in.

I point my gun at him. "And we both know how that came to happen. Don't make me rid you of your kneecaps this early in the game. Come clean."

"Or I'll make you," Ethan adds, equally determined to hurt Jake.

I hear a familiar clicking sound and look over my shoulder. My stomach instantly drops at the sight of two more cartel fellas coming in, both sporting AK-47s and some nasty looks on their faces.

The first goon chuckles dryly. "You boys should've planned this better. I don't go anywhere alone."

Ethan looks around, realizing the monumental pile of shit we walked into. "Where did they come from?" he grumbles.

"Inside, probably," I reply. We're screwed.

"Might as well pop 'em," one of the men says.

But Jake intervenes. "No, you need them. They're the ones with the money."

"He's not as dumb as he looks," the second goon chuckles.

"There were three of them. These two can rot, for all I fucking care. Maybe it'll incentivize their brother to pay up."

Jake is about to object. But Ethan moves faster. In a single split-second, he shoots one of the men in the shoulder.

I immediately turn around and start firing. I get goon number two in the stomach. The third one fires back, but Ethan and I are already on the move. Jake hides behind his car, taking cover, while my brother and I run along the north side of the building.

"Move! Move!" I shout.

"Cover me!" Ethan says.

Without hesitation, I fire a couple more rounds. The third goon tries to catch up, but I manage to shoot him in the leg.

Ethan picks up speed, and so do I.

We turn the corner and bolt as fast as we can. The pavement is partially frozen. There are patches of snow, too. It makes it difficult for a clean run, so our boots slip now and then, slowing us down.

I hear someone shouting an order and Jake contradicting him. But their voices fade as we reach the front of the storage complex again. We don't stop until we run past the gates and return to our truck.

"You drive," I tell Ethan and toss him the keys.

He catches them, then slips the gun back into his holster and gets behind the wheel.

Just in time, too.

Another guy catches up, firing shot after shot.

I dodge two of his bullets, then retaliate and empty the clip, forcing him to take cover while I slip into the passenger seat.

The engine roars to life, and before I even shut the car door, Ethan floors it.

We screech onto the road and leave this hot mess behind.

My heart's in my throat.

Something tickles the side of my neck.

"Are you okay?" Ethan asks, panting as he keeps an eye on me and an eye on the road. "I'm gonna go around to the next highway exit and circle back," he says. "Are you okay, Mitch?"

"Yeah," I mutter, checking the side mirror. "It's just a graze."

It's starting to sting, but it'll be fine. That second round almost got me.

"Jake is still in business with them," Ethan says. "What the fuck is going on here?"

"He framed Melissa," I reply. "Nothing else makes sense. He planned everything that night. He had evidence and witnesses to incriminate her. Plus, his own testimony. He was probably hoping to get the drugs out of lockup after Melissa's sentencing. Something must've gone wrong."

"And Jake is trying to save his own ass by playing the game," Ethan says. "We need to get to the bottom of this," I tell my brother. "Or cough up the money and find someplace safe for Melissa to stay until it blows over."

Ethan shakes his head, hands gripping the wheel so tightly, his knuckles turn white. "It's never gonna blow over. Sooner or later, they will get to her, and they'll hurt her. Nobody wrongs the Esparza cartel and gets away with their life. Nobody. That much we know for a fact."

And it presents us with the inevitable.

We have no choice but to dig into Melissa's past to get to the bottom of Jake's lie and machinations in order to prove our theory. Jake wanted Melissa framed so he could run away with the cartel's money. He almost got off scot-free, too... but something happened. Likely with evidence lockup.

"We need to talk to her," I say.

25

MELISSA

It's hard to keep a panic attack at bay when Mitch and Ethan come home from a literal gunfight. Luckily, they're alive and well, with the exception of a graze on Mitch's neck. All I can do is sit in my armchair by the fire, wondering if I'll have any sense left in me to cook their dinner later tonight. My brain is ablaze. I'm still trying to wrap my head around everything.

Colton stands near the window thinking while Ethan tells us what happened.

"And so, we think Jake planned the whole thing," Mitch concludes. I can't take my eyes off the Band-aid on his neck.

"The whole thing," I mumble, hands discretely cradling my belly. I'm not showing yet, especially underneath this over-sized hoodie, but my baby is growing, my secret lingers beneath, and I could've lost both Ethan and Mitch today. The thought brings tears to my eyes.

Mitch rushes to kneel before me. "Hey, hey... Melissa, it's okay," he says, gently caressing my face. "We're okay, see?"

"But you could've—" I hiccup.

"We could've, but we didn't," Ethan adds and sits on the armrest of my chair, lovingly squeezing my shoulder. "We survived, and I have zero regrets about going there in the first place. We figured it out today. The whole thing."

"The whole thing," I say it again. "Make it make sense because it sounds like one hell of master plan."

Colton nods in agreement. "It kind of is if you think about it. Jake was making pennies compared to what the cartel was pulling in from their drug deals. He wanted more, but he didn't want or couldn't get involved any deeper with them. My guess is they're too dangerous, too easy to cross. So, and I'm just theorizing here… he figured he'd move some more cocaine for them. He'd get you arrested, charged, and imprisoned for it. If he had someone on the inside…"

"With Ainsworth PD, you mean," Ethan replies.

"Yeah. If he had a buddy or some accomplice in uniform over there, it might have seemed like an easy gig. They'd simply wait until Melissa was in prison, and then the confiscated drugs would just disappear."

Mitch sighs. "The cops have a protocol for these narcotics. They sit in evidence lockup for a predetermined period of time, and once that term expires, they destroy the drugs. If Jake's inside guy could swipe them before the term expired, he'd get himself a nice cut, and Jake would walk off with the rest. Melissa's in prison, fooled into pleading guilty because of overwhelming evidence and testimony against her."

"The cartel blames her, and here we are," Colton continues. "But something went wrong somewhere along the way. You're right, Mitch. Something happened with his inside guy in Ainsworth, and Jake found himself cut off from his stash. He can't get the drugs out of evidence lockup, which is why he came back to find Melissa, to scare her... to push her into figuring out a way to save his sorry ass."

Ethan scoffs. "He heard about the Path to Freedom Initiative. Probably did a little bit of digging beforehand. Saw the ranch, how big it is. He must've thought we're sitting on piles of cash out here."

"Truth be told, we're not poor," Mitch chuckles dryly.

"Yeah, but you can't pay off the cartel," I say, shaking my head in dismay. "We've gone over this one too many times. It's not an option. And it's not your mess to clean up."

"And we've gone over that, too," Colton cuts in. "It isn't your mess either, Melissa. You're our woman, our partner. We're not letting you take more of this fall for Jake Miller."

I take a deep breath, daring to imagine a future where there's no Jake, no cartel. Just me, holding my baby Wrapped in the arms of my men, thanking God for having brought me this far. It fills me with a sense of hope, an idea slipping into the back of my head—maybe, just maybe, all isn't lost yet.

"What can I do?" I ask the guys. "How can I help?"

"I'm glad you asked," Mitch says, a smile blooming across his dark, handsome face. I reach out and run my fingers over his growing stubble, loving the prickly feel against my skin. "We need to take a trip to the past, Melissa. We need to investigate the very incident that got you arrested, starting with the people who testified against you and your old friends from Lincoln."

"While you do that, Ethan and I will look into Ainsworth PD to see if we can find out who Jake's inside guy was," Colton says.

The idea of going back to Lincoln doesn't thrill me, to be honest. It's a part of my life I've long since said goodbye to. But if I have to do this in order to protect myself, my baby, and preserve what future I have left, then I guess I don't have a better choice. It's the right thing to do, especially after everything Colton, Ethan, and Mitch have already done for me.

Besides, my life here on the ranch won't go any further unless we get the cartel off my back.

It means throwing Jake to the wolves, but... I realize I have zero hesitation in that sense. They'll kill him. If we get to the truth, if we get the evidence we need against him, not only will my name be cleared and my sentence vacated—it will set Jake on a direct path of Hurricane Esparza. I've paid enough for his crimes. It's time to turn the tables and set things right.

"Okay, we'll go to Lincoln," I tell Mitch with a slight nod. "We'll get to the bottom of this and help the truth come to light. There's no other way."

"We're with you, baby," he replies and kisses me softly on the lips. "Every step of the way, we'll be right there with you."

It's what gives me the strength to push forward.

* * *

"Kyle and Jason are going to help Sammy with the cooking side of things. Darla's handling the cleaning," Mitch reassures me as we head to Lincoln.

We're using one of the ranch's older pickup trucks in order to keep a low profile, but I don't mind as long as I'm with Mitch. Ethan and Colton are headed to Ainsworth, in the meantime, following a similar strategy.

"It feels weird," I tell Mitch as the road opens ahead, "not being at the ranch."

"You've gotten used to it. Personally, I don't mind. In fact, I like it. It means you really have become one of us," he replies, half-smiling.

His phone is mounted on the dashboard, and I catch glimpses of Colton's updates coming in. They'll be in Ainsworth by nightfall. They haven't had any issues so far but the issues will start the minute they walk into the police station and start asking questions. If Mitch's theory is correct, they'll ruffle a few feathers and stir up a lot of trouble.

"I can ride a horse, too," I say with a little giggle, but I don't feel too peachy.

The pregnancy is taking its toll on me, an added discomfort to the preexisting stress and anxiety. I'm constantly queasy, trying my best to stay hydrated and keep my vitals in the above-average range. I take the prenatal vitamins every day, and I've even adjusted the ranch menu to fit my needs without explaining it to anyone. Hell, the guys have actually enjoyed the new recipes and fruit additions.

"Melissa, it's going to be okay," Mitch says after a while, noticing my greyish state.

I can't bring myself to tell him it's more physical than emotional, so I nod instead. "I know, babe. I trust you and your brothers completely. I just… I just wish we didn't have to do all this."

"We kind of do," he replies. "Yet another thing I don't mind, to be perfectly honest. You deserve to have your name cleared and your life given back to you in full. There's no turning the clock back, but we can still try and fix what we can." He pauses and takes a deep breath as we drive past a sign that says we're about fifty miles from Lincoln. "Now, tell me about those witnesses Jake found. What were their names again?"

"Laurel and Bruce," I say, glancing at my notes app on my phone.

"And you said you'd never met them."

I shake my head. "Laurel sort of looked familiar but I have no idea why. Bruce was a complete stranger to me. When they took the stand and claimed we were all friends, I kind of froze. I just couldn't believe they would just swear on the Bible and lie through their teeth like that."

"Did you and Jake have any common friends?"

"There was Lyle, a former foster kid like me. We hung out a lot while I was with Jake. He disappeared for a while," I say, trying to remember my friend. His shaggy blonde hair and brown freckles come to mind, his wiry frame and crooked smile. He lost a tooth during a bar brawl. I wonder if he ever got around to fixing that. "A good guy, but he didn't really like Jake."

"And looking back, why do you think that was?"

I chuckle bitterly. "That's a good question. Jake used to say it was because Lyle had feelings for me. I always thought Lyle was playing for the other team, though he never… you know, officially came out in that sense. I guess I chose to believe Jake." I frown and shake my head. "Oh, God, I need to go over every conversation I ever had with Jake and remember how much of his crap I actually bought."

"You were in love," Mitch replies. "And you have a way of seeing the best in people. Stop beating yourself up over it. We've all done stupid things; we've all believed our share of lies over the years. Okay, so, Lyle. He could be a good starting point for us. Would you be able to find him?"

"Let me see. We were connected on social media. On my old account. Hold on…"

A few minutes later, and as we get closer to Lincoln, I manage to log into my old social networking account. There's Lyle, posting a recent update to his profile. He looks a lot better to my delight. He's grown a lot over the past few years. The shaggy hair is gone and the scraggly blonde beard is trimmed. And his eyes look bright in the photo.

"Lyle Sanders," I say. "Yeah, he's active, still in Lincoln. Says here he works at the Troubadour. I know that place. It's a nice bistro downtown. Great food."

"We should stop by and grab some lunch, what do you say?"

I give Mitch a broad smile. "You keep reading my mind, babe. I could definitely eat something."

Lincoln is almost the same. Not much has changed in the handful of years since I've been gone. Storefronts look the same and so do the buildings. I see the same neighborhoods with townhouses and tiny front yards, picket fences, and curious neighbors watching every car that passes by. Not much has changed, but I certainly have. I feel like a stranger in my hometown.

We find the Troubadour and it's looking better than I remember it. The front of the building has been repainted and there's an added a splash of white on the giant window frames. It makes the whole place look brighter, cleaner. A hostess welcomes us at the door, and I notice the new uniforms: black pants, white shirt, dark red vest with a brass-colored nametag.

The young hostess takes us to a table and hands us menus.

"Is Lyle still working here?" I ask.

She smiles and nods. "Yep. He's actually here right now. Would you like him to wait on you?"

"That would be amazing. Thank you so much."

She nods politely and walks off.

"You're nervous," Mitch says, watching me intently.

"I don't think I'll stop being nervous until this is over," I reply. "But in the meantime, I could eat. Ah, quiche. They have quiche."

"You make the best quiche," he says.

I look up to find him smiling, his loving gaze drinking me in. I would like nothing more than to jump in his lap and hold him close for the rest of my life. He deserves all the love I can give him and his brothers alike.

"I certainly don't make the best quiche. Pretty sure the French beat me a very long time ago," I quip, and he laughs lightly.

A presence to my left makes me turn my head. As soon as we see each other, the air in the room changes completely.

"Melissa... Is that you?" he asks, his voice but a whisper.

"Lyle. Yeah, it's me. I can't believe this," I gasp and jump from my seat to hug him.

He welcomes the affection, albeit with slight reluctance. "You look fantastic," he says once I sit back down. "I almost didn't recognize you."

"It's me." I laugh lightly. "How've you been? How is everything?"

"Better than the last time we saw each other, for sure," he says, giving Mitch a second glance. "I'm Lyle, by the way. I'll be your server today."

"You're going to be our best friend today, Lyle," Mitch replies and politely slides a couple of hundred-dollar bills across the table.

"Wait, what?" Lyle is understandably confused.

I take the money and slip it into his vest pocket. "I need your help. Can we talk? When's your next break?"

"Um… Wow, okay, ten minutes?"

"Perfect. Meet you in the back garden?" I reply.

He nods slowly, then proceeds to take our order. "I'm glad to see you're okay, Melissa. Really. I'd heard some stuff, but I didn't think it was true. I figured they were confusing you with somebody else."

"And I heard this place makes the best quiche in town. So, please, don't prove me wrong," I reply, smiling as my gaze wanders across the restaurant.

Ten minutes later, I leave Mitch at the table waiting for our food. I head out into the back garden. It's too cold for anyone to sit here, and the terrace itself is cleared, the tables and chairs stacked in a corner under the roof overhang.

Lyle waits for me in the corner, next to the stack of rattan chairs and tables, looking rather nervous. His eyes keep darting back to the patio door.

"Hey, thanks for taking the time—" I try to speak but he cuts me off.

"Nobody here knows about my past, okay? Please, Melissa."

"Whoa, wait a moment. Hold on," I reply, my eyes wide. "I'm not here to cause you any trouble, Lyle, I swear. If anything, I'm just so glad to see you're doing okay."

"I am okay," he sighs. "Better. So much better. I'm renting an apartment. Can you believe it? I can afford rent. No more jumping from one couch to another, no more twisted relationships for a bit of food and shelter."

I give him a warm smile. "Good. You deserve it. And I'm sorry for bailing on you the way I did."

"Oh, long forgotten," he scoffs, almost smiling. "I figured Jake had you hooked on his loving. I couldn't do anything about it."

"You did try to warn me. I should've listened."

"What happened to you?" he asks, and I bring him up to speed, as briefly as I can, without mentioning my relationship with Colton, Ethan, and Mitch, and without mentioning my pregnancy. The less he knows about the most intimate layer of my current life, the better. But as he listens to me talking, as the details sink in, I can see the color draining from Lyle's face.

"Jesus, Melissa. That man is the fucking devil."

I nod in agreement. "Right now, our working theory is that it was all a frame-up. He planned to screw me over the way he did. And I have been digging into my past, trying to find some common points, some leads to follow. You were around at the time. I'm hoping you might be able to remember something I may have missed."

"Who were these witnesses again?" he asks, his brow furrowed.

"Laurel Buchanan," I say, remembering my notes from the trial. "And Bruce Jonesy. I might have known Laurel, but—"

"Hold on," he gasps, eyes wide as something clicks in the back of his mind. "Laurel. Tall and skinny? Long, black hair and tattoos everywhere?"

"Yeah."

"Yeah, I remember her. She had the word 'Blessed' tattooed across her neck. The guys at the cabaret and I used to make fun of it. We called her 'Little Miss Limited Employment Opportunities'. She was a raving lunatic. Beautiful but dangerously dumb, that girl."

My heart skips a beat. "You know her."

"Yeah. Went around, bouncing from one sugar daddy to another. She made ends meet as a working girl sometimes. She was one of us, Melissa. And I think we were all in the same foster home at one point. I was fifteen, you were maybe sixteen. The Frampton house. Yeah, that's it. We were in the same foster at the Framptons."

The more he tells me about those times, the more memories emerge from the darkness of my past. Moments I left behind and decided to forget because they were too dark, too miserable and painful. I didn't want to carry them into my future, into my life as a free woman. But Lyle is right. Laurel and I did cross paths. It wasn't for long, but we knew one another.

"What possessed her to lie in court about me?" I ask my friend.

Lyle offers a dry smile. "Isn't it obvious? She was sweet on Jake Miller. And Jake Miller was probably sweet on her. Come on, Mel... The bastard can be charming; let's give credit where credit is due."

"Do you know if she's still around? Or still in Lincoln?"

"No, but you could check the streets around the cabaret," he says. "They're still active. You might find her there if she's down on her luck."

"We'll try that, sure... What about that Bruce guy? I really have no idea who he is."

"Do you remember what he said during the trial?"

"Well, I remember Laurel saying she knew me from when we were kids, that we used to be friends, even though I couldn't remember her, not really. But Bruce... I can't for the life of me remember even meeting him."

Lyle thinks about it for a moment. "What did he look like?"

"Bruce was a big, burly guy. Receding hairline, dark hair. Looked like the kind of guy who spent most of his time catfishing women on the internet. Unkempt. Didn't have much regard for personal hygiene."

"Beady, brown eyes and the kind of sneer that made your insides squirm," Lyle groans and rolls his eyes. "Ugh, I know the guy. He used to run the laundromat up on Fourth Street. Where did he say he knew you from?"

"He claimed to be our friend. Mine and Jake's. Jake confirmed his story, so it was the two of them against me."

Lyle shakes his head again, this time in sheer disgust. "Bruce used the laundromat as a front to move drugs through Lincoln. We all knew about the place. I stayed away because... well, you know..."

"How long have you been clean now?"

"Four years," he says.

"I'm proud of you. I really am."

"And I'm proud of you for doing what you're doing now. It can't be easy, especially with the cartel trying to slit your throat. Jesus, Melissa, you sure drew the short stick on this one."

I shrug lightly. "It's not like I even saw it coming."

"Bruce was working with Jake. That much I can tell you for sure. If Jake was moving drugs for the cartel, then he must've passed them through Bruce's laundromat more than once. They did business together. That's why he testified against you."

"He knew details about me," I reply.

"He knew what Jake probably told him," Lyle says. "I guess you were right about him. You have a better chance of getting the truth out of Laurel if you find her and give her a good shakedown. Bruce will never fold."

"I agree. If he was in business with Jake, he certainly won't want to cross the cartel."

"But Laurel..."

"I might be able to persuade her. She'll need some incentive, though."

Lyle gives me a cold smirk. "Do your cool ranch bosses have friends in the Justice Department? 'Cause y'all can just offer her some kind of deal, like no jail time if she confesses to perjuring herself in court. It should be enough."

"Enough to aid in my case, but not to exonerate me. I need to bring Jake down altogether. I need proof that he planned the entire operation to frame me."

"Well, Laurel may be dangerously stupid by nature, but even she has her limits. She kept some kind of evidence of Jake's evildoing as an insurance policy. That girl's a rat. The streets raised her, the Framptons abused her... she's learned how to cover her back over the years. Find her, Melissa. Find her, and you might get closer to what you need."

"I can't thank you enough, Lyle."

"I wish I could do more."

"You've done plenty."

He glances back at the patio door. "My break is almost over. You should go back in. I'll bring your dishes in just a bit, alright?"

"Okay. You take care of yourself, yeah?" I tell him. This is probably the last time we're going to see each other for a while or maybe forever. "I'll leave you my number, in case you ever want to reach out, in case you need anything."

Lyle cups my cheek and gives me a soft, warm smile. "You take care of yourself first, honey. Don't you worry about me. I made it this far, right?"

The rest of our lunch at the Troubadour is quiet but delicious. Once we're done eating, we bid Lyle farewell and leave him a generous tip along with the tab, then head out.

With all the information we've gathered so far, Mitch and I decide to survey the cabaret neighborhood and see if we can get a line on Laurel. Maybe, like Lyle said, she's down on her luck again.

"How does it feel meeting up with an old friend like Lyle?" Mitch asks as we're cruising through the neighborhood in the late afternoon. It's getting dark, and the street lamps have come on, casting their warm glow over the snow-covered streets. It's getting colder, too, as the moon is swallowed by winter clouds.

"It was weird at first," I say, comfortable in the passenger seat next to Mitch. "I felt guilty, to be honest, for leaving him behind, for letting life get between us. Lyle is a wonderful guy. Stayed true to himself despite his slipups. I'm just happy to see he made it and that he found balance and is doing better."

"You're doing better, too."

"I'm serving what's left of a five-year prison sentence cooking on a ranch," I reply, then immediately burst into wholehearted laughter. "Granted, I'm also in love with three amazing men and trying not to get myself killed by the cartel. We can agree it's sort of a mixed bag, right?"

"That's one way of looking at things. Hold on," Mitch replies and pulls over.

Up ahead, on the right side, I see the main entrance of the former cabaret.

The strip club is still open. Red lights adorn the front door along with stylized posters of the current dancers. I see two big, brawny bouncers standing outside and plenty of people moving up and down the street. Some stop by, a few manage to get in. The rest just glance at the doors, admiring the posters before they continue walking.

Farther down the road, on the corner of 12th Street, I recognize a deal going down. One guy slips a roll of cash to another guy. Something else reaches the first guy's jacket pocket. It's all too familiar. Sickening. Sad.

"What did you just say?" Mitch asks, pulling me out of my silent analysis of a street I used to roam many winters ago.

"Huh?"

He leans closer, smiling softly as his eyes settle on my lips for a moment. "You're in love with three amazing men?"

"Well, yeah," I mumble, my face feeling hot. I didn't even register the impact my words would have in this situation. But I won't take them back. It's how I feel, and life is short and messy enough. I'm not going to lie, especially given the secret I'm carrying in my womb. "I'm in love…"

"I had no idea Sammy, Kyle, and Jason would touch your heart like that," Mitch replies.

I gasp and playfully slap him across the shoulder. He laughs and pulls me into a deep kiss. The kind of kiss that tells me more than his words could ever convey. I feel him, I feel his heart beating next to mine. Hell, I feel Colton and Ethan through him as well. I feel them all in my very soul, turning me inside out and making me a better woman with each passing day.

"I'm sure you know the feeling is mutual," Mitch says, his lips brushing mine. "We're head over heels for you, Melissa."

"What men in their right minds would go on this wild goose chase with me?" I laugh lightly and kiss the tip of his nose. "I kind of figured it out the minute you told me I'm one of yours, then you proceeded to refuse to let me run away, even though it would've saved you a heap of trouble."

"Oh, you figured it out then," Mitch raises an eyebrow.

I can't help but smile. "I might not seem very bright, but I can put two and two together."

"Melissa, you are one of the sharpest women I've ever met. Don't ever sell yourself short," he says, then kisses me again. This time, I feel his hunger and his longing, too. Were it not for our location and our mission, clothes would be flying off without a care in the world.

"We're going to do everything in our power to keep you safe, you hear me?" he asks, as if reading my mind.

"I hear you, babe," I reply with a loving smile.

 By midnight, we meet Colton and Ethan in Ainsworth.

There's a bar open late, and it's pretty empty at this hour. The weather isn't too friendly, as snow keeps falling and adding a new crisp layer of white on top of everything. But we have a few moments before we hit the road again, and we do need to go over all the intel we've gathered throughout the day.

"No trace of Laurel, but we did talk to a few guys. They said we should come around on the weekends, when business picks up a bit," Mitch tells his brothers. "In this cold-ass winter, even the working girls stay off the streets."

"Everything's done online anyway," Colton scoffs. "Pimps and hookers are getting with the times. We'll have to try that angle, too."

Ethan nods slowly. "We'll talk to Sheriff Kavanaugh as well. If Laurel's still in the business, then she's probably gotten herself arrested a few times. There should be a record, an address, some lead to follow until we find her."

"And Bruce?" Colton asks.

I shake my head. "No luck. The laundromat shut down shortly after the trial ended. And no one's seen the guy around. It's like he vanished."

"Chances are he did, in fact, vanish," Mitch mutters. "The cartel might've cut him loose, so to speak, or Jake."

"I don't know. Jake is a terrible human being, but I can't imagine him killing anyone," I say.

"Do not underestimate a desperate man, Melissa," Ethan warns me.

"What about Ainsworth PD?" I ask Ethan and Colton. "Any luck there?"

"Actually, yes," Colton replies and shows me a few photos he took on his phone. "Meet Officer Orlando Reyes."

I remember him. He was one of the arresting officers in my case. Just the sight of him makes my stomach churn and my blood run cold. "I know him," I say with a trembling voice. "He and his partner were the ones who arrested me."

"He was also the co-captain of the Star Spanglers, Ridgemont High's football team," Colton replies, his eyes on me. "Guess who he co-captained with."

"You're kidding," I gasp. "Jake?"

"Jake Miller himself, yeah."

"That was our inside guy, then," Mitch concludes. "What do we know about Officer Reyes?"

Colton goes through his phone, but I'm not sure I like the sour look on his face. "Not the most exemplary record. He got a few citations and complaints filed against him, but he was in charge of evidentiary lockup for the Ainsworth Police Department until a few months ago."

"What happened?" I ask.

"He's had a fatal accident," he says. "Died in a car crash. Horrible way to go, I imagine. I think that's why Jake was so desperate to get to you, Melissa."

"We spoke to Reyes' colleagues," Ethan adds. "That cocaine was destroyed at the end of the year. He missed his precious window, so was short with the cartel and was trying to survive because it all went to shit."

"It blew up in his face," Colton says. "Had Reyes gotten the drugs out before they were destroyed, Jake would've had his ticket out of here."

"But he didn't because he died," I mumble.

"So Jake had to figure out another way to get out from under the cartel's heavy boot. Once he learned about you getting into the Path to Freedom Initiative, he knew he had one last shot to keep the whole thing pinned on you while also keeping the cartel off his back," Colton says. "He's probably still moving drugs for them, facilitating deals and whatnot, but the cartel is short two million dollars' worth of cocaine. Jake is playing a stupid game here."

"You know what they say about stupid games," Ethan sighs, glancing down at his glass.

"Stupid prizes or not, I'm still legally responsible," I say. "How do we get closer to the truth, then? I need to find Laurel, right? That has to be it."

"Or we find a way to comb through Reyes' personal life, his bank accounts, his home," Mitch suggests. "There's got to be something there."

Time is running out.

Colton covers my hand with his. "Don't despair, Melissa. We're getting closer to the truth."

"Are we, though?" I scoff, lowering my gaze. There is comfort in his touch, yet the dangers surrounding us are too imposing, too frightening to overlook. "We have no witnesses, no physical evidence. We have stories, memories, but nothing that will hold up in court, especially with Reyes. The last thing Ainsworth PD will ever corroborate is that they had a corrupt cop on their payroll."

"We are closer today than we were yesterday," Colton insists. "We may not be able to find Bruce, but we still have a chance to find Laurel. Rest assured, we're going to dig through Reyes' stuff, too, until we find something. Jake is anything but a criminal mastermind, Melissa. He caught a few lucky breaks, that's all."

"We'll find something," Ethan says. "They're not invincible, not the cartel and certainly not that cowardly prick. We'll bring him down one way or another."

And while I would like nothing more than to blindly believe them, part of me knows there's always that one chance, no matter how slim, that things will not go the way we want them to go.

Running away is still an option, but it's also the worst option. I'd be putting myself in too much danger on top of the danger already there. At least I'm relatively safe at the ranch. We've got neighbors who are willing and eager to help, the sheriff and his deputies, too.

"What about that DEA investigator?" I ask, remembering snippets of our last conversation with Kavanaugh.

"He's tripping over red tape with the Justice Department," Mitch mutters. "But he is trying to open a RICO operating point in Long Pine. If he gets that going, we'll have a few more boots on the ground to work with if the cartel tries to come after you again."

I need to go to church and light a candle for my sorry ass. For all the progress Colton says we've made, I feel like we're struggling up a creek without a paddle.

26

MELISSA

Back at the ranch, nothing feels out of place. Everything is precisely the way we left it, and the days that follow bring us closer to February. Kyle and I take the tree down, return the decorations to their boxes, and carry everything upstairs to the attic. But I leave the colored lights on the windows as well as the decorative snowflakes. They speak of winter, not just Christmas, and I need as much seasonal cheer as I can possibly get under these wretched circumstances.

"Well, here's to hoping this winter's out of blizzards," Darla says as she wanders into the kitchen. "I can't wait for spring."

"It's still January," I chuckle softly as I take the dishes out of the washer and put them away in the cupboards.

"Upside is we only lost two heads of cattle throughout," Darla says. She stops by the coffee machine and brews herself a cup. I find comfort in the gurgling sound. "It's better than last winter, for sure."

I give her a curious look. "Did you do something different in the barns?"

"We upgraded the insulation and added a few more heaters on a separate power line," she replies. "It was worth the investment."

"Still, it's nice of you to make such an effort for a few cows."

"Colton wants us to care for each of them as though they're just as important as the family dog. And I see a lot of sense in that. A lot of ranchers don't bother."

I smile softly. "Colton and his brothers aren't like regular ranchers, though."

"You're right about that, and it shows. Their daddy would be proud. Their momma, too."

"You miss them."

Darla laughs lightly. "Oh, you bet. We had our arguments. Plenty of times we knocked heads and whatnot. But the ranch always thrived when there were more Averys around. Maybe I should've had some kids just to keep the numbers up. I don't know."

"Do you regret it?"

The last of the plates are safely put away. All that's left now is to wipe the counters down and go put my feet up for a while. At least my room doesn't feel as small as it used to, not even when I feel an episode coming. I call that progress.

"Not having kids?" Darla replies, and I nod slowly. "No. I mean, I wish I had a husband to have them with, but I guess it just wasn't meant for me. I don't regret a single day of my life, mind you. I love what I do."

"What about you and Sammy? What's going on there?"

Darla sighs and takes a seat at the table, slowly sipping her coffee. "Honestly, I don't know anymore. We were happy in the years past. It ended abruptly. I threw a hissy fit, he threw one as well, we let our bruised egos get in the way, and then it felt like we were drifting farther and farther apart."

"Yeah, but that was then. What about now? I can tell he loves you, Darla. He loves you deeply," I say.

"I'm all he's got in a way," she replies, lowering her gaze. I notice the pain in her eyes. I hear the longing in her voice. "He's all I've got in a way. I don't know what to tell you. I guess I'm too tired to mend that fence. If Sammy were to come up to me and tell me he wants us to give it another go, I wouldn't turn him down."

"Well, you haven't made it easy for him in that sense," I reply dryly.

Darla gives me a hard look.

For a moment, I worry she's going to tear me a new one. Instead, she scoffs. "You're right. I've been prickly and gnarly. A little too much, even for my own taste. I should do something about that, huh?"

"I mean, I don't blame you," I say, offering a smile. "Maybe... I don't know, try to reconnect with Sammy on a deeper level. Give him an opportunity to try again. A smile here, a touch on the shoulder there... you know, the subtle things that tell a man you're open to him. I think Sammy's worried you're gonna turn him away."

"I do have a history in that sense."

I sit at the table and listen to her spin her tale. She tells me about what it was like for them growing up on the ranch. Working together. Sharing this place and this life with Tamara, Sammy's wife. They were so close, maybe a little too close for Darla's liking. The more she speaks, the clearer it becomes that she's been in love with Sammy for most of her life, yet unable to do anything about it because she loved Tamara like a sister, too.

I don't have any advice or really anything I can say that will help her. She knows what she has to do. She just has to decide to do it.

"You should listen to your heart, Darla," I tell her. It's the only thing I know for sure.

"That's harder than it sounds."

"Don't I know it!"

We laugh together. I stand quickly to retrieve the coffee pot to fill her empty mug. But I suddenly feel lightheaded. Something comes over me, and I freeze, hand on the counter, gripping the towel tighter and tighter. My breathing is shallow. My skin tingles all over. I feel weak and as though my legs are going to give out. A sharp pain cuts through my body, my belly.

"Melissa, what's wrong?" Darla asks.

"I... I think I need to go to the clinic," I manage, then my knees give out.

I fall to the floor with a heavy thud, but I manage to absorb some of the shock with my hands. Sweat drips from my face. I'm hot and cold at the same time.

"Melissa!" Darla yelps and jumps from her seat and kneels beside me. "Honey, what's wrong? Talk to me."

"I need... I need to go to the clinic. Dr. Hartman..."

"Dr. Hartman? Oh..."

I give her a terrified look, but her gaze softens as it meets mine. She puts her arm around my shoulders and helps me get up.

"Come on," Darla says in a soft voice, "I'll drive you."

"Please," I mumble as I lean into her, cautiously leaving the kitchen behind. "They can't know. Not yet. Don't tell them. Please."

"Let's get you to Dr. Hartman first, honey," Darla replies. "Your health is the most important right now. Nothing else."

I'm humbled by her self-control, by her ability to react and take care of me when I clearly can't manage my condition. Whatever is happening feels wrong.

"You're gonna be okay," Darla says, once we get into the doctor's office. "I got this feeling."

"Gut feeling?" I ask, almost laughing. "Ow..."

The pain in my belly comes back, though not as sharp as the first round.

"Not like what you're dealing with right now, but yeah," Darla replies, giving me a worried look. "How far along are you? And why haven't you told anyone, especially the boys?"

"Given everything we've been dealing with, do you think they'd be able to focus if they knew about this?" I ask with a flat tone.

"Fair enough," she grumbles. "Plus, you're still an inmate."

"Yes, there's that, too," I sigh deeply. "I don't know what the hell I'm going to do. I just... I just want us to be safe, Darla."

Dr. Hartman comes in. "Good to see you again, Melissa. Nurse Hadley said you feel sick?"

"Hey, Doc. Yeah, pain, weakness..."

"Where's the pain?" he asks.

I describe my symptoms in as much detail as possible while he sets me up next to the ultrasound machine and checks my vitals again with a furrowed brow. "Mmm... Okay, let's not panic just yet," he says, then gives Darla a look. "Family?"

"She's the closest thing I have to a mother," I tell the doctor with a trembling voice.

"And Melissa's the closest thing I have to a daughter," Darla swiftly replies.

Dr. Hartman smiles and proceeds with the ultrasound. I lift my sweater and shudder when he applies the cold gel, then hold my breath as I wait for the image and sound to appear. My eyes are glued to the screen, though I have no idea what's on the screen.

"Any bleeding or spotting?" he asks.

I shake my head. "No, sir. My appetite's increased. There's still plenty of morning sickness, and not just in the morning... I get dizzy, sometimes."

"Oh, God, that's why you keep tuning out when one of us is talking to you," Darla groans. "I should've seen the signs. I should've put two and two together."

"I'm sorry," I mutter, giving her an apologetic smile. "No more secrets, though… I promise."

"You hear that?" Dr. Hartman interjects, ultrasound device stopping somewhere below my belly button. He turns the volume up, and I hear it.

"Oh, wow," I whisper.

Dr. Hartman narrows his eyes at the screen, and I tense up.

"What is it? Is something wrong?" I ask.

He smiles and shakes his head. "No, nothing is wrong. I just saw a little something on the screen here I want to confirm." He points to the image on the screen.

"Wait, is that…" Darla pipes in.

Now they're both looking at me, waiting for me to catch on. Suddenly it dawns on me. "Wait, two?"

"Yes, there's two," Dr. Hartman says. "And both look healthy."

"But there was only one the first time," I say, my brain struggling to process.

"It's not uncommon for one twin to hide behind the other when they're this small. We often don't catch twins until the second or even third ultrasounds."

"Oh, God, I'm having twins." It's even more overwhelming and twice as exciting and insanely challenging. How the hell am I going to manage?

"You're going to be okay," Darla replies. "I'm going to say it until you get it through your thick, beautiful, stubborn head, Melissa. You're going to be okay."

"Am I, Darla?" I'm on the verge of tears, and I don't even know if they're tears of joy or despair. "How do you know?"

Dr. Hartman clears his throat. "Well, health-wise, the little ones seem to be within their parameters. The cramping can be normal as your uterus expands to accommodate the growing babies. As long as there's no intensive bleeding or any other symptom that requires hospitalization, you should be alright."

Once we're in the car, neither of us moves or says anything. Darla sits behind the wheel, staring ahead. I sink into the passenger seat, my face flushed but my heart a tad lighter knowing my baby—correction—babies are okay.

"I need to eat more," I mutter, remembering Dr. Hartman's advice. "Didn't think that was possible, but here we are."

"You've been sneaking food upstairs, huh?"

I nod slowly. "Had to keep a low profile."

"Well, you're eating for three, it seems." Darla exhales sharply. "By the stars, when God gives you a challenge, He does not go easy on you, does He?"

We laugh despite the shock.

"I don't want to go back to the ranch yet," Darla says after a while. "In fact, I think we should eat something. The Cavalier is open. How about a pizza?"

"My mouth is watering," I bluntly reply.

Darla turns the key in the ignition, and it's as if my soul restarts along with the truck engine. We need to get some food in our stomachs, then we can think about what I'm going to do next. One thing is clear. I can't hold out on this pregnancy much longer. Darla already knows. It's only a matter of time before the guys find out. They should hear it from me.

Just as Darla is about to pull out onto the road, a car blocks us. "Hey!" Darla shouts. "Move it along!"

But the driver gets out.

"Oh, no," I manage as I recognize Jake. "It's Jake."

He's smiling the most obnoxious smile as he approaches our truck. "We need to talk, Melissa. Right now."

"You need to get the fuck out of my way," Darla replies, but he blatantly ignores her, pointing a finger at me.

"Melissa, get out of the truck. We need to talk. You're running out of time, and I'm the only one who can help you."

My hand reaches for the door, but Darla stops me. "You sit right there, honey. You're not going anywhere with this fool."

"I have no intention of going anywhere with him," I say. "I just want him to leave me alone."

"Then sit the fuck down and let me handle this." To my surprise, she reaches for the glove compartment and takes out a shiny Colt revolver.

"Darla..." I whisper, but she cuts me off.

"Relax, kid. I know what I'm doing."

She gets out of the car, and Jake starts laughing. "Lady, I have no quarrel with you. I just need to talk to—WHOA!"

"You need to get behind the wheel of that vehicle," Darla says, pointing the gun at him. "You need to drive as far away from this town as possible. Don't look back. Don't pass go. Don't collect 200 dollars, you miserable son of a bitch."

"Hold on, ma'am, I'm trying to help Melissa!"

"You're only trying to help yourself," she hisses and takes a step forward.

Jake moves back, hands up as his eyes widen with the realization that Darla is not kidding. She has every intention of shooting him in the face if he doesn't do as he's told.

"Melissa, please," he tries to reason with me again, but I don't budge.

Instead, I cradle my womb and find comfort and safety in Darla's presence. All the Averys are hardcore and insanely protective of their family and loved ones. I see it now. The drive, the fierceness, the fearlessness. It's in their blood, and I sure as hell hopes it gets passed down to my babies.

"Hey!" she shouts again. "What did I just say?"

"Alright, alright!" Jake concedes and moves farther back. "I'm leaving."

"I don't see you leaving just yet," Darla replies. "Get in the car. Drive. Leave Melissa alone, or I swear to all that is holy in this world I will empty this gun into your sorry ass."

I hold my breath as I watch him get back in his car and drive off. He makes a sharp left turn and disappears around the block. Once he's out of my sight, I exhale slowly and welcome Darla behind the wheel.

"Thank you," I say, my voice uneven with emotion. "And I am so sorry."

"What the hell are you sorry for?" she asks, putting the gun back in the glove compartment.

"This! This whole frickin' mess. Jake, the cartel, guns every-where... I'm so tired. I never asked for any of it."

Darla gives me a long, hard look. "Of course you didn't ask for any of it, nor could I blame you. I get it, now. You are a victim of that asshole's scheming, pure and simple. You just happened to cross our path, and I know with unshakable confidence that God didn't bring you to us willy-nilly. This was meant to happen. This bubble had to burst."

"This is more than a bubble," I sigh deeply. "It's a nightmare."

"And you're not dealing with any of it on your own, alright? I've got you. The boys have got you. Hell, Sammy and Kyle and Jason have your back, too. You've seen all those neigh-bors patrolling the ranch, covering our asses... this is what we do out here, honey. We look out for our own."

"I still feel responsible."

"You'll feel less responsible once we get some food in you."

Fifteen minutes later, we're at the Cavalier, getting comfy at one of their corner tables. It's nice and warm in here. Rela-tively quiet, too. The lunch rush is over, and only a few customers are hanging around the bar at this time.

Louisa comes over with our menus. She's just as pretty and as obnoxious as the last time I saw her.

"Oh, look what the cat dragged in," the girl says, then gives Darla a flat smile. "How are you doing, Auntie D?"

"I've seen better days," Darla replies. "What's with all that makeup?"

"Huh?" Louisa is taken by surprise. She doesn't know how to react. "What do you mean? What's wrong with my makeup?"

Darla scoffs. "You're barely legal, honey. No need for cakey foundation and way too much eyeshadow, especially in this line of work. What are you tryin' to do, hit menopause before you turn thirty?"

"Oh, wow, that's… harsh."

"It makes you look old."

"I would really love a chicken and mushroom pie with the flaky crust, if your kitchen is open," I cut in with a soft smile, almost feeling sorry for the girl. "And some sparkling water, please."

"Huh? The chicken and mushroom pie," the girl says, then starts jotting it down. "Right. Yeah, kitchen's open, we can get that done for you. Anything to start with?"

"Um, maybe a cheese and tomato salad?"

"Okay," she replies, taking my order. "And sparkling water, you said."

"Yes, please."

"How about you, Auntie D? What do you wanna eat to go with that nasty attitude you dragged in today?" Louisa says, finding her voice again.

Darla laughs lightly. "You could never take criticism. Makes you more like your uncle than you care to admit. Alright," she pauses and glances through the menu. "Actually, you know what? I'll take the same as Melissa. Chicken and mushroom pie. Salad starter. But add a coffee with my sparkling water, please. I need the caffeine fix."

Louisa nods slowly and walks off, likely muttering a slew of curses that would make a nun blush.

"What?" Darla asks, raising an eyebrow at me. "She had it coming."

"I wasn't going to say anything," I chuckle softly. "But I do appreciate it."

"Don't worry about it. That girl's been carrying a torch for Colton ever since she was in pigtails. I warned Sammy, but he said it would pass." She shakes her head slowly. "Colton told me about your date night and Louisa's behavior."

"Oh."

"Well, nothing stays a secret for too long at the ranch," she replies. "Speaking of. You do need to figure out how you're going to tell them about the babies."

"I'll tell them tonight," I say, nodding with newfound determination. "I'll sit them down and just... lay it out. Oh, Darla, what if they don't want any of this?"

She smiles broadly. "Are you kidding? Those boys are dying to be fathers, to start a family. They just so happened to get lucky enough to stumble upon a woman like you. If that ain't God talkin', I don't know what is."

"But the cartel—"

"Auntie Darla, can I talk to you for a moment?" Louisa cuts in. I didn't even see her coming over. "It's important."

Darla looks up at her. "What is it?"

"It's private. Please."

"Go on, Darla, it's cool. I'll wait," I say.

"Alright."

The minutes roll by, and my thoughts continue to swirl, ideas brewing, fears unlocking. I become restless as the salads arrive, courtesy of the other waitress. I look around, but I can't see Louisa anywhere. Darla, either. I check the time on my phone. It's been twenty minutes. That can't be right.

"What the…" I mumble and get up from the table.

I'd rather focus on my salad and toasted bread, but something feels off. I walk out of the Cavalier, hopefully finding Darla and Louisa, but they're nowhere to be found. The street itself is almost empty. Barely a soul outside. It's close to freezing, and it looks like it's going to snow again.

"Where are they?" I ask and go up the road. There's an alley to my right that leads to the back door of the pub.

There's a car parked a few feet away, wedged between the building walls. No one else can get in or out. The headlights come on, temporarily blinding me. "Motherf…" My voice trails as I hear the car door open and the rushed footsteps.

My heart starts racing. My instincts kick in as I realize the engine is running. I turn to run back up the alley, but I react too late.

Jake covers my mouth with his hand to stop me from screaming. His arm snakes around my waist, and I'm hoisted off the ground. I struggle as hard as I can, trying to kick and hit whatever I can, but I'm no match for a desperate man's strength.

He drags me out of sight and shoves into the trunk of his car.

"Jake!" I cry out when he pulls back.

"Shut up!" he snaps and smacks me so hard across the face, I see stars for long enough for him to close the trunk.

"Oh, God," I mumble, fear and dread eating me up from the inside. I'm trapped in the trunk of Jake's car. I listen to him get back behind the wheel.

The car starts moving, and I'm screwed.

27

ETHAN

It took us a while and a few favors pulled from former Army buddies, but we found Laurel Buchanan. She's working at a pizza restaurant, bussing tables, and making considerably less money, but she looks at peace from where I'm sitting—which is the passenger seat of Colton's truck.

"It's her," I confirm, taking another look at the photo we have of her.

Colton follows my gaze, using a pair of binoculars. "She's a redhead now."

"Spoke to one of her colleagues. She goes by a different name these days."

"Which is?"

I didn't get much out of the pizza cook when I interviewed him an hour ago, but what I did get does qualify as useful information. "Melissa," I say. "Melissa Hancock."

"That's a little on the nose, isn't it?"

"The audacity is something," I grumble. "How do we do this?"

Colton thinks about it for a moment. "We can't arrest her. We don't have the authority. We can't spook her either. But we do want to bring her in for Kavanaugh to put just enough pressure on her to get her to confess."

"Look at her," I tell my brother. "She switched up her whole life to keep distance between herself and Jake Miller and the Esparza cartel. The moment she realizes who we are, Laurel's gonna run for the hills. We'll lose her."

"We can't afford to lose her."

"We need to entice her with something," I say. "Otherwise, she won't tell the truth."

Colton nods slowly. We need a smart approach if we're to convince her to testify under oath again.

Colton's phone rings. He picks up while I keep an eye on Laurel.

"Hey, Darla, what's up?"

I hear her frantic voice, but I can't make out the words. At the same time, Laurel carries a large pizza over to a table, then refills their coffee mugs with a flat, lifeless smile plastered across her face.

"Whoa… Darla, deep breath. Where are you?" Colton asks.

He has my full attention.

"Stay there, we're on our way. And call the sheriff," Colton says, then hangs up and starts the engine. "We need to get back to Long Pine right now."

"What about Laurel?"

"She's not going anywhere. She doesn't know we were here," he replies, then gives me a look I haven't seen in a very long time. He's scared, the blue in his eyes darkening with concern. "Melissa's been taken."

I thought I could weather any storm, any blizzard. I could take on an entire cartel of bloodthirsty Colombians and a thousand Jake Millers. I fought insurgents and terrorists, craven lunatics and warmongers. I stared death in the eyes, more times than I could count, yet all I ever had to do was take a deep breath, count to ten, and then let the monster inside me take over.

This time, however, I'm lost.

As Colton races toward Long Pine, the town rising ahead with its gloomy greys and white roofs, I realize I wasn't prepared for this, for the real possibility that we might lose Melissa. She's gone, and we don't know what happened. Colton doesn't have much information either. Darla was too frantic over the phone.

"There they are," Colton says, pulling up outside the Cavalier.

Sammy is present, talking to his niece Louisa, while Kavanaugh pulls Darla away from the crying girl. The sheriff's car is parked right in front of the diner's massive doors, red and blue lights flashing, while curious onlookers try to hang around to find out what's going on. Kavanaugh waves them away.

"Move it along, folks, nothin' to see here!" he barks.

"I'll smash her face!" Darla snaps, and the sheriff has to literally position himself between her and Louisa, aided by an equally befuddled Sammy.

"Thank God you're here," Sammy says upon noticing us. "Get her under control," he adds, pointing at Darla.

"She's to blame!" our aunt shouts, red with fury.

Colton steps in and unceremoniously drags her farther away from Sammy and Louisa, while Kavanaugh sticks by our side.

"Okay, what the fuck is going on here?" my brother asks, giving both the sheriff and Darla equal shares of glaring attention. "Where's Melissa?"

"Louisa said she wanted to talk," Darla says with a trembling voice. "So, she takes me out of the pub and down the road. But it was all a ruse. She wanted me distracted so they could take Melissa."

"I had nothing to do with it!" Louisa cries.

"I will smack the shit out of you!"

"Darla, focus!" I snap. "Talk to us, come on!"

Darla takes a deep breath, shaking like a leaf. "I brought Melissa into town. We stopped by the Cavalier to eat. We're waiting for our order when Louisa comes over and says she wants to talk to me in private."

"Okay, we're with you so far," Colton says. "Go on."

"I go out, Louisa's with me. She keeps inching away from the pub until we reach the Pink Flamingo coffee shop—"

"That's almost a block from here," Kavanaugh mutters.

"Aunt Darla, you said Melissa's missing," Colton cuts in.

"I turn around, and I see Melissa coming out of the restaurant." She points at the diner. "She was looking for me. Next thing I know, I'm running toward her... and I see Jake Miller pop out of the service alley. He drags her in. I'm shouting, calling out his name and Melissa's, but I was too late. By the time I got back here, he had her in his trunk and was swerving out onto the road."

She breaks down crying, and Colton holds her close.

"Shit," I mumble, understanding precisely what this means.

"I put out an APB on Miller's car. I've got the deputies combing through and around town, looking for them," Kavanaugh assures us. "But I don't understand what Louisa's role is in any of this."

Darla curses under her breath. "She was in on it. I don't know if Jake was going to go into the diner and get Melissa out, or if Melissa simply walked into the trap, but I wasn't supposed to be there. Louisa said so. She kept shouting after me to let it go, to get out of his way."

And then it hits me.

I open my phone and do a quick search on social media. It doesn't take long to see it. The subtle relationship-hinting posts. The obscure selfies that show enough but not everything—just enough for me to recognize half of Jake Miller's face as he smiles and holds Louisa close. I show Colton the feed.

"Keep Darla away," he tells Kavanaugh.

The two of us switch focus and walk over to Sammy and Louisa. Sammy is understandably annoyed and confused. Louisa's crocodile tears don't impress me, though. I can tell from the way her gaze keeps darting around that she knows she's about to be found out, whether she likes it or not.

"What the hell is going on here, fellas?" Sammy asks. "What's gotten into Darla?"

"How long have you and Jake been hooking up?" Colton addresses Louisa directly.

"What… Who? I don't know what you're talking about," the girl replies, her eyes wide with faux innocence.

Colton shakes his head and shows her the social media feed. "This isn't a joke, Louisa. A woman's life is at stake."

"Oh, you mean the skank you've been shacking up with," she blurts.

Immediately, Sammy's protective demeanor changes. "Excuse me, miss? What did you just say? Is it true? Is it? You and Jake Miller?"

"He's a good man! it's not his fault that bitch ruined him!" Louisa insists.

Colton can't help but groan with frustration, running his fingers through his hair. "Oh, God, Sammy, you need to do something about this, 'cause I'm about to lose my damn mind."

"So, it's true, then," Sammy says to Louisa, then grabs her by the arm. "Listen to me very carefully, little girl. That man has been feeding you lies, and you're gonna tell us everything you know, every goddamn detail, or I swear I'm gonna let Kavanaugh arrest you!"

"Arrest me? For what?"

"Conspiracy to commit kidnapping for starters," the sheriff replies, one ear on our conversation and one eye firmly on Darla. "Melissa Carson was taken against her will."

"Yeah, because it's the only way for Jake to clear his name!" Louisa insists.

"Melissa went to prison because of Jake's lies," I yell, then lower my voice as I continue. "He brought the Esparza cartel to our doorstep. We're sleeping with one eye open and shotguns under our beds because of him. You're gonna tell us precisely how you got involved with that fucker and everything else you know, or I swear I'm going to make your life miserable. Your uncle Sammy won't be able to help you if I get my hands on you, you little brat."

Whether it's the tone of my voice or the glare in my eyes, but it works.

Quivering with fear, Louisa starts singing like a nightingale on a sweet summer night. She tells us all about how Jake first approached her, how he love-bombed her—though she calls it courting because she's still too young and inexperienced to tell a lie from a truth as long as she gets a man's attention. Kavanaugh then takes her in for questioning.

"I'm gonna take Darla back to the ranch," Sammy says as we watch Louisa being ushered into the backseat of the sheriff's car. "She gets a phone call, anyway. She can call her no-good parents to bail her out. I'm done here."

"Sorry you got involved, Sammy," Colton replies.

"That piece of shit Jake Miller really got around, didn't he?"

"Yeah, and he got way too lucky, too," Darla chimes in. "Melissa had no idea what was happening, the poor soul."

"They're a few hours ahead of us, but we can still catch up," I tell Colton. "We do need to get Laurel over here, though. We can't let her slip away."

"We can't go after her ourselves either. We need to find Melissa," my brother says, and I completely agree. "I'll reach out to our friends. One of them will come through. They just need to pick Laurel up and drop her off with Kavanaugh. We'll explain everything once she's secured. We can't risk her disappearing like Bruce, not when we're so fucking close."

Sammy nods and offers to drive Darla back to the ranch. "The boys might need your truck to split up while they go out lookin' for Melissa," he says. "Colton's got his ride, but Ethan—"

"Yeah, that's fine," Darla concedes and gives me the keys. "You drive safe, boys. And don't get into any more trouble."

"Will do, Auntie," I reply with a stern nod. "Thank you for trying to keep Melissa out of harm's way."

She tears up. "I did, I swear to God I did."

"We'll find her," Colton says. "I'll get Mitch down here as well."

"There's something you need to know, though," Darla adds. "I wasn't gonna tell you before she had a chance to sit you boys down."

"Tell us what?" I ask.

The look on Darla's face fills me with a new kind of dread as the words spill out of her mouth. "Melissa's pregnant. That's why we were in town earlier. She got sick, really sick. We did an ultrasound and everything."

"Was she okay?" Colton gasps, his eyes wide with shock.

I can barely fucking breathe as reality sinks in.

"Yeah, for the most part. It's mostly stress-related, and I can't blame her. She's scared, boys. Scared of prison, scared of the cartel, scared she won't survive, or worse, that she'll end up back in Ridgeboro and they'll take her babies away," Darla says, trying hard not to cry.

"Babies?" I mumble.

Her eyes widen, then she sighs. "She's having twins."

Colton and I exchange glances. We know what this means. Or what it most likely means. The twin gene runs strong down the Avery bloodline. That's our seed growing in Melissa's womb, and she was thrown into the trunk of Jake Miller's car, taken away. Fucking hell, as if things weren't complicated enough, I can't even rejoice in the exhilaration of learning that we're going to be fathers.

That we're going to be a family.

We need to find her. We need to protect her.

Now, more than ever.

28

MELISSA

I'm sick to my stomach before the trunk lid opens again.

It's still light outside, and after maybe an hour spent in the darkness, it smashes into me. I'm temporarily blind as my nose registers a slew of different smells, my brain trying to learn as much about my surroundings as possible in the shortest span of time.

"Get out," Jake says as he forcibly pulls me out.

"Jake, what the hell are you doing?"

When my boots hit the ground and I wobble in a desperate attempt to remain upright, I realize we're far away from Long Pine. It's some kind of abandoned farm by the looks of it. Heaps of brambles and unkempt bushes sit under heavy layers of hardened snow. There's a rickety old farmhouse with broken windows and a crumbling roof and miles and miles of empty land. It's all white and there's nothing else in sight, except for a few patches of naked trees here and there.

"Where are we?" I ask.

"Move. We're going inside," Jake shoves me, and I stumble forward.

I'm shaking like a leaf, damn near close to fainting as I slowly regain my focus and self-awareness. I'm okay. I'm alive and breathing. I can still do something about this situation. First, however, I need to understand what Jake's play is here.

He pushes me again. "Come on, move!"

"I'm going!" I snap and trudge up the creaky wooden stairs.

I push the door open. For a moment, I worry it might fall off its hinges as threads of snow and dust fall into the semi-darkness. No one has lived here for a long time. The windows are cracked and too filthy to see through. There's grime and dirt everywhere, and years' worth of dust mites must be hiding in the old sofa—one of the few pieces of furniture left in this place.

The fireplace has dull embers in it, though. There's a hint of warmth lingering about it. I notice the footprints through the dust on the floor and the crumpled sleeping bag next to the fireplace. An empty coffee mug is on the table. There's a duffel bag on a chair in a corner.

"You've been squatting here," I mutter, my eyes darting and registering every possible detail. "Jake, what the hell is going on?"

"What's going on is you're not doing your part, and now the cartel's after me for not following through on my promise," Jake hisses and slams the front door.

He takes deep breaths and pulls a flask out of his coat pocket. He sets the gun on the windowsill, watching me like a hawk as he unscrews the cap and takes a swig. The smell of cheap whiskey and sweat and fear hits me. All I can do is shake my head slowly.

"I told you to get the money out of your rancher fuckboy," Jake says. "That's all you had to do. Cry a little, explain what's at stake. I know they have it."

"If they pay the cartel on my behalf, it changes nothing," I reply. "You know it, and I know it. They're still going to kill me."

"Like I give two shits about what happens to you!" he snarls. "This is about me! About *my* survival! If you pay them off, I can move on. I can't even leave the fucking state. They're always following me around, always figuring out where to find me."

"Are you hearing yourself?" I gasp, trying so hard not to laugh in his face. His audacity is unbelievable, and I'm starting to think he has slipped into some kind of psychotic delusion. "You blamed everything on me. You had me thrown in prison to serve a sentence meant for you. You told the cartel that I stole their drugs, and now you're mad because I won't pay you back for the drugs you had me transporting, unbeknownst to me? Are you insane?"

He shakes his head, chuckling bitterly. "It wasn't supposed to turn out this way. I had a plan."

"Tough titties, Jake. You're in this mess because of you and you alone."

"You're gonna stay here until the Averys pay me two million dollars," Jake replies. "I'll make sure they get that message, loud and clear. And if they don't come through for you, I'm gonna have to kill you myself. If I kill you, at least the truth will die with you."

My blood runs cold, but I can't let him see my fear. I cannot show him the slightest hint of vulnerability, especially in my condition. "Are you hearing yourself, Jake?"

"Oh, yeah, I've thought about it a lot. These are my only options," he says, staring out the window for a moment. "The ranchers pay, and I get to walk out of this mess without the cartel coming after me for not going harder on you." He faces me. "'Cause I promised them, Melissa. I promised them I would get the money out of you, one way or another."

"Right, because they think I stole those drugs."

He rolls his eyes. "Again, with that. It doesn't matter anymore. Point is, I can't have you walking around, playing the victim, and giving anybody enough information to revisit your arrest. The last thing I need is the cartel suspecting I might've lied to them."

"Might've," I scoff.

Jake grabs the gun and points it at me. "I swear to God I'm gonna shoot you right now if you don't stop talking."

"Your lack of self-awareness is truly spectacular," I reply, my stomach tight, my heart pounding with dread. "This is what it's come to, huh? After such an elaborate ploy to have me take the fall for you—"

"I didn't think it would go wrong! I was supposed to get my drugs back!" he shouts. "Okay? I was supposed to get them out of lockup. But that idiot had to fucking die and I was stuck on the outside looking in. That money would've secured a clean escape."

"Isn't that what you wanted the two million for when you first came to the ranch?"

He nods once. "Yeah. That was the plan. Finish what I'd started."

"What happened?"

"What I told you would happen if you didn't move fast," he replies. "The cartel caught up with me. So I had to play my part some more. I had to try to at least get them their money so I wouldn't have to spend the rest of my life hiding or looking over my shoulder."

"While I rot in a shallow grave somewhere, right?"

He can't possibly be this thick or self-absorbed because that would mean I was completely blind and incredibly stupid throughout our relationship. I can't even fathom not spotting any of the signs. Jake must've lost his marbles somewhere along the way. This egregious callousness must be the result of some kind of psychotic break. The cartel caught up with him, and now he's overwhelmed, trying to untangle himself from a potentially deadly situation.

I'm in no position to further antagonize him, though.

He's the one with the gun, and he'll probably kill me if he doesn't get what he wants. I can only pray that Darla realized I didn't leave on my own. I can only pray they're out there looking for me, trying to get to me. Colton, Ethan, Mitch. My heart aches as I think of them. They must be worried sick. I need to find a way to get myself out of here.

"What's the plan, then?" I ask Jake. "I'm going to stay here until when exactly?"

"I'm not sure. This wasn't exactly organized. I had to take advantage of Louisa's disdain for you. She texted me; you know? As soon as you and that crabby bitch walked into the diner. Louisa's a good girl. Loyal. Proactive. Not like you, constantly bitching and moaning. She understands me."

"She's a child who's miffed that her little crush won't give her the time of day," I mutter. "You're Louisa's consolation prize at best."

He laughs. "Oh, right. 'Cause her crush is too busy boning you. See how it worked out? In my favor. The universe loves me, Melissa. That's why we're here, why I had to do all this." He grins like a madman. "After I heard about the cartel visit, after I saw your ranch hands patrolling the fence, I knew my options were limited. I had to act."

"So you figured you'd take me and hold me hostage, hoping the Averys will pay."

"Precisely. I saw the way Colton looked at you. I saw how far his brothers are willing to go in order to protect you. I don't know what you did to them, honestly, but kudos to you. You had a nice thing going over there. It's a shame you had to ruin it."

"*I* ruined it?"

"Yeah, by not complying with my terms and conditions," he replies with a cold sneer. "I told you, didn't I? Get the money and you might survive. You insisted on playing the victim, and here we fucking are! You forced me to do something I honestly didn't want to do."

He steps closer, gun still pointed at me. I take a step back.

"What are you doing?" I ask with a trembling voice.

He takes a pair of cuffs out of his back pocket. "I need to make sure you stay put while I run some errands. My cartel contacts have gone dark, and I'm worried they're going to do something drastic before I have a chance to squeeze your boyfriends for their cash and get ahead of the problem."

"You're joking."

The gun's cold touch sends chills from my cheek all the way down my spine. "No, Melissa. I'm done playing nice. Do as you're told, or I will blow your brains out. It's an option. Not my first choice, but I will make it if you push me."

29

ETHAN

Searching the streets of Long Pine got us nowhere. No one has seen Miller or his car.

"He was smart, and he was careful," Colton says as we meet outside the sheriff's office. "Figured out how to avoid any traffic cameras."

"Chances are he took her out of Long Pine," I reply. "What did the sheriff want?"

It's dark, now. The night is deep and black above, while the town is bathed in the golden glow of streetlamps. I would've considered it beautiful, even worthy of a midnight stroll with Melissa hanging from my arm—but given the circumstances, everything feels bleak and ominous.

"Our Ranger buddy came through," Colton says. "They've got Laurel upstairs in one of their interview rooms. I was thinking we might talk to her, see what she knows. The deputies are still out there, patrolling and working their way out of Long Pine. It's all they can do without any reports or tips coming in."

"They've got Melissa's and Jake's photo posted everywhere. Someone will spot them eventually," I exhale deeply. "Yeah, let's see what Laurel can tell us."

I check my phone. Darla and Sammy have yet to call us from the ranch, but my guess is there's nothing new going on over there either. Melissa's in the wind, and every second that goes by without us knowing where or how she is feels like fucking torture.

We head upstairs and find Kavanaugh standing outside the interview room waiting for us. The station is close to empty, with every man searching for Melissa and Jake. It feels odd. Eerie, even, to see this place so wide open, not a uniform in sight. But it feels good to see Laurel sitting at that table, fear imprinted on her tired face. There's a ketchup stain on her diner uniform. The mark of a hard day at work that just went from bad to worse.

"Has she said anything?" Colton asks the sheriff.

"Nope. She wants a lawyer. I figured I'd let you have a crack at her as civilians before I inform her she's not under arrest," Kavanaugh replies. "Might as well play the card without breaking the law."

"Smart thinking." My brother smiles. "Though I'm surprised Laurel didn't realize she's not under arrest."

Kavanaugh chuckles. "A girl with her background? Yeah, I agree. She's been Mirandized plenty of times before. You'd think she'd know the drill by now." He glances around and takes a deep breath. "I'm gonna go get myself a cup of coffee from the kitchen. That should give you five, maybe ten minutes to get something out of her."

"What about the DEA?"

"Oh, I've rung the alarm. They're sending more agents and a SWAT team to assist us. I'm probably gonna have to hand over Melissa's case to them when they arrive, but we still have a few hours to ourselves here."

"We'll put said hours to good use," I assure Kavanaugh and make my way into the interview room. As soon as I walk in, Laurel looks up. "Good evening, Miss Buchanan."

"My name's not—"

"Cut the crap, Laurel," I cut her off. "We know who you are."

I take a seat across the table from her, while Colton slowly closes the door and remains standing, hands behind his back as he watches me work. There's no time, so there's no point in going too easy on this wretched creature.

"I don't understand," she mumbles. "What am I doing here? I didn't do anything."

"Melissa's missing. Jake took her. We assume it has some-thing to do with the Esparza cartel and the drug money they're owed. Drugs Jake lost. You know what I'm talking about. The drugs you helped him pin on Melissa."

Laurel freezes in her seat, slowly shaking her head. "I don't know what you're talking about."

"Perjury is a serious crime, but lying to the cartel is even worse. Imagine what's going to happen when they hear you lied about the whole thing. That they're two million dollars short because of a scheme Jake Miller fumbled," I say, following her every micro-expression, watching as the fear and the despair gradually set in. I can almost hear the wheels turning in her head. The stupidity evaporating as the truth comes to light.

"The Esparza cartel," she mumbles.

"Oh, yeah. You see, Melissa works for us at our ranch. Part of a prison program meant to help her and others like her start new lives once they get out," I say. "I'm Ethan. That's Colton over there."

Laurel glances at him, then looks at me again. "Okay. What does that have to do with me?"

"It's got everything to do with you, Laurel. We know Melissa is innocent. She's serving five years for a crime Jake Miller committed. And you helped him destroy her."

"I told the truth—"

"I will smack you if you try to lie to me again. Don't think for a second I give a shit that you're a woman," I snap. It's a lie. I won't hit her, but she doesn't need to know that. "Melissa is in danger, and trust me, if anything happens to her, if you don't help us set things right, I swear I'll deliver you to the cartel myself and tell them what you did."

Laurel gasps. "I didn't do anything!"

"Had you told the truth in court, we wouldn't be in this position," I remind her.

Laurel takes another deep breath and steals a glance at my brother. "What do you want from me?"

"I spoke to the sheriff, and he's willing to help you out. Confess. Tell the authorities about the perjury, give them all the information you have on Jake Miller and his movements, his cartel associations, everything." I lean closer. "Laurel, I mean *everything*. Because a judge will need to believe you after you tell him you lied. You get me?"

She nods slowly. "What then?"

"They'll provide you with protection."

"For how long?"

"Throughout the trial, for sure. And then you'll probably go into WitSec," I say, though I'm not sure they can arrange that for her unless the information she provides is essential. "It depends on how good your intel is. Either way, if you don't cooperate, you're fucked because Melissa is missing, and we want her back."

"Fucking Melissa," Laurel sighs, lowering her gaze. "I knew this was gonna come back to haunt me someday."

"Whose fault is it, though?" I ask Laurel. "You're the one who placed a hand on the bible and lied your ass off."

"It wouldn't have been my first choice, in hindsight."

"But it was a choice you made, nonetheless. What are you going to do about it now? Because you know you're not walking out of here until you start telling the truth," I reply. "It's not about five years in prison for Melissa anymore. It's about her life, and you don't want that on your conscience. If you think the cartel is scary, wait until I have to cope with losing her. Nobody's going to save you from my wrath."

She's perfectly aware. It's written all over my face. It's embedded in the tone of my voice. She understands the repercussions. And I certainly am not joking, nor am I trying to scare her. I have every intention of making her life miserable if she doesn't come through for Melissa.

"We're tired of fending off cartel drug lords," Colton politely chimes in. "And Melissa feels the same way. Whatever issue you had with her, it cannot be worth putting her through this hell, especially when there are consequences to your actions. As you can see, the past is now catching up with you. Sooner or later, we will get enough evidence to bury you and Jake Miller—if the cartel doesn't bury you first, just to cover their asses. We're pretty sure they already did away with that Bruce fella."

The blood drains from her face. "Bruce?"

"The other false witness," Colton says. "Surely you remember him."

She nods silently.

"He's nowhere to be found. And trust me, we dug deep. We have connections throughout the government. A man who vanishes like Bruce did is not breathing anymore. So do yourself a favor. Help us, and we'll help you."

"These are your only options," I add.

"Dammit, fine," Laurel replies, resting her face in her bare hands. "I'll write a statement, whatever."

"Excellent," Colton replies. "We'll get the sheriff in here to do a proper recording of your statement. And any information you have that can back up your new testimony will come in handy. I'll personally make sure you're safe until the federal authorities take you into custody and move you into WitSec."

Laurel gives him a hard look. "Wasn't Melissa under your care when she was taken?"

I ignore her jab as I get up and join my brother outside. We leave Laurel behind and in Kavanaugh's custody. He goes in and takes over the conversation. He knows what to do next, and we know we're one step closer to clearing Melissa's name. If only we could also find her before it's too late...

"It's better than nothing," Colton says.

"I agree. I just—"

His phone rings. I notice Sammy's name on the Caller ID. Colton answers, a stern look casting a deep shadow over his eyes.

"What is it? Wait… What?" He looks at me. I see a whole new kind of horror in his gaze, his lips slowly parting. Dread. Devastation. My stomach drops and my insides tighten as I hold my breath, as I expect to hear the worst possible news. I'm not ready to lose this fight, dammit. I'm not ready to give up on Melissa and our babies. Our future. Our life together. No. "Okay, Sammy. We'll be there soon."

"What's wrong?" I ask as he hangs up.

"The cartel is at the ranch"

We drive back to the ranch in the dead of night, darkness swallowing the snowy hills around us. The moon hides behind thick clouds, nary a star in the sky. I suppose it's befitting how we feel, how this entire situation is unraveling in darkness and endless fear.

Any moment, now, we could either win or lose.

Melissa could survive or we might have to bury her. And our unborn children.

"I don't like this," I tell Colton as we pull up outside the house. "We should've told Kavanaugh."

"He's getting us a location for Jake," my brother replies. "We need him focused on that. Besides, if the cartel is here tonight, what does that tell you?"

It hits me harder than the icy, midnight air as we get out of his truck and count four silver Escalades parked right in front of the porch.

"What did Sammy tell you?" I ask.

"That the cartel is here, and they want Melissa or the money."

"Shit," I say. That's the suspicion I've been nursing on the way here. "They don't know what Jake did today."

"Nope."

"You lead. I follow," I tell my brother.

I always let him lead in situations like this. Frankly, I'm better with the physical side of things. If he needs me to scare the shit out of someone, push someone into submission or needs me to hurt or kill, I'm his guy. In this case, however, a different approach is necessary. I am always the last resort. Clearly, we're not there yet.

"Alright," Colton says. "We keep calm and—" His voice ends as he walks through the front door. "No..."

"Don't move," a man says.

I hear the guns clicking before I see them, but the two bodies on the floor capture my full attention. My heart is breaking. Bile rushes up to my throat.

"Kyle... Jason," I whisper.

Darla is in the armchair, sobbing and afraid to even react at the sight of us. Sammy is on the sofa, seething and wiping tears with the back of his sweater sleeve.

Six men are present, making the living room look a whole lot smaller than it actually is. I spot the leader quickly—his demeanor makes him easily recognizable. He's dressed well, in neutral tones of beige and cream, his hair combed, and his eyes filled with confidence as he looks at us.

"Gentlemen, glad you could join us," he says.

The other five are goons: big and burly, clad in mostly black and carrying semi-automatic weapons. The smell of gunpowder and fresh blood invades my nostrils as I give Kyle and Jason another glance. They were shot dead and judging by the crimson pools in which they lay, by the warm color of their cheeks, it didn't happen too long ago.

"You didn't have to do this," I say, cold-burning hatred dripping from my voice.

"I think I did because you fellas didn't take us seriously," the leader says. "It's regrettable, and I cannot say I enjoyed it, but it had to be done."

"Darla, Sammy, are you okay?" Colton asks. I can feel his rage blazing underneath that calm demeanor.

"Yeah... but Colt... Kyle... Jason..." Darla mumbles, then bursts into another wave of tears.

"We're fine for now," Sammy says, giving Darla a long, worried look. "We're fine. We're gonna be fine, honey."

I notice Sammy lean toward a still-sobbing Darla. "Baby," he whispers, "I swear, if we make it out of this alive, I'm gonna make an honest woman out of you."

"You mean it?" she sniffs.

"Ring and everything, darlin', I promise. Fresh start. Just take a deep breath for me, I don't want you getting sick or passing out. Please."

"He gets through to her, and I can almost feel Darla's relief subtly flowing through her as she inhales deeply, then slowly lets the air out.

"Who the fuck are you?" Colton asks the leader.

"Ramon Esparza," the leader replies. "I'm sorry we're having to meet under these circumstances. But my patience has run thin."

Ramon Esparza. I remember the name. The entire cartel is named after him and his brothers.

"You want Melissa," Colton says, "or the market value of the drugs you claim she lost."

"I'm not claiming anything. She did lose it. To the police," Ramon replies. "You know, I met her. Sweet girl. I swear I hate having to do this."

"Wait, what?" I blurt out. Ice fills my veins as he flashes a smile.

"Melissa. I met her in town not that long ago. I wanted to see what she was like. Jake didn't have any kind words to say about her, but I could see it in her eyes. The ability to deceive, to lie in order to cover her ass. Sweet girl, like I said, yet capable of bending truths and hiding secrets. So, how good does that make a person?"

"This is your ultimatum, then," Colton replies. "You come into our home. You kill two of our own. This is it? The finish line?"

"I have to finish what Melissa started," Ramon says. "I could've dropped her when I met her, you know? But I decided to give her a chance, to give Jake a chance to come through. Yet here I am, with no money and no Melissa, long after I explained the terms and conditions. I assume either Jake is being inefficient or you fellas don't understand the gravity of the situation."

"Oh, we understood," Colton sighs. "But you have a problem, Ramon."

"What's that?"

"Jake lied to you," Colton says. "About the drugs, about who stole them."

"I suspected as much from the beginning, but he made a compelling case. Plus, there were witnesses. I was at the trial, discreetly hiding in the back, watching everything, and making sure I had the right culprit," Ramon replies with a wry smirk.

"Except those witnesses committed perjury," my brother insists. "We couldn't get a hold of Bruce, but we found Laurel. She's with the sheriff and the DEA as we speak, recanting her testimony."

Esparza lifts an eyebrow. "What does Laurel have to say?"

"You'll read about it in the news," my brother replies, layers of confidence added to his voice as he picks up on the same body language cues coming from Esparza. His goons don't move an inch, but I can tell they're just as confused by this conversation. "If you'd come to us peacefully, without your guns and threats, we might've spared you the trouble. Jake lied to you. He planned the theft. He wanted Melissa to take the fall for it because he was able to easily frame her. Some evidence planted here, a false witness there.

"It was all fine and dandy. She got arrested and the merch was confiscated. All Jake had to do was play the innocent with you and with law enforcement, which he did. He played his cards right; I'll give him that. Only, he was supposed to get the drugs out of lockup with the help of an inside guy, a dirty cop. Said cop died in an accident, and Jake was hung out to dry."

"He needed the drug money to get out of the country," I add. "He had no intention of giving the drugs or the money back. That was the point of the whole shtick. Steal your product, have Melissa go to jail for it, sneak the product out of evidence lockup, give the crooked cop his cut, sell the rest, and move to another country. Disappear without a trace."

Darla gasps, her eyes widening as she looks at us. "Poor Melissa."

"That's right," Colton replies, taking advantage of Esparza's stunned silence. The man's ego is about to explode, so my brother needs to drive his point home quickly and effectively before it blows up in our faces. "Melissa had absolutely nothing to do with your drugs. She was always innocent. And if you want to ask why Jake went to such great lengths to hide the truth, think about it this way: My two close friends are dead on the floor. He knew what he was doing and how he was going to do it in order to avoid a similar fate. Jake wanted the money and the freedom, and he knew he'd never get both while transporting drugs for you."

Esparza looks at my brother, then looks at me. The silence that fills the house is tomb-like, cold, and heavy, pressing down on my shoulders and making my stomach feel like it's packed with lead. Every second we spend here trying to convince the head of a deadly cartel that Melissa is innocent is a second we're not looking for her and getting her as far away from this fucking hell as possible.

"Jake's been playing you and your people for complete idiots."

"How trustworthy is that Laurel woman?" Esparza asks, his gaze on me.

"I made it clear that I will not rest until she pays if anything happens to Melissa. Let's just say Laurel is motivated to survive at this point," I say.

"Ah, so you're the scary one."

Mitch's voice comes through from the kitchen. "We're all scary ones."

By the time Esparza's goons realize he's here, it's too late. His sniper rifle is pointed at their boss's head. It's a semi-automatic, too. They're not going to take him down before he kills Esparza.

"Well, then," Esparza sighs and slowly lifts his hands in the air. "I guess I underestimated you. But none of you will live if anything happens to me."

"I'm not here to kill you," Mitch says. "I'm here to make sure nobody else dies tonight because of Jake Miller's bullshit. That, and I want my woman back."

Esparza smiles, looking at each of us with newfound interest. "You're Special Forces. I see it, now. The grit, the self-righteousness... any other man would've come in, guns blazing and shooting everything in sight."

"Army Rangers," I reply. "And we deliver on our promises."

"We're at an impasse, but I'm willing to mend this fence and offer a solution that satisfies each of our needs," Colton politely says.

"A solution, you say?" Esparza is curious.

As if summoned by the heavens themselves, my phone pings. It's a text from Kavanaugh, with the information we've been waiting for. I give Colton a subtle nod. He knows what to do next.

"Yes," he tells Esparza. "We'll take you to Jake Miller. Work your shit out with him and leave us out of it. Leave Melissa out of it."

"You know where he is."

"His little side piece in Long Pine finally gave him up," I say, glancing briefly at Sammy. "We know where he took Melissa. We just need to get her out of there. Safely."

"And if you're lying? If this is all a ruse? No Laurel, just bullshit to keep me away from my retribution?" Esparza asks, raising an eyebrow.

"You know where to find us," Mitch says. "We'll always be here. Always ready."

"And fearless, I see," Esparza chuckles.

"Determined," Colton says. "But my brother is right. We're here. We're not going anywhere because we've got nothing to hide. Neither does Melissa."

It's a gamble, but Esparza doesn't strike me as a fool. Jake did spin quite the web for the cartel to believe him regarding the drugs and Melissa's arrest. His most recent actions have raised a red flag with these people. Esparza wants his money, and he wants to protect his reputation. The only way that's going to happen is if the responsible thief is punished. The real thief.

"I don't think you want word to get out that Jake Miller bamboozled you and your associates," Colton adds. "Because if you let that fucker walk, if you go after Melissa, that's what's going to happen. Jake will figure a way out of this state and out of the country, and the world will know what went down here tonight. You'll be the stooge."

"That's not going to happen," Esparza bluntly replies.

We're playing with fire.

We might get burned. But from the moment we got Sammy's call, we knew it would get to this. There's no other way.

30

MELISSA

When Jake returns, I've yet to figure out a way to get myself out of this mess.

I'm cuffed to this stupid chair, shaking and terrified, trying to come to terms with the situation. It's particularly infuriating to want to do more and not be able to even move.

My wrists hurt, so I tell Jake as soon as he walks in, "The cuffs are too tight. You have to loosen them a bit."

He gives me a crazed look as he starts pacing across the room. Outside, it's dark and cold, the winter slowly and steadily creeping into the old house. Shivers run down my spine. I'm not sure if it's because of the drop in temperature or because of Jake's terrifying expression.

"Your comfort is the least of my concerns, Melissa."

"What happened? Where were you?"

Jake stills in front of the fireplace, slowly turning to face me. Only now do I see the anger, the fear, and the insecurities bubbling to the surface, overwhelming an already over-whelmed man who still has a gun in his hand.

"Here and there. Listening. Watching. Eavesdropping. Real-izing that your boyfriends screwed me over before I even had the chance to really drive my point home."

"What do you mean?" I ask hearing the tremor in my voice.

"I was going to get word to them, to let them know they can get you back if they pay me," Jake says. "I figured I'd find them at the sheriff's station, moping around, waiting for a ransom call. But no, I found Laurel and Louisa there, both in custody. Laurel. How the fuck did they find that bitch when I couldn't?"

"They have Laurel?" I gasp, a splinter of hope cutting through my heart.

"Of course, which means everything is off the table," Jake says. "If she's in custody, I'm fucked. They got to her before I could."

The realization slams into me, damn near knocking the air out of my lungs. "Laurel disappeared before you could kill her after she testified on your behalf," I mumble. "Like you killed Bruce. That's why nobody could find him."

"You have no idea how much work I put into this project," he scoffs. "How many hours, how much energy I burned to make this whole thing happen, from the planning stages and all the way down to the execution. Yet every fucking time, somebody had to get something wrong along the way. And here I am, fucked sideways."

"I don't understand."

"It wasn't supposed to end like this!" Jake snaps and points the gun at me. "I was hoping I wouldn't have to do this, but…"

"Whoa, whoa, hold on, Jake, talk to me," I say, desperate to live. "Maybe Laurel didn't say anything to the cops. I mean, she lied for you once, didn't she? Did she know you'd try to kill her after the trial?"

He takes a moment to think about it, then slowly shakes his head. "I don't think so. We parted on somewhat friendly terms. I paid her. Told her not to be a stranger."

"Was she in contact with Bruce?"

He shakes his head again. "No. Not that I know of."

"So technically speaking, Laurel might not even be aware of what's going down here. Maybe Colton and the sheriff found her, but she's not saying anything. How close were you able to get to her?"

"I stole a janitor's uniform. I snuck in. But I couldn't get in to see her or talk to her. Some of the deputies came back. My photo is plastered everywhere. I barely snuck back out without getting caught."

Jake is wading through a mess of his own making, and he's running out of solutions, out of ideas, out of reason.

"Jake, don't get yourself in deeper," I manage. "You don't have to do this."

"I do, actually. I can't have you telling the truth. Someone might believe you."

"I think we're a little past that, don't you?"

"It won't matter anymore," he says, raising his weapon once more.

Staring down that dark hole, I feel… nothing. It's as if everything inside me has come to a sudden halt. I'm frozen. Speechless. All I can do is hold my breath and wait for it.

A honk rather than a gunshot tears through the silence of the night. It rips the whole universe apart, accompanied by rumbling engines and scraping across the half-frozen snow outside. By the time Jake realizes we're not alone anymore, boots thud across the porch. The door bursts inward, splinters flying everywhere.

I scream at the sight of one too many men clad in black.

So many weapons.

"Melissa!" Colton's voice finds me.

Jake is about to shoot, but a familiar face pops into my hazy field of vision and smacks him hard across the face. It's not Colton, though. It's not Ethan either, or Mitch.

"Ramon," I whisper, looking at them all, confused. "What is going on here?"

"I can explain!" Jake starts sobbing. His gun lands on the floor and slides farther away from him. Suddenly, he's alone and helpless, mewling and whimpering like a lost kitten.

I gasp as I realize that Ramon, the nice man I bumped into the other day, is Ramon Esparza. Holy shit. I was mere feet from him a few weeks ago.

"We need to talk," Ramon tells Jake. "But first, you're going to let this poor girl go."

"Let her go? I caught her for you!" Jake tries to spin this back in his favor.

Ethan whips out his gun, prompting Ramon's people to point theirs at him. Ramon curses in Spanish and motions at Ethan. "Put that down. We had a deal, Mr. Avery!"

"Fucking hell," Ethan hisses and puts the gun away.

Immediately, Ramon's men focus on Jake, while Colton and Mitch flank Ethan—their eyes searching my face. I'm dazed and beyond confused, trying to wrap my head around what just happened. Seeing Colton and his brothers in the company of the cartel, while Jake is out of excuses and lies... I admit, I did not see any of this coming.

"Alright, Jake, so here's where we stand," Ramon says, glaring at him with dead eyes. "You need to remove Melissa's cuffs first."

"Ramon, I—" Jake tries to object, but Ramon smacks him across the face with the butt of his gun. It's the second blow, and it draws blood, splattering it across the dusty, grimy floor.

"Uncuff her."

Jake nods and does as he's told. With trembling hands, he fishes the key out of his jeans pocket and rushes around, getting behind me. As soon as I'm free, I jump out of the chair and bolt right into Colton's arms.

"Are you okay?" he whispers.

I feel Ethan's hand on the small of my back.

"Yeah," I whisper back.

"Ramon, hold on, you got things wrong here. I was planning to bring Melissa to you," Jake tries to weasel his way out of this, but it's not going to work the second time around. "I had her in cuffs for you."

"You were going to kill me before the cartel got anywhere near the truth," I say, my tone flat, my sympathy in shambles. "Had they not come in…"

Ethan pulls me closer to him. "It's alright, baby. He's not going to hurt you anymore."

"Jake, I don't like being played for a fool," Ramon says. His calmness is eerie, reminiscent of the quiet before a devastating storm. "What's this about Laurel and Bruce committing perjury in court? I listened to their stories. I believed what you told me about Melissa because I thought to myself… No, Jake can't possibly be stupid enough to even consider playing me."

"I never played you, Ramon, Melissa was going to run off—"

Ramon cuts him off. "Say that lie one more time, and I'll put a bullet in your head right here. I heard Miss Buchanan's revised statement. Here I am, terrorizing these good folks, hounding this poor woman, thinking she's going to get me my money back, while you've been doing what, exactly? Laughing behind my back? What the fuck are we doing here, Jake?"

"I… I never… Ramon, you gotta believe me…"

"You wanted Melissa to go down for you. You made me believe this girl tried to pull off one hell of a brazen heist. Truthfully, in hindsight, I shouldn't have bought into it. You were the one transporting my merchandise. You're the lazy, greedy little fucker. And you made me look like the ultimate stooge," Ramon sighs. "Honestly, at this point, I'm too tired to start from scratch and try to get my money back."

"What do you mean?" Jake mumbles, the color draining from his face.

I can feel his dread almost echoing within me as Ramon raises his gun and points it at Jake. "I need to make an example out of you. My honor demands it. Nobody plays Ramon Esparza for a fool and gets away with it."

"Ramon! Wait!"

The bullet pops through his head, throwing him backward.

My scream is muffled as I hide my face in Ethan's coat, averting my gaze. I hear Jake's body drop with a pathetic thud. I can almost hear the last breath escaping from his chest. He's gone. It's over.

31

MELISSA

Flanked by Colton and Mitch, hiding still in Ethan's arms, all I can do is look around and listen as the aftermath of Jake's murder unfolds in steady, heavy tones. I watch Ramon's goons get Jake's body out and carry him to the trunk of one of the Escalades.

"Use a tarp. It'll take forever to clean that blood, otherwise," Ramon instructs his men, then turns his attention to us. "An apology won't be enough for everything that has happened between us," he adds, focusing on me, in particular. "But I don't regret letting you live when we first met, Melissa. I followed my instinct. I wanted to see what you were like. In a way, I suppose, I was already having doubts, but it wasn't until your friends put things in a different perspective that I realized how far Jake had gone with his scheme."

"I never stole a thing," I tell him.

"Yet you took the fall for Jake."

"It was the only thing I could do. My court-appointed attorney told me to confess so I could maybe get a shorter

317

sentence. Turns out that wasn't the best advice, but I didn't have any evidence to counteract the prosecution's either."

"Yes, I was there," Ramon says. "It's in the past now. You can't undo any of it, just as I can't undo what happened earlier. Please, Melissa, accept my apologies. Rest assured, the cartel will never bother you again." He glances at Colton. "I believe your friends procured the evidence they need to clear your name."

Colton scoffs. "Provided you leave Laurel Buchanan alone."

"I have no business with that girl. I already got my retribution," Ramon replies. "Our business here is concluded."

"Is it, though? You killed Kyle and Jason," Mitch cuts in.

I gasp, horror crushing my very soul. "Oh no!"

"The truth had yet to reveal itself, and I needed to make sure you all understood the stakes," Ramon sighs. "I am sorry, but there is nothing I can do to change that. I will pay for proper burial, and I will instruct my lieutenants to keep this entire district clear and safe on top of the local police."

"The best thing you can do is take your cartel business and get as far away from Long Pine as possible," Colton says.

"Consider it done." Ramon gives him a cool smirk. He walks out, accompanied by the rest of his goons.

Colton watches him like a hawk, while Ethan and Mitch analyze the situation through the dirty windows. A tremor takes over my body, but Ethan's firm grip keeps me grounded as I let the adrenaline flow through me. As I try to ascertain my condition overall—aside from the horrific fright of everything that just happened, I feel... fine. Relieved even. At peace. The nightmare is coming to an end, and while I don't like the way it happened, I am thankful for it.

"Give me a ten-minute head start before you call the sheriff," Ramon says over his shoulder. "It will be better this way."

As soon as they're all in their cars and driving off, Colton turns around and comes closer, cupping my face with both hands while I'm still tucked away in Ethan's arms.

"Is it over?" I ask with a trembling voice.

"It is," he says.

"Really?"

"We got Laurel's confession on tape, enough leads to follow up and make a case before the judge. You'll be cleared, Melissa. Your conviction will be overturned, and your sentence will be vacated. It'll be okay," he replies.

Mitch plants a soft kiss on my cheek. "You should've told us you're pregnant."

"Oh," I mumble, my face burning red. "I didn't know when or how to, given everything that was going on. I'm sorry."

"Don't be," Colton says and kisses me on the lips. I welcome the heat; I welcome the love pouring from him like ambrosia from the gods themselves. "In retrospect, I think it was wiser to keep us in the dark. Had we known, we would've made ourselves vulnerable, desperate, prone to deadly mistakes."

I glance back at the window. The Escalades' red taillights shrink in the depth of the winter night. "I thought I'd lost you. All of you," I whisper, tears stinging my eyes.

"You're not going to get rid of us that easily," Colton chuckles softly.

Lost in their embrace, I find comfort and peace again. This time, however, it feels whole. Permanent. So real I can never deny it.

"Come on, there's a lot we need to do before dawn," Mitch says.

Ethan pulls away for a moment and takes out his phone. "I'll handle the sheriff. We need them at the ranch, too."

"Oh, God," I say, tears flowing freely down my cheeks at this point. "Kyle and Jason... Did they really?"

"I'm sorry. There was nothing we could do," Colton says, then tells me about how everything went down from the moment they learned I'd been taken. "By the time we got to the ranch, they were already dead."

"That bastard," I grumble, anger working its way through my heaving chest.

Colton sighs deeply. "We'll give the boys a proper funeral, help their families. We'll need some time to recover, to regroup, to figure out what we're going to do next."

"We're going to get Melissa's name cleared, first and foremost," Ethan says as he gets off the phone with the sheriff. "Kavanaugh is sending a crime scene unit over to the ranch and two of his deputies over here to draw up an incident report. They'll take all of our statements first. We'll head down to the station tomorrow for the full interview and whatnot. He's already processing Laurel. The DEA is in town. A whole team."

I shake my head slowly. "I can't believe this. It really is over."

"And you're not going anywhere," Colton says, then takes me in his arms. "We need to redefine your role on the ranch. Your role in our lives, too."

I glance at the puddle of blood on the floor, already congealing and darkening into a thick reddish brown. "He nearly ruined my life."

"He's gone now," Ethan says.

"Are you hearing me, Melissa?" Colton interjects.

"Huh?" I give him a curious frown while simultaneously melting in his embrace.

"Okay, let me try that again," he laughs lightly and gives me another kiss. I feel it differently this time. It's infinitely more profound, reaching my soul on a deeper level. "I love you, Melissa. *We* love you. We love you so much, it almost fucking killed us to lose you, even if it was just for a few hours. And that right there," he adds, gently placing a hand on my belly, "that's our child…"

"Children," I reply.

"Right. 'Cause you had to make it extra challenging," he jokes, and I giggle. "Our children, Melissa. We're going to be a family. If you'll have us, that is."

"Of course, I'll have you. I'll have the three of you for the rest of my life."

Mitch smiles gently and tucks a lock of hair behind my ear, his touch almost electric, sending pleasant chills down my spine. "Good," he says.

"We'll figure the rest out, one day at a time," Ethan exhales sharply. "Right now, I just want to put this whole fucking nightmare to rest."

Once we've given our statements, the sheriff's deputies let us go back to the ranch. We arrive at a gloomy scene, somewhere around four in the morning. The CSI van is pulled up outside the house, while two police vehicles are parked next to it. Another deputy guards the main gate, letting us through.

"Sammy and Darla are inside," Kavanaugh says as he meets us on the front porch. "They're okay. Shaken aplenty, but the doc checked them out before he helped the coroner with your boys. I'm sorry, fellas. I really am."

"So am I," Colton replies, staring at the front door for a moment. "Are they still in there?"

"No, we got their bodies out, but the living room is off limits for a few more hours. The rest of the house is yours, though," Kavanaugh says. "I'll have my deputies keep an eye on the place for forty-eight hours. The DEA is already expanding their search for Ramon Esparza and his crew."

"You won't find them," Ethan says. "They're long gone, and they have no intention of showing up in the area again. They got what they came here for."

"I'm guessing that's Jake Miller," the sheriff grumbles.

"Yeah. Melissa's safe, and we have everything we need to push forward with her exoneration. That's all that matters right now," Colton says. "I doubt we'll get anywhere with bringing Kyle and Jason's killers to justice."

It feels wrong and it makes me sad.

It breaks my heart altogether when Darla and Sammy come outside. It's so cold, and they don't even have their coats on. I'm wrapped up in my parka and glued to Mitch's side. I'm warm and calm, but they're shivering and reeling from a horrendous tragedy. They saw their friends get killed, and they will never be able to forget that.

"I thought I'd lost you all," Darla bawls and throws her arms out.

Mitch and I are the first to catch her, while Ethan and Colton hug Sammy so tight, I can hear his bones crackling.

"Are you two okay?" Mitch asks.

"It's so good to see you boys." Sammy pats them both on their shoulders. "We're as well as we can be all things considered."

"The crime scene fellas will send a cleaner in the morning," Darla sobs in my arms, then gently kisses my cheek. "Gosh, Melissa, I'm so glad you're okay. We were fucking mortified. I am so sorry; I had no idea what that idiot was planning. Louisa, the little shit, she was in on it."

"Yeah, it's okay, Darla. I know it just happened, and it happened fast," I tell her. "What matters is we survived, and we're going to honor Kyle's and Jason's memory."

"We're going to take care of their families, too," Colton adds. "They deserve that much for getting caught in the crossfire like that."

"Those poor boys," Darla mumbles, then gives me a worried look. "How are you feeling, honey? Babies okay?"

"I think so, yeah," I reply. "It was scary as hell, but I kept it together for these two little lives."

Sammy comes closer. "That's your survival instinct, kiddo. We all have one, even when we think we're gonna freeze up and get ourselves killed. You did what you had to do to protect those precious ones."

He hugs me, and I hug him back. I welcome the fatherly affection, too. I bask in Darla's loving cuddles. And every second that goes by reminds me of how lucky I truly am to be a part of the Path to Freedom Initiative. I wouldn't be where I am today without these incredible people.

"Our guys are going to finish up with the crime scene by dawn," the sheriff politely interjects. "Like I said before, y'all have the rest of the house to yourselves. Just don't touch the living room until I give you the go ahead."

Sammy clears his throat and turns to Darla, prompting the rest of us to go quiet. There's a sense of anticipation swirling through the biting January air.

"I made you a promise, you firecracker of a woman," Sammy says with a trembling voice. "I don't have a ring on me right now, but I'll get you one as soon as the jewelry store opens, I promise. But I gotta ask you…"

"Sammy," Darla gasps. "You're crazy."

"No, I just love you. I've always loved you, Darla, even when I wasn't supposed to. Maybe that's why I acted the way I did when we finally got together. Part of me didn't feel like I truly deserved you. Like it was too good to be true, after so many years of yearning… I love you, honey, and what's left of this life, I wanna spend it with you."

"Oh, Sammy." She tears up again, but this time, the most beautiful smile blooms across her face. "You've lost your goddamn mind to shack up with a crabby old lady like me."

He chuckles and takes her in his arms, and it's the sweetest thing to witness, as they finally surrender to one another, as they finally accept each other as they are—as they've always been. "I may be old and rickety, I may have a foul mouth and a few bad habits I'm never gonna lose, but you know I love you; you know I'm loyal. You know I'll take a bullet for you, baby."

"Fine, I'll marry you. Just don't bust out into a song," Darla jokes and rolls her eyes, then laughs as Sammy lights up like a firebug and gives her a long, heartfelt kiss.

I look with joy as Colton, Ethan, and Mitch happily congratulate the newly engaged couple. Kavanaugh chuckles and slaps Sammy on the back.

"You've finally done it, old pal. You finally got the nerve," he says.

"I promised her," Sammy quips. "I promised Darla that if we survived tonight, I'd make an honest woman out of her. I'm a man of my word, y'all know that."

"You most certainly are," Darla says, softening in his reassuring embrace.

This is the closest we'll ever get to a happy ending, considering everything that happened here tonight. I wasn't sure I'd make it back. Staring down the barrel of that gun... all I could think about was the future my babies would've missed out on. For a second, I prayed their souls might find their way back into this world.

I lock my arms around Colton's waist, feeling his heart thud against mine.

"I'm home," I tell him softly.

"Yeah. Yeah, you are," he says.

And I believe him.

32

MELISSA

As spring comes rolling over the hills of Nebraska with cherry and apple blossoms aplenty, I find myself preparing for a whole new chapter of what has already been a rather eventful life. Melting into my seat, I gaze out the window of the courtroom. In the distance, past the town, I can see the hills with their patches of crude green and pale pinks, whites, and yellows galore. The world is coming out of a long and heavy slumber, and so am I.

"Your Honor, we'd like to call one last witness to the stand," my attorney, Mr. Wilkes, says.

His voice pulls me out of my thoughts, my mind having wandered somewhere far over those beautiful hills. I should be more focused on what's going to be my full exoneration, but I've been so strung out over the past few years, I'm actually glad I'm able to let my mind fly away like this. It's been three months since I've had a panic attack. It's amazing what true peace can do for a person.

I glance across the courtroom. The prosecutor, Mr. Vaida, gives me a long, regretful look. It's better than the contempt with which he treated me the last time we met—the day I was sentenced to five years in prison for a crime I did not commit. Time has not been too kind to this man. His brown hair is thinning. His eyes seem more tired than ever.

"Laurel Buchanan," my attorney replies.

"Wasn't she a witness for the prosecution?" Judge Hennesy mutters.

Ethan leans in and whispers in my ear. "Keep cool, baby."

He's not alone. Mitch and Colton sit with him, right behind me, and it's the greatest feeling in the world to be here and know that I have their full support. Cradling my growing bump, I give him a soft, over-the-shoulder smile. "I'm as cool as cucumber," I whisper back.

"Yes, she was," Mr. Wilkes says. "She has, however, recanted her testimony and agreed to a deal with the prosecution in exchange for leniency on the perjury charges."

"I can confirm," Mr. Vaida sighs deeply. "This case was an absolute sham. We have no objection to Ms. Buchanan's revised testimony."

"Then you may call your witness," Judge Hennesy says.

I hear the courtroom doors open and glance back and watch Laurel as she enters the courtroom. She combed her red hair in a tight bun, and she picked out a simple but neat black outfit for this occasion. She looks at me for what seems like forever—just enough time for me to see the regret, the guilt swirling deep within her soul.

"Here we go," Colton mutters.

Laurel takes the stand, and the bailiff swears her in. This time, I know she's telling the truth. Mr. Wilkes gets up and begins his questioning while the judge and the prosecutor watch in silence. There's no jury for this hearing. There are hardly any people in the courtroom, except for my men, a handful of town reporters taking notes, and a couple of lawyers who knew about my case from the papers. It's fine, though. I don't need an audience for this.

Laurel gives her testimony, and the prosecutor nods his approval.

"We rest our case, Your Honor," Mr. Wilkes says, giving me a quick but confident smile. "And it is hereby our most ardent request that Melissa Carson's sentence be vacated, effective immediately, and all charges removed from her record altogether."

"The prosecution seconds that motion."

"Of course you do, Mr. Vaida. This was your mess to begin with," Judge Hennesy scoffs, then nods my way. "Miss Carson, I cannot begin to express how sorry I am that you had to spend three years in prison for the crimes of another. The justice system may be flawed, but it worked with the evidence and the testimony available at the time. While we cannot give back the time you lost, we can only offer our sincerest apologies and immediately proceed to vacate your sentence. As of right now, you are a free woman, clear of any and all charges."

Suddenly, an ocean of relief washes over me.

I've been waiting for this moment for so long that I didn't even register its magnitude and its importance until now. As I take a deep breath and stand up, I can feel every ounce of fear and misery, every sliver of anger and sadness leave my body. It's over. It's finally over, and all I can do is smile and nod and let Mr. Wilkes shake my hand.

"Congratulations, Melissa," he says.

"Thank you," I mumble, tears filling my eyes.

Colton is the first to take me in his arms, while Ethan and Mitch give Mr. Wilkes their thanks. He's one of the ranch's top lawyers, of course. They wanted to make sure I had the best representation after everything that happened with Jake and the cartel.

"Well done, honey," Colton says to me. "You made it to the end of the tunnel, huh?"

"It's so bright and warm now." I am laughing and crying at the same time.

He gently wipes the tears from my cheeks and plants a kiss on my lips. In public, he's the one I'm with. We agreed on this in order to keep our relationship safe, especially with the twins on the way.

"You're a free woman," Mitch says as he steps closer, leaving Mr. Wilkes to have a final exchange with the prosecutor and his assistant. "What's the first thing on your to-do list?"

"I'd kill for a burger," I reply, prompting a hearty laugh from my men.

Ethan offers a wink and a smile. "We could stop by the Cavalier before we head home."

"Home," I mumble.

"It'll be your home for as long as you want it," Colton lovingly reminds me.

I give him a fluttering kiss on the cheek, reveling in the feel of his sandy stubble against my lips. "I absolutely want it forever, Mr. Avery. Our children will love growing up there."

* * *

AFTER A GENEROUS LUNCH at the Cavalier, where Louisa is no longer working, since she's serving a one-year prison sentence for helping Jake with my abduction, much to her family's chagrin, we head back to the ranch.

As soon as Colton's truck passes the front gates, it's as if the world is finally opening itself up to me again. Everything looks better. Everything smells fresher—including the manure. It's ridiculous, what true freedom can do to one's senses. You don't even realize how precious freedom truly is until you're stripped of it.

Darla and Sammy come out on the porch to greet us

"So?" Darla asks, her eyes wide with excitement as Ethan helps me out of my seat. I've gotten heavier, sluggish at times. Carrying twins takes a toll on the body. "How'd it go?"

"All good," I say with a bright smile. "I've been exonerated. My record cleared. My sentence vacated. It's truly over."

"Oh, honey, I'm so glad," she exclaims and rushes to hug me, albeit careful so as not to squish me and my growing bump.

"We were just about to take the lasses out on the pasture," Sammy tells the guys. "If you care to join us, that is. The ranch hands are at the stables, getting our horses ready."

"How are they coming along?" Colton asks Sammy, a tint of sadness lingering in his gaze. The memory of Kyle and Jason is still strong on the ranch. They were good men who didn't deserve what befell them. Not a day goes by that they're not missed. "Are they giving you any trouble?"

Sammy scratches the back of his head. "Not really. Omar's a tad slow, but he's a hard worker. And Jessie's a real fire-cracker. I reckon he'll break the grey filly by next month. Something tells me she's gonna let him ride her before summer comes around."

"That's good to hear," Colton replies with an appreciative nod.

"We're not going to be able to join you, though," Mitch says, snaking an arm around my waist. "We just had a monstrous lunch at the Cavalier, and we'd like to put our feet up for a while. It's been a long morning, to say the least."

Sammy chuckles and gives me a gentle pat on the shoulder. "I can't blame you. Y'all rest up, Melissa, and what can I say? I'm glad you're free of all that nonsense. I'm also glad you're stickin' around with us, sweetheart. You would've been missed. This place ain't the same without you."

"Thank you, Sammy."

* * *

THE HOUSE still feels strange at times.

I expect to bump into Kyle or Jason at any hour, but then I'm immediately reminded that they're no longer around. It'll take a while for this sadness to wash away, but the prospect of little kids darting about, laughing and squealing, quickly brightens my mood.

My room was recently turned into the master bedroom—our safe haven away from the world. It's still my space, but I spend my evenings here in the company of my men.

"Gosh, you're so beautiful," Colton says, smiling as he and his brothers walk in.

I'm fresh out of the shower and wrapped in a delicate, rose-pink robe made of fine silk, one of the many gifts they've been gracing me with since the whole nightmare with Jake and the cartel came to a drastic end. My hair flows freely over one shoulder, capturing rays of sunlight in its dark waves. For the first time in a long time, I feel like my truest self.

"You fellas are quite easy on the eyes as well," I say and laugh lightly.

With slow but sure steps, I walk up to them just as the door closes behind Ethan, his gaze shifting from a light blue to the very night sky that will soon grace the heavens above.

"Take that off, darling," he says.

"Yes, sir," I reply with a playful smile and let the robe fall to the floor.

I watch as their eyes travel from my head to my toes while they remove their clothes, one layer at a time. First, the shirts and the boots. I'm graced with a splendid view of their gorgeous torsos, muscles bulging and stretching seamlessly as heat gathers in my core.

Without hesitation, I touch myself as they get out of their jeans.

My breasts are swollen and tender. My hips have widened, and my baby bump is growing beautifully. Yes, I feel heavy and sluggish most of the time, but my men make sure to also make me feel like I'm the most beautiful woman in the world, their most prized possession, theirs to love and share until the end of time.

"I'm afraid none of us will last long," Mitch says, stroking himself as he watches me. He's big and hard and aching for me, much like his brothers.

Their cocks are twitching, veins pulsating along the shafts as pearls of precum gather at the tips. I get on my knees and take each of them in my mouth, tasting them, enjoying them and memorizing each of these extraordinary men to the deepest detail.

Ethan runs his fingers through my hair when it's his turn. "I didn't think I'd be able to love someone as much as I've come to love you."

"Then we're in luck because it's more than mutual," I reply.

Colton slides deep down my throat, and I welcome all of him, relaxing my jaw to fit as much as possible. His cock throbs furiously against my tongue, causing liquid heat to trickle down the insides of my thighs.

"You're perfect," he whispers.

"And you taste like heaven," I tell him.

This is my first time with them as a free woman, and it hits differently. Mitch pulls me up and moves us to the edge of the bed, showering me with kisses as Ethan and Colton run their hands all over my body.

"Come here, baby," Mitch says as he lays on his back.

I climb on top and straddle him, letting him stretch me and fill me to the brim. "Oh, yes," I groan excitedly as all my nerves endings light up. "You're precisely what I needed."

"Got more for you right here," Ethan says and gets behind me.

He joins Mitch inside me while Colton stands next to the bed and holds on to the canopy frame as I part my lips and let him glide down my throat again. It's incredible precision and a feat of perfection as I'm claimed by my men, hard and deep and insanely intense.

A rhythm builds between us.

My breasts bounce, but Mitch makes sure to lovingly tease each, taking my nipple in his mouth and letting his tongue flick over it. Again and again, until an orgasm builds up within my core. I let my hips move back and forth, moaning with a mouthful of Colton while Ethan goes faster, deeper. I come hard and gushing all over them, panting and sweating as they take me straight to heaven.

"Welcome to the first day of the rest of your life, Melissa," Colton grunts as he tightens his grip around the base of his cock.

I suck him harder, shuddering in the aftermath of my climax while Mitch exhales sharply and comes with a brusque jolt. Ethan's hand comes down, slapping my ass before he lets loose and fills me with his seed.

"I love you so much," I whisper as Colton leans down to kiss me. "So, so much."

"And we love you," Ethan rumbles in my ear, nibbling on the side of my neck. "Just as much. You're ours, Melissa."

"You're mine, too," I say.

Mitch puts on a lazy smile, while I linger on top of him. "Damn right we're yours."

EPILOGUE I

MELISSA

"Welcome home, kiddos," I say as I walk through the front door.

Behind me, Colton and Ethan carry each of our newborn sons, while Mitch has his arm around my waist, keeping me close. It's the sweetest haze, and I've been in it for the past couple of days since my boys came into this world.

"There they are!" Darla cheers as she and Sammy hurry out of the living room to greet us. They're both crying tears of joy, positively overwhelmed by the view. Frankly, I'm close to weeping, too. "Oh, my gosh, look at those little angels."

"Averys through and through," Colton chuckles, beaming with pride as he shows the firstborn off with a huge, glimmering smile. "I'm just glad we were able to bring them home so quickly."

I'm sore as hell. My whole body is recovering from a fast but insanely intense labor. It was the scariest and, at the same time, the most beautiful experience. I'm not going to tell the guys just yet, but I secretly can't wait to do it all over again someday.

"You're right, they look like angels," I say with a laugh as I watch the boys sleeping in their fathers' arms. Ethan and Colton have commandeered both armchairs, while Mitch joins me on the sofa. He hasn't left my side, and I couldn't love him more for this.

"Do we know who the daddy is, specifically?" Darla asks while Sammy pulls up a couple of stools for the two of them.

I shrug. "We do. Dr. Hartman did a test strictly to check the father's medical history," I tell Darla. "We're keeping it to ourselves, though."

"It doesn't really matter," Sammy replies. "They're lucky little fellas. Coming into a big family like this. I can't wait to teach them both how to ride."

"Right now, we plan on taking advantage of a few days of quiet," Colton quips. "Then we've got the shifts organized. Feeding, changing, the whole shebang."

Ethan chuckles dryly. "Yeah, my boy Colt here set up an entire system."

"I just want to make sure Melissa gets enough sleep," Colton replies.

"I got lucky, what can I say?" I chime in, melting in Mitch's embrace. He's been such a comfort over this past couple of days. I'm truly blessed. "Three strapping fellas taking good care of us. You two and Jessie and Omar, too. One big, happy, unconventional family."

"Add twins into the mix and brace yourselves," Mitch laughs. "They're going to be a handful. I hope you're all fully aware of that particular nugget."

Darla shoots him a cool grin. "Aren't you the optimist."

"Avery boys were never not troublemakers," Sammy says. "Even Mitch. He came to us a tad later, but he grew into the name quickly. Didn't you, Mitch?"

"And then some."

"How are you feeling, Momma?" Darla asks me.

There's water and coffee on the tray. I spring for the coffee, first. Decaf, of course, since I'm nursing. "I'm in need of a good cup of coffee and a lifetime's worth of sleep, but other than that, I'm good," I tell Darla. "Frankly, I'm both proud and humbled. I don't know what I was expecting the labor to be like, but the way it unfolded, man, it was incredible."

"Oh, I can only imagine," Darla says.

Colton gives me a soft smile. "You were a veritable warrior, honey."

"Have you picked out their names yet?" Sammy asks.

"Kyle," Colton says, nodding at his little bundle of joy. "And that's Jason over there." He looks at Ethan's charge. Both sleep soundly, wrapped in white and pink-nosed, still wrinkly and coming to terms with life outside the womb. "We figured it was the best way to make sure we'd honor their memory while giving our sons names they could be proud of."

Darla tears up again. "That's incredible. I swear, your momma and daddy are smiling down on you all from heaven."

"Couldn't have done any of this without you, without Sammy," Ethan cuts in. "Wanna hold these two?"

"You don't have to ask me twice," Darla says.

Gingerly, Colton and Ethan give our sons to Darla and Sammy. The former gets Kyle and the latter has Jason, and they're both over the moon, eyes shining with awe and joy as they get a closer look at the babies. I swoon over Kyle and Jason all the time, too. I can't blame them. They're beautiful and pure, innocent and sweet. They're mine. Ours. And it fills my heart with the purest form of joy, knowing our children will grow up on this ranch, out in the open, surrounded by hills and forests and all of Nebraska's splendiferous wilderness at their bare feet.

"Jason looks like he's going to be the top troublemaker," Sammy says, practically melting as he gazes at twin number two. "I got a feeling."

"That's 'Imma teach this boy to piss everybody off' in Sammy speak," Darla grumbles, half-smiling. "And I'll bet little Kyle here is going to be the leader of the pack. He's got a certain poise."

"Pretty sure that's his pooping face," Mitch chimes in.

Darla crinkles her nose. "I guess you're right. The new medication didn't just give me my taste back, it sharpened my sense of smell, too."

We all laugh, but something feels different. I look around and notice the subtle glances Colton, Mitch, and Ethan exchange. I'm filled with love and golden sunlight when their eyes meet mine, yet this moment, right here... it's a signal of change. I'm not sure how to put it into words, except that my instincts have yet to fail me.

"It's time," Colton says.

"Couldn't agree more," Mitch adds.

"What are you talking about?" I ask, my curiosity piqued, while Darla and Sammy shrug at each other in honest confusion.

"In between labor and diaper changes and feedings, we figured we'd make room for something really important," Ethan tells me.

At the same time, he and his brothers get up and kneel before me. I'm glued to the sofa, unable to move as I quickly realize what's coming. My heart is already racing, my whole body bracing for the explosion of overwhelming joy as Colton takes out a small, pale grey velvet box and opens it.

"We've been itching to do this for a while now," he says. "But we could never find the right moment. Life here on the ranch has kept us busy. The events that led up to this moment were just as time and energy consuming. But rest assured, Melissa, we've given this every thought…"

"Oh, my God," I gasp, covering my mouth with both hands at the sight of a superb diamond ring. Teardrop-shaped, brilliant cut, and mounted on a delicate crown of pink rubies. "Oh, my… Wow…"

"In the eyes of the law, only one of us will get to be your husband, but the three of us are asking you. With Darla and Sammy as our witnesses, with the heavens shining down on us and the rest of our lives unfolding ahead," Colton says. I catch the slight tremble of his voice, the emotions surging through him.

"You're the only woman we want or need," Ethan adds. "You, Melissa. Our friend, our lover, our partner."

"Our soulmate, through and through," Mitch says. "Never did any of us imagine that a day like this would come, but here we are."

"Marry us, Melissa. Let us make you our wife. In sickness and in health, for better or worse, 'til death do us part," Colton says. "Marry us and give us the honor of spending every waking day and night making you the happiest woman on this earth."

"I'll marry you, all three of you," I add, bursting into tears.

Colton slips the ring on my finger, then pulls me into a kiss. Ethan's next, then Mitch, then next thing I know, I'm wrapped in their arms and showered with loving pecks. My lips, my cheeks, my closed, tearful eyes… they kiss me all over, they hug me and hold me tight, while Sammy and Darla hold on to our children and bear witness to one of the most beautiful memories I'll have to look back on many years from now.

It will always be yes.

EPILOGUE II

MELISSA

"Your glamorous ranching idea is starting to pay off," I tell Mitch.

It's been two years since the twins were born. Two years since our lives changed forever and only for the better. To my surprise, the ranch itself joined us on this fantastic voyage. We're atop our horses, way up on the hill, watching the glamping area from afar. Cosmos neighs delightedly, and Mitch pats him on the neck, while Isabella shudders as I stroke her beautiful white mane.

Below, Colton and Ethan carry our sons on their shoulders, gently introducing them to their horses, Apex and Elias, respectively. Soon, Kyle and Jason will learn how to ride the beautiful mustangs, so it's good to establish these bonds from an early age. The twins are growing fast, but I am pleased to be able to cherish every single moment, every new discovery and milestone along the way.

"Yeah, we're getting more and more people coming in for the rancher's experience," Mitch muses, smiling as the sun sets in deep shades of pink and red somewhere behind us.

I doubt there's anything more beautiful than late summers in Nebraska.

Then again, it'll be winter again soon. We'll gather around the Christmas tree. Relive the nights that brought us together. A golden wedding band joined my diamond ring in the meantime. I still smile as I remember the wedding. A small affair so we could do it properly, the four of us in the heart of the world itself. It was all we needed.

"Sammy did a fantastic job with the glamping site too," I say. "It looks fantastic."

"Darla had a say in it," Mitch reminds me with a dry chuckle. "Or more than a say in it. Remember the project stage?"

"My God, she wouldn't let the man sleep without making her amendments to the design," I laugh. "How could I forget? We were secretly placing bets on how long before they'd file for divorce."

"But they didn't."

"They're still going strong," I mumble. "I'm glad, though. They're quite the pair."

"Frankly, they deserve each other. He's the patient one. She's the blizzard. A match made in heaven."

We have more staff on the ranch, too. Six ranch hands in total, plus a dozen seasonal workers for spring and fall with their respective harvests. Soon, in maybe a year or two, we're going to open a winery as well. Colton and Ethan worked hard on those western hills, and the vines have grown tremendously. We're expecting our first grapes to hang from them in September. Almost there.

But it's the glamping project that has brought the ranch a surprising new and generous source of revenue. More and more of the city folk have turned to our lands for a reconnection with nature. With each passing year, the ranch yields more potential. With it, the town of Long Pine also grows. We're getting more tourists in the area, which has opened up new hospitality opportunities. The Cavalier is practically overwhelmed these days.

"There she is," Colton exclaims from the foot of the hill, pointing up at us.

"Momma!" Kyle calls out.

"Wee!" Jason shouts, waving excitedly from Ethan's broad shoulders.

"Hey, babies!" I laugh as I wave back at them.

Mitch clicks his teeth, prompting Cosmos to move. "Come on, gotta tell you something," he says. Isabella joins them before I even issue the command.

"Whoa, tell me what?" I ask.

"Give it a second," he laughs.

I'll give it a few more as we ride down the smooth hill, hooves thundering across the ground. The smell of grass and wildflowers fills my lungs, the wind brushing against my face and through my fingers. There's nothing I love more than this.

"Fellas, it's time," Mitch tells his brothers.

"Okay, I'm getting worried now. What is this about?" I frown slightly.

With one hand keeping Kyle on his shoulders, Colton chuckles and takes out an envelope from the back pocket of his jeans. He hands it to me. "This came for you earlier in the morning."

"What is it?" I ask as I get off my horse and turn the envelope over.

There's an official stamp from the Michelin Culinary Academy branch of Lincoln, Nebraska. They're one of the top culinary schools in the Midwest and it's always been a secret dream of mine to attend. My heart skips a few beats as I look up at Colton, then Ethan, then Mitch while the twins eagerly smile at me. Of course, the boys have no idea what this is about, but I'm pretty sure they picked up on their fathers' excitement.

"Guys?" I ask again.

"Open it," Mitch replies with a cool grin.

I tear the envelope open and take out a letter. "Dear Mrs. Avery, it is our pleasure to inform you that…" I lose the rest of my words as I read the whole thing, my heart now performing acrobatic somersaults in my chest. "Oh, wow… What… How? I never applied."

"We applied for you," Colton replies. "Back in the spring. Remember that weekend when we had you cooking a six-course meal for a few videos?"

"Yeah… you had a professional crew filming the whole thing," I mumble. "You said it was for the ranch's website. For the glamping promos."

"We had an ulterior motive," Ethan admits, his lips curling into an innocent smile. "We sent the videos and a few samples of your baked goods to the school in Lincoln."

"Why would you do that?"

"Because you deserve to take your skills to the next level," Colton says. "Don't you want that?"

I nod enthusiastically. "Of course I do. I just didn't expect this. Wow. I don't know what to say. When do I start?" I pause, the reality check quick to smack me over the head. "Hold on, it's in Lincoln. What about the boys? The ranch? I'm still your chef, remember? Wait, I don't know. How's that going to work?"

"Come here," Mitch laughs and takes me in his arms. "Relax, babe. We've got you. We already worked the details out with Sammy and Darla."

"The courses last for about a year, but they're segmented in two semesters. And structured accordingly," Colton says. "We rented a nice house in Lincoln, starting in mid-September. Mitch will go there with you and the boys, and Ethan and I will join you as often as we can. We'll switch places depending on our work with the ranch, too, but Sammy and the crew have most of it handled."

"And the vineyard?" I ask.

"That, too. We'll have the seasonal workers, remember?" Colton replies.

"What about the kitchen?"

"Already taken care of," Ethan interjects. "Marty's daughter and his cousin will handle the cooking for the whole year. All you have to do is go to school and get your degree."

I keep staring at the letter, stunned and beyond exhilarated. I'd almost given up on this idea. With the boys and the ranch constantly evolving, I was already busy and stimulated enough. Deep down, I did feel a little sad about it because cooking still is and will always be my first love.

"I can't believe this," I say, tears of joy tickling my eyes. "You did this for me?"

"I really want to open a new restaurant in Long Pine," Mitch says. "I'm not going to do it without you by my side. And you really want to get your Michelin degree. It felt logical. Two birds, one stone. We're going to rule over Long Pine, honey. There's nothing left standing in our way."

"So, what do you say?" Colton asks me.

I look at the letter again, then plant a sweet kiss on each of their lips. I take a deep breath and smile. "Let's do this, then. Let's build something amazing together. We've made it this far, haven't we?"

"You're damn right," Colton exclaims.

"Dam' light!" Kyle mimics his father.

Mitch scoffs. "Setting a great example, as usual."

"Shut up," Colton chuckles.

"Shut up!" Jason also rushes to imitate him, prompting a hearty laugh out of Ethan.

"Alright, then, we're doing this," Mitch says, lovingly hugging me. "I can't wait to see what you do with what they teach you over there, Mrs. Avery."

"And I can't wait to knock your socks off with the menu for your future new restaurant in Long Pine, Mr. Teller-Avery," I reply, eagerly softening in his embrace.

Our boys cheer and giggle. Their fathers rush to join Mitch, and so I'm once again wrapped in strong arms, kept warm and happy by the purest, most powerful kind of love. Come September, a new chapter begins. One I didn't expect, but one I fully welcome.

And to think I came here with a hint of shackles on my wrists and ankles.

But I found the truest, purest freedom.

The End

Printed in Dunstable, United Kingdom